THE GOLDEN GIRLS' ROAD TRIP

ALSO BY KATE GALLEY

The Second Chance Holiday Club

THE GOLDEN GIRLS' ROAD TRIP

Kate Galley

An Aria Book

First published in the UK in 2023 by Head of Zeus Ltd,
part of Bloomsbury Publishing Plc

9 7 5 3 1 2 4 6 8

A catalogue record for this book is available from the British Library.

ISBN (PB): 9781804542262
ISBN (E): 9781804542248

Cover design: HoZ/Jessie Price

Typeset by Siliconchips Services Ltd UK

MIX
Paper | Supporting
responsible forestry
FSC® C171272

Printed and bound in Great Britain by
CPI Group (UK) Ltd, Croydon CR0 4YY

Head of Zeus Ltd
First Floor East
5–8 Hardwick Street
London EC1R 4RG

WWW.HEADOFZEUS.COM

For Leo ♥

I

Sometimes I try really hard not to think about the summer I turned eighteen. On other occasions I allow the memories to engulf me, the pleasure and the guilt to wrap themselves around me. From time to time it comes at me unexpectedly, like a slap or a kiss. Today it's in the form of a book and makes me smile. How could it not, because today is our birthday. Today we are both seventy years old.

I open the box of books and pull out a few dusty paperbacks. The donations have been pouring in over the last few days and I have a lot to get through. I would have thought the heatwave we're experiencing at the moment would put people off clearing out their cupboards and shelves, but it would seem not.

I begin to flick through the pages, checking for anything left behind. It's odd what some people use for a bookmark. A till receipt is one thing, or maybe a five-pound note, but I've found shoelaces, pressed flowers, important documents and once, on page seventy-eight of a battered copy of *Pride and Prejudice*, a Curly Wurly wrapper with half the chocolate bar still inside.

So far today there is nothing more than a train ticket for

the Brighton to London, dated a year ago. I stand up, feeling that pull in my lower back, reminding me I missed yoga this week, and begin to fill the space I've made on the shelves.

'Sharon is coming in later, Connie. She has something she wants to discuss with us, apparently.'

My colleague, Gita, a slight and super-efficient woman, is hanging freshly steamed clothes on a rail by the door. She likes to group items into sets, everything perfectly matched, the same way she dresses herself. If you like the red skirt you may like the blouse to go with it, and the handbag, shoes and scarf. I'm not overly keen on this approach. I prefer things grouped into sizes – no point loving a garment if it's not going to fit you. I don't like to contradict though, and, anyway, Gita's perfect grouping makes the shop look less like a jumble sale.

'What does she want to discuss?' I ask.

'Do you remember, she mentioned a bit of a shop refit a while ago, so, I imagine she wants our input. Maybe she'll ask us to do a few extra hours to get it done. I don't mind; I've got some great ideas. The jewellery isn't selling well and I think it's that old cabinet; it's off-putting. We should get a low display table with lights and a glass top, make it look more desirable.'

I think this is a good idea. The jewellery brought into our charity shop is probably not worth much. Sharon always takes out anything valuable for auction, so it's only the beads and bangles that are left behind, and I can see that Gita's suggestion would make them look a little more appealing.

'Sounds like an idea worth exploring,' I say.

I reach into the bottom of the box for the last couple of books and turn one over in my hands. It's a copy of Katie Fforde's *Highland Fling* and it makes me stop in my tracks. All these years and it still affects me. Any reminder of that summer I spent in Scotland in 1970 and I'm right back there, the years disappearing instantly. I allow myself a moment, breathe deeply and then, after checking for anything undesirable between the pages, I place it onto the shelf where it seems to stare at me, so I turn quickly away and try to squash the fluttering that has begun in my chest.

'You all right, Connie?' Gita asks, as she ties a silk scarf around the neck of a coat hanger to finish an outfit.

'Yes, yes, fine,' I reply brightly, and am saved any further probing by the arrival of a customer.

An elderly woman with a pram pushes her way through the open doorway and I rush over to help her and her wheels up the step. She's wearing a blue summer dress with spaghetti straps and the skin on her reed-like arms looks so thin I worry it might tear with any sort of contact. She is fragile and for a moment I'm reminded that today I am seventy and then I'll be eighty, and possibly ninety. This will be me, and it's coming sooner than I'd like.

'It's sweltering out there,' she says, as I lift the pram into the shop. Only then do I see the tiny Chihuahua curled up inside.

'Oh, how sweet,' I say, surprised, reaching out to stroke it, but draw my hand back when the dog's lips lift and curl. 'Shall I fetch a bowl of water for him?'

'Her,' the woman says. 'Penelope Jones, that's her name. Penny-pops for short. She's such a love, I don't know what I'd do without her. Water would be very kind, thank you.'

Penny-pops' lips continue to curl around her little needle teeth and I take a large sidestep and retreat to the safety of the staffroom, catching Gita's grin as I go.

With a bowl for the dog and a glass for the customer,

I leave her to rummage through the bargain bin and turn my attention to the stack of donations that need sorting.

I've volunteered at the hospice charity shop here in Brighton for almost three years – two days in the week and Saturday mornings. My son, Simon, suggested it as a way to settle me into civilian life, as he calls it. He says it keeps me out of trouble. I think that what he means by that is he doesn't want a repeat of what happened with the keys for my van. It really wasn't my fault that they slipped down through the slats into the drain. It could have happened to anyone. Simon had agreed, but unfortunately, because I was in Snowdonia, he had to drive up with the spare set.

'Maybe it's time to slow down,' he'd said. 'Perhaps you're getting too old for this lark, Mum.'

A lot of my life I've spent travelling and working on the go, pleasing myself. I've been very lucky, he reminds me. As I'm supposed to be in my retirement years it's time to offer what I have while I still have it. I think Simon is right, and he seems happy that I've settled close to him – his wife, Diana, not so much.

'Connie Fitzgerald!' a voice booms from the front of the shop, making me jump. I put down the crockery I was beginning to sort through and see my friend Victoria with a bottle of champagne in her hands. 'Happy birthday, old girl!'

Vic is the person I've known the longest in Brighton, after meeting at a yoga class and being the only two to dash off for a glass of wine straight after. She's much taller than me and willowy, with graceful arms and long fingers. I had asked if she was a pianist when we first met and she'd laughed and said *pickpocket*. In truth, she looks after her elderly parents now – one with dementia, the other with Parkinson's. I can't even imagine how difficult that is, but then, I haven't seen or spoken to my own parents for many years.

'You didn't say it was your birthday,' Gita says. 'I'd have brought in some cakes if I'd known.'

Not one for a fuss, I wave off Gita's concerns, take the bottle offered to me and pop it behind the counter.

'Thanks, Vic,' I say, giving my friend a quick hug.

'Can you believe that this woman is seventy today?' Vic asks Gita, Penny-pops' owner and the young man hovering in the doorway, unsure whether it's safe to come in or not. They all offer murmurs of surprise.

'Ignore us,' I say to the young man. 'Please, do come in and have a browse if you'd like.'

He smiles sheepishly, ducks inside and heads for the CDs. This surprises me and it must show on my face because he laughs and says, 'For my mum.'

Gita moves quickly away to help Penny-pops' owner with a purchase and I turn my attention back to Vic.

'I'm serious, you know. You do not look seventy, my friend. What's your secret?' she asks, peering closer at my wrinkles. 'Drinking the blood of virgins?'

I try not to wince and say, 'Drinking the heck out of a good Rioja more like.'

'Are you out tonight?'

'Yes, meeting Simon and Diana for dinner with Leo,' I say, and Vic shudders theatrically.

'Good luck with that. How is the poisoned little witch?'

'Vic! She's my daughter-in-law. She's not that bad and anyway, I'll find a way to win her over, eventually.'

'I hate to break it to you, but it's been eight years already and I don't think you're winning.'

I sigh, knowing she's right, but without any way to rectify the situation.

'I've put by a few bits I thought you might like,' I say, changing the subject and reaching behind the counter to pull out a carrier bag. 'There's a book about train journeys in the UK that I know your dad will love. The pictures are amazing. And there's a sparkly top for your mum with some bangles. I've paid for them; I haven't just taken them,' I add, seeing her face drop. But, it seems I've misunderstood, because she grabs my hand and squeezes it.

'Thanks, love,' she says.

The young man is walking towards us with a stack of CDs.

'I'd better…'

'Of course,' Vic says. 'See you on Friday morning?'

'I'll be there.'

'Have fun tonight. Just get drunk and ignore the flak.'

I smile at her, but I won't be able to get drunk because I'm driving. Leo has decided he wants to meet me there for some reason. Simon has chosen a restaurant near their home in Lewes, so I suppose it is easier for Leo to come independently from Pevensey Bay.

'And give lovely Leo a big kiss from me,' Vic says and then she's gone.

The closed sign is on the door and we're tidying up when Sharon arrives at five. Gita has spent the afternoon working on her refit intentions and I've been jotting them all down for her. Some are actually pretty good suggestions, but others are dubious. I'm not convinced that Sharon will go for a kids' ball pit alongside a high-end jewellery display.

Sharon breezes in as if it's not thirty degrees outside. She's wearing a white linen dress without a single crease in it and her complexion is clear and cool, nothing like the red sweaty-faced customers appearing in the shop all afternoon. There is definitely something other-worldly about her. As the manager, she takes the shop very seriously, but I sometimes think that no matter how much she says she appreciates what us volunteers do, the truth is, we're a bit of a nuisance.

'Ladies,' she coos, taking a sip of her iced coffee. I recognise the logo from the café up the road and try not to stare at it longingly. 'Lots to discuss,' she says. 'Shall we have a seat in the staffroom?'

This is most definitely a first. I have never been invited to sit down in this shop. Despite the heat, the hairs on the back of my neck begin to prickle.

'Ooh, yes,' Gita says. 'I have ideas.'

'Ideas?' Sharon looks confused.

'About the refit. I think you're going to love my suggestions.' Gita has the list clutched to her chest and looks like a child on Christmas morning. I have a very uneasy feeling.

'Ah, I think we're at cross purposes,' Sharon says. 'Perhaps we ought to go and have a chat.'

2

Heat waves are radiating from the bonnet of my camper van. The paintwork is the colour of raspberry jam with seats, trim and curtains to match. There are cream-coloured cupboards with a sleek black top covering the gas burner and the sink. I even managed to find a carpet with a raspberry stripe running through it. She's called Ruby and even though my daughter-in-law thinks she's an abomination, I adore her.

Ruby is the only vehicle on this open-air level of the multi-storey because I'm the only one, it seems, foolish enough to have parked here. Inside, the steering wheel is melting in the late afternoon sun and my faux leather seats are scorching to the touch. Maybe I should have closed the curtains.

I slip into the suffocating confines, turning the key in the ignition and the dial for the temperamental air con simultaneously, and even though I know that, for it to be truly effective, I'll need to close the door, I can't bring myself to do it. Eventually a coolish waft of air begins to register on my face, and the sweat running down my spine slows. I close the door and slump in my seat, the word *redundant* still ringing in my ears.

It wasn't about the refit, or certainly not a refit that involves me or Gita. Apparently, a new and more dynamic team are being brought in to liven things up, which is shop talk for, anyone over the age of sixty is getting the boot. I'm not sure on the ethics of making a volunteer redundant, but then we hadn't really been given much choice. Sharon had asked us if we might stay on to train up some of the new girls and I had considered it until I saw Gita's grim stare. I recognised the look, and it was, *don't you bloody dare*. Instead, I had wished Sharon and her new team well, picked up my hessian bag, pulled my plait over my shoulder, and with an air of bruised pride, walked out of the shop. Gita had told Sharon to go and do something unmentionable to herself and had slammed the door.

After pulling out of the car park I make my way to the restaurant at speed, the emerald in my engagement ring catching the light as I change gear. I glance down at it, still surprised to see it there even after three months of it decorating my ring finger. The green stone is flanked by pear-cut diamonds, art deco in style, a little old-fashioned perhaps, but I love it.

My fiancé is meeting me at the restaurant. Lovely Leo he's referred to by most, due to his generous and good nature. He also seems to be able to charm my daughter-in-law and take the edge off her acerbic words. He's a man who manages to soothe a heated situation, to defuse an argument, to comfort and calm. He is kind and gentle, and yet, still I have surprised myself by deciding to spend the rest of my life with him, because I've never been married before. I have managed to make it to my seventieth birthday with a small handful of flings, but only one significant relationship to my name. Of course, I really mean two, because now I have Leo.

I'm ten minutes late to the restaurant because of the embarrassingly long time it took me to find the place. For a person so well travelled, I have to be honest, I sometimes lack a sense of direction, and the heat has made me flustered. There's an unpleasant stickiness across the back of my neck because of the gallant sprint from where I had to park Ruby. Actually, it was more of a huffy-puffy walk, but still, an effort all the same in this unbearable heat.

It's the beginning of July and the heatwave has taken everyone by surprise. June was a washout, and no one seemed prepared for the blistering atmosphere that has settled over the south-east like a heavy, scratchy old blanket. Every day seems to have less air than the last and everyone moves in slow motion. An alarming amount of chalk-white flesh has been liberated from spring clothing and is on ready display. You can't buy an oscillating fan anywhere, and suntan lotion is in short supply. It's beginning to feel very much like the summer of my youth, which just makes me feel discombobulated.

I notice the flowers first, a huge bouquet in lilac and coral tones, and then a pair of Leo-shaped legs in navy chinos underneath, finishing in his favourite suede brogues. He has his phone in his hand and is frowning at the screen, but he pockets it when he sees me.

'Hello, sweetheart,' he says, lowering the blooms as I cross the road. 'Happy birthday, Connie.'

'They're gorgeous, Leo, thank you,' I say, taking them and hanging them upside down so I can kiss him. Something falls to the pavement from inside the flowers. I bend to pick it up, assuming it's a card, but when I open the envelope I find theatre tickets for a courtroom drama at the Devonshire in Eastbourne. 'What a lovely gift, that's really thoughtful, thank you.'

'Brenda used to love the Devonshire,' he says, wistfully.

I kiss him again and try not to make anything of the fact

that *my* birthday present was perhaps chosen as a favourite venue of his dead wife. He holds the door open for me and we step inside the restaurant. I desperately want to slip into the loo to freshen up, but can already see them waving from a table by the window. Well, Simon is waving, Diana looks as if she has something nasty stuck in her swan-like throat.

I rest the flowers behind my chair and Simon gets up to greet me. I envelop him in a warm and slightly sticky embrace – my terrific son. It's ridiculous how much I love him. Despite his fifty-one years, he will always be a boy to me. I've always supposed it was because I was young and single when I had him, there had been an extra special bond we'd shared from the start. It probably helped that he'd been such a good baby and I was quite a laid-back mother, in defiance of my situation. Because of the unpleasant circumstances surrounding my pregnancy, I'd vowed to work that bit harder to make sure he felt loved and wanted, but despite all that had occurred, really it had come so naturally to me.

Diana clears her throat behind us and Simon peels himself away.

'Hello, Diana.' I lean in, intending a warm embrace, but I'm usually met with her cold and unyielding body, so I opt for an arm squeeze instead. She offers up an air kiss so far from my cheek that she may as well be greeting the woman sitting at the table next to us.

'Is that another charity shop find?' she asks, picking at the cream-coloured cheesecloth of my sleeve.

'No, actually it's vintage; I bought it in 1970. Only bring it out on the odd occasion so it doesn't fall apart. It's just about all I can bear to wear in this heat today.'

Diana gives it a grudging nod, but doesn't go so far as to

congratulate me on being able to fit into clothing I bought when I was eighteen.

Simon and Leo begin their usual back slapping and man hugging. They've known each other for a few years as they used to work together. Simon is the European sales manager for a computer software company and Leo worked in their accounts department before he retired. They have a close relationship and Leo is like the father Simon never had.

Slipping into my seat, I help myself to a glass of water from the carafe on the table and gulp it down in noisy gasps.

'Are you okay, Connie?' Diana asks. 'You look like a sweaty tomato. You're all shiny.' She smiles, her sweet, pink lipsticked lips curved perfectly, her eyes full of malice. 'Hello, lovely Leo,' she purrs, before drawing him close for a hug.

I wish I liked my daughter-in-law, but I don't. Perhaps I should have tried harder at the start, but I was disappointed when Simon divorced his first wife, Hazel. She was such a sweet girl, but for some reason, Simon treated his marriage like a bit of a fling rather than the solid institution it's supposed to be. Then he met Nikki, his second wife. Nikki I liked very much – apparently more than Simon did, because she tired of his inability to commit much past saying, *I do*. I began to worry I hadn't set a good example, having never been married myself. Third time lucky, he'd told me, but every time I look at Diana, I'm less than convinced. A woman fifteen years younger than him with, what seems to be a shard of ice in her, but Simon seems obliviously happy, now. It's as if he was warming up for the main event. I have had to make my peace with his choice, but it hasn't been easy.

Diana once accused me of clinging onto my son so I didn't have to bother forming intimate relationships with others. She said that I had been selfish to drag him around on my travels when he was younger, when a father and solid foundations would have been better. I had been understandably hurt and also confused, because I had a horrible feeling that Diana was right.

Eight years on, my daughter-in-law and I are still playing a game where we pretend to like each other, but neither one of us is fooled.

'I'm fine, thank you,' I say.

'That's good. I do worry about you sometimes.' She looks at me over the top of her menu, and flips a swathe of blonde hair away from her chestnut-coloured eyes. She's wearing a pretty, off-the-shoulder dress that perfectly showcases her delicate clavicle. I catch Simon gazing at his wife in silent regard. He doesn't seem to hear any of the snippy comments; he's too much in love.

'How does it feel to be seventy?' Diana asks me with an innocent expression. 'I can't even imagine. I mean, it's such a *huge* number.' She says *huge* while moving her hands apart to better show how *huge* she means. She looks a little like a fisherman, over-exaggerating his catch.

'I wouldn't know. I wasn't born until ten-thirty at night, so technically I'm still in my late sixties,' I retort and earn a winning laugh from Leo.

The waiter arrives then to take our order, and I choose a chicken Caesar salad and a large Viognier; it has been quite a week. I ignore Diana's steely gaze as she opts for a mineral water herself.

'I think this calls for Champagne actually,' Leo says decisively, but I notice the tiniest gulp as he turns the page on the wine list. He looks across at me, and there's a moment where he seems to weigh up which bottle I'm worth. I hold my breath while he decides. 'A bottle of the Dom Perignon 2008... vintage,' he adds. 'Oh, and the mushroom risotto please.'

Simon leans across the table and places a small package down in front of me. It's beautifully wrapped with a perfect bow in silk ribbon. I have to give Diana her due, she does do lovely presentation.

'Happy birthday, Mum,' says Simon.

The package is light and I hesitate with my fingers on the ribbon. It could be jewellery. Seventy is considered a significant birthday.

'Diana chose it,' Simon says with a shrug. 'She's so much better at gifts than me.'

I pull away the ribbon and pick off the Sellotape slowly, buying precious seconds to prepare my face. There have been gifts from Diana in the past, chosen specifically to make me feel old: blankets to wrap myself in when watching the television, a heated mattress topper, an odd combination of tartan slippers and a matching scarf. I'm hoping it is jewellery. How old could Diana possibly make me feel with a necklace or a bracelet?

'This gift was chosen because there is something we want to tell you,' Diana says at the moment I pull off the paper and lift the lid of the velvet box inside. There's a gold brooch, which spells out a word, nestled on a padded cushion.

Grandma

I'm very aware suddenly of a buzzing in my ears. It muffles out the sounds of the restaurant. I can see that people are talking, but can't hear what's coming from their mouths.

Simon and Leo are embracing again and Diana is looking at me expectantly. I know I'll have to pull myself together; a lot hinges on this moment. If I don't say the right thing, it won't ever be forgotten. But there's no denying that little stab of fear. Will it be this that brings me closer to my daughter-in-law, or drives us further apart? Babies change everything; this I know from experience.

'I'm overwhelmed and completely excited for you both.' I have no idea where the words come from, but luckily they arrive fully formed and the buzzing stops in time for me to hear that I actually sound quite normal. I push back the chair on some kind of automatic pilot, knowing I'll have to make a gesture, and I turn to Diana, my arms open wide. She looks baffled and then realisation dawns. She gets out of her chair and steps into my embrace. It's just about the most awkward act between two people, but when I see the look of pleasure on Simon's face, I pull her in a little closer.

'I'm thrilled for you,' I say into her hair and unwittingly take in a mouthful of her hairspray.

'Goodness, thank you, Connie.' Diana sounds a little choked, so I loosen my grip.

The waiter arrives with the bottle of Champagne, so we all sit back down and wait for him to pour. I take Simon's hand across the table and give it a squeeze.

'I wasn't sure if a brooch was your thing really, but Diana insisted you'd love it.'

'I do,' I say, running my fingertips across the letters, hoping no one suggests I try it on. I love the sentiment, but perhaps not the brooch itself. Now desperate for a drink, I raise my glass of Champagne before Leo has the time to toast, and knock half back in one go. I look up to see the three of them with their glasses raised.

'Sorry, so thirsty,' I say, drinking the rest and reaching for the bottle to top up my glass. Suddenly remembering Ruby waiting patiently in the car park for me and the drive home, I reluctantly push my drink just out of reach.

'Well, congratulations all round then,' Leo says. 'Happy birthday, Connie, or should I say, Grandma!'

I feel overwhelmed at the thought of a baby in the family. I didn't really think it would happen for them. Of course, it is wonderful, but it also raises lots of conflicting feelings.

'And such great news, you two. When's the baby actually due?' Leo asks.

'December,' says Simon. 'Can't believe I'm finally going to be a dad. I'm certainly going to be a better one than mine was.' There's no edge to his words. Simon always accepted what I had told him; that he was the result of a fling, and it was always just going to be the two of us. Of course fling sounds so much more acceptable than assault. But that is something I have managed to bury. It seems that if you repeatedly tell yourself something didn't happen, after a while it's just possible to believe it.

'Of course you will be, darling – there's no competition at all,' Diana says, and then with a sideways look at me: 'I chose wisely.'

'You'll be a fantastic father, Simon,' I say, steadfastly ignoring Diana's gaze. 'The trick to being a good parent is to always have your child's best interests at heart, even before your own.'

'Travelling around the country in a camper van?' Diana snorts.

'Maybe,' I say. 'We had a wonderful time.'

'Well, we want good family foundations for our child. I appreciate you enjoyed your lifestyle back then, but two parents and a permanent home is our way. To be honest, Connie, I'm not really sure I'd take advice from someone who doesn't speak to her own parents.' This last is delivered quietly and with a little giggle as if she's really only joking, but it cuts into me in a way that her other jibes haven't before. It makes me squirm in fact. Is it her pregnancy hormones or is she upping her game? After all, there's more at stake now: a baby. I look across at Leo to see his reaction to this sharp barb, but he's busy looking at his phone again. Simon is reading the label on the back of the Champagne bottle. Love really is blind it would seem.

'If you had known my parents,' I say quietly, 'you wouldn't have talked to them either.'

She doesn't say anything to this, but a knowing smirk briefly touches her face.

The food arrives then, lifting the lick of tension that's beginning to creep in, but as the waiter places each plate down, Leo's phone begins to ring and even though he's staring at the screen he still manages to look surprised.

When I first met him at Simon and Diana's summer barbecue last year, I saw an uncomplicated man, three years widowed and ready to find someone new to spend the rest of his life with. That was certainly how Simon had portrayed him to me. Simon was always bringing Leo's name into conversation. Even before I'd met him in person I felt as if I knew him. He was a *top bloke at work* and then *a top bloke who'd lost his wife*, then *it's so sad that Leo is on his own* and *he'd love to meet you*. By the time I was standing in Simon and Diana's garden, sipping an ice-cold gin and tonic and navigating a plate of charred chicken wings and coleslaw, I was fairly sure we were being set up. But, when Leo invited me out for dinner it seemed like the most reasonable thing to say yes, even if it had been orchestrated by my well-meaning son. And we had a nice time; he's a nice man.

Before I knew it we were on another night out and then another. There was hand-holding and yes, kissing too. I hadn't had any sort of relationship for quite a few years. In fact it had been a good ten years since I'd had the pleasure of another person's lips on my own, the joy of waking up in someone's arms and the talk of when we would do it again. And I was becoming a bit lonely, returning from each of my trips away to an empty flat, feeling a good deal older, a good deal more weary.

And then there'd been sex, which came as a bit of a surprise. It had been lovely and I was glad to see that I was still desired, but Leo had cried afterwards and said he felt as if he was being unfaithful to his late wife. I tried so hard to reassure him, but we went back to holding hands, which flew directly in the face of what my mother had always told me was possible.

We slipped into a sort of friendship that somehow worked, which for a while was enough for Leo, but then, this Easter, as we walked along the promenade on Eastbourne seafront, he'd manoeuvred himself with one knee down to the ground. I thought he was tying his shoelace, but the beautiful emerald ring suddenly appeared and much to the delight of passers-by, he proposed and I said yes.

It's time to settle down, I'd told myself. *The right man at just the right time*, Simon had said and perhaps he already knew about the baby and maybe he was hinting. And maybe I could finally shake off that overwhelming guilt I'd dragged around with me for the last fifty-odd years. Could Leo be my clean slate? With a little time, I imagined that we would become closer, that the physical side of our relationship would reignite, that we might use the word *love* to one another. It didn't occur to me, for some reason, that those things should really have been in place before a proposal, and certainly before an acceptance.

'Sorry,' he says now, looking at the screen. 'I've got to take this.' He slips out of his seat and also out of the restaurant. I watch him pacing and talking through the window. I wonder if he's talking to his daughter, Fiona, the woman I have yet to meet.

'How are the wedding plans going?' Simon asks as he tucks into his steak. 'Only two months to go; you must be all set.'

'Pretty much,' I say. 'Still have to choose things like the wine and I haven't sorted the cake or the flowers yet.'

'Chop, chop, Connie, you probably should have done this already,' says Diana. 'What about your flat? Are you going to sell up and move into Leo's place in Pevensey Bay, or buy something together?'

'Not sure yet, lots to think about,' I say dismissively. In truth, Leo says he wants me to move in with him, but I don't really like his bungalow. It's a little claustrophobic, and his wife is everywhere.

'Are you getting cold feet?' Diana asks, just as Leo appears back at the table.

'No, of course not,' I say quickly. 'Everything okay, Leo?'

'No, not really. I'm so sorry, Connie, I'm going to have to go. Fiona's husband has left her. She's distraught and, you know, not having her mother, it's all a bit too much for her.' Despite what he's saying, there's an excited edge to his voice, although I can't see why he'd be thrilled about a family break-up.

'Sit down for minute.' I get up and take his hand. 'You're not thinking of driving to Peterborough now, are you?'

'I have to; Fiona needs me. I'm going to help her in the café for a few days. Sorry, love.' He pulls his jacket from the back of his chair and slings it over his arm.

'I'll come with you,' I say, but Leo shakes his head.

'No,' he says quickly. 'I don't want to spoil your birthday meal.'

It's probably for the best; these might not be ideal circumstances to meet my future daughter-in-law. I have tried to orchestrate a get-together, but Leo says she's a sensitive girl who misses her mother. She isn't actually a girl – I'm pretty sure she's in her late thirties – but I understand what he means. I've held back and let Leo and his daughter dictate the pace, but this now feels like a mistake. I should have insisted on a meeting and we could be going together to offer comfort and practical help. Fiona and Paul opened the café together, so it won't be just the marriage he's left, it will be the business too.

'I'll phone you later,' Leo says. 'Enjoy the Champagne and don't let this spoil your evening.' He kisses my forehead as if I'm a child and then after tucking a handful of notes under Simon's side plate to cover the bill, he practically skips out of the restaurant.

3

My phone rings at eight and I grapple for it on the bedside table as my brain registers I'm no longer in my dream state. Leo's name is flashing on the screen and I swipe to answer. I sat up until gone one, last night, in case he called, but he didn't, and now I wipe the sleep from my eyes and the memory of an intoxicating dream from my mind. I don't seem to be able to get that Katie Fforde book out of my head.

'Leo! How's it going, how's Fiona?'

'It's not good. Paul has gone off with a woman who lives over the road from them. Turns out he does actually want to have children, because she's pregnant. Bloody fool, I could throttle him. And now Fiona is saying that she would have liked to have had children but went along with Paul's wish for it to be just the two of them.'

'Oh, poor girl,' I say. 'But, you know, perhaps she could still have a child if she's quick.'

'If she's quick! It takes time to find the person you want to be with, Connie, and Fiona is thirty-nine.'

'I was thinking more about a sperm donor actually,' I say and hear Leo choke on the end of the line.

'That's not the way we do things in this family,' he says

indignantly, and I'm not sure if it's a reprimand of my lack of morals or a reminder that I'm not part of the family; not yet anyway. He has an edge to his voice that I haven't really heard before.

'Just a thought,' I say, quietly.

'Well, she's really feeling the loss of Brenda right now – nothing quite like a mother's hug.'

My mind slips briefly to my own mother and to what Diana had said last night about our lack of communication. It's always there hovering over me despite my attempts to rid myself of thoughts of Elizabeth Fitzgerald.

'They had a rock-solid marriage, no problems at all and then this, out of the blue, bam!'

'I could get in the van right now and be with you in a couple of hours. Perhaps she'd accept a hug from me?'

'No, Connie, she wouldn't,' he says and I try not to hear the scathing tone in his voice. 'It's kind of you to offer,' he adds, 'but I think she's happy with it just being me here.' His voice is softer now, but the message is clear. I'm not wanted.

There are so many things I want to say to him now: is it okay to be marrying a woman who you don't feel you can introduce to your daughter? Is it normal to still parent that daughter like a child when she's an adult? What will my role be within his family? What does he really want from me? The words line up on my lips ready to spill out, but now doesn't seem like the right time, with him being so far away.

'Perhaps you could give her my love then and tell her I'm very much looking forward to meeting her. And, if there's anything I can do…' I trail off, convinced that even if I had wise words to impart, Fiona wouldn't want to hear them.

'I really just wanted to check you got home okay and your

dinner wasn't totally ruined,' he says without sounding as if he needs answers to those questions. He's always a little distant when he visits Fiona.

'I'm going to pop into the florist today to arrange the wedding flowers,' I tell him and he doesn't ask me why I'm not at work, although I remind myself that Leo doesn't take my volunteering job all that seriously.

'Right,' he says distractedly, 'I've got to go, speak later.' And then he hangs up.

Leo, I decide, is more complicated than I first thought.

I flop back onto my pillow and contemplate the two men in my life and the two women doing their utmost to undermine those relationships. How did I get here? Fiona is easy to work out, but Diana is much more complicated; also much more important. If I want to see my grandchild, I'm going to have to find a way to agree a truce. I allow myself a small smile at the thought of impending grandmother-hood.

Simon and Diana have been trying for a baby for years and after many failed attempts, this round of IVF has obviously been successful. Did I come across as supportive enough when they announced it last night in the restaurant? I'm pretty sure I did, but Diana makes everything so difficult. I wonder if she might soften a little when the baby comes, but I doubt it.

Diana's mother, Linda, had her when she was forty-eight, and once described her daughter as an inconvenient and unexpected shift in her life's plan. She'd been suspecting the menopause but ended up with a baby instead. Linda is certainly not the fussing type and her husband the same. I can't imagine either of them spoiling Diana – quite the opposite. Perhaps because of this, she was always going to be a tense and demanding wife, looking for the attention she never received from her parents. Simon told me he was determined to make this his last marriage and embraced it wholeheartedly. One thing is incredibly clear to me; my son adores his wife and I believe she feels the same way about him. I see it in the way she looks at him and the way she talks about him. I think that, really, they have something pretty solid and that gives me pause for thought.

I pick up the gift box from where I'd left it on the bedside table and pull the brooch out again. The gold shines in the morning sunlight coming through the gap in the curtains. If Diana did really choose this gift then surely that's a start – an olive branch in gold letters – *Grandma*. I just can't reconcile that name with Diana being pregnant somehow. For now, simply, my son and his wife are expecting a baby, and I will become a grandmother at some point, although that rather depends on what sort of grandmother Diana will allow me to be.

My thumb instinctively goes to my engagement ring and I spin it around on my finger. A grandma and a bride in the same year, two badges to declare my age and my status. I sigh and pull back the covers. I have things to do today and perhaps Leo will be pleased with me if I can tick a couple of wedding items off the list.

Picking up my phone again I hesitate with my finger over my contacts. I briefly consider asking Diana to come to the florist and help me choose my flowers. That might be a perfect bonding opportunity. Without Simon or Leo around, we might be able to bridge that gap. I don't really feel I can take the rejection though, so I chicken out and scroll through for Gita's number instead.

★

The florist is in St James's Street and Gita is waiting outside. The sun is already intense for only ten-thirty and I can feel sweat on the back of my neck. I pull a clip from my bag, grab a handful of hair, twist it up into a messy bun and secure it in place. Leo asked me if I was planning on getting it cut for the wedding, but the thought hadn't crossed my mind. I love my long hair and how easy it is to look after. He had suggested a short bob, but I had said it wasn't really for me. The next time I was at Leo's place I had taken a closer look at a photograph of his late wife. It was a holiday shot in Venice with Brenda standing in St Mark's Square, the sunlight shining on her short, neat, beige bob.

Gita is one of the happiest people I know and has been married since she was in her late teens to the love of her life. I have met her husband, Farin, a couple of times and can see how suited they are. When I asked her what the secret was to their long happy life, Gita said she married her best friend and then shrugged as if it was obvious. It made me want to cry.

'Can't believe you haven't done this yet. Aren't you leaving it a bit late?' she says as I cross the road to meet her.

'The flowers or getting married in general?' I say, and Gita laughs.

'Connie, if you've found the person you want to be with more than any other, then surely it's never too late.'

I smile at her while my insides squirm as I remember my dream from last night – stretching out on the banks of Loch Ness, the sun warm on my bare skin, fingertips tracing circles on the inside of my forearms. Although, that wasn't just a dream, it was a memory and one that I will never forget.

'Shall we go in then?' Gita asks.

'Yes, yes of course,' I say, pulling myself back to the present.

The bell jingles as I push open the door, and we step inside. The smell of the flowers is overwhelming, all the blooms competing with each other, the lilies most discernible. I suppress a sneeze.

'Gorgeous,' Gita breathes. 'Look at those peach peonies, stunning!'

'Morning!' The florist beams at us from behind the desk. He's wearing a knitted tank top with embroidered daisies on it and I wonder how he can bear to in this heat, but actually, the atmosphere in the shop is cool and I notice the floor-standing air con unit keeping the buckets of blooms from wilting.

'Hello,' I say.

'How can I help?' he asks.

'I'm Constance, Connie Fitzgerald, you're going to be doing my wedding flowers, and I'm here to choose them. This is my friend, Gita, and she knows far more about flowers than me, so I brought her along to help.'

'Ah, lovely,' he says. 'I'll get my book of ideas and we can have a look to see what you fancy.'

He disappears behind a beaded door curtain to the back of the shop and returns moments later with a huge photo album.

'So, what's your theme, colour wise?' he asks, as he lays the book on the desk in front of us.

'Um, I don't have one. I just need something for me to hold, not too big, and buttonholes for two men,' I say, and Gita tuts before she begins to flick through the pages.

'And will you have flowers in your hair?' he asks, waving his hands in windmill motions. I have no idea what he's trying to suggest with the gesture, but it becomes clear when he pulls out some photos from the back of the book. The images are of young brides, hair tousled and hanging long with flowers threaded in among the locks. I suddenly feel every one of my seventy years and a bit foolish. Am I too old to be a bride? The whole thing is beginning to feel faintly ridiculous.

'I shall have my hair plaited and coiled round I expect; simple and neat. I think flowers might make it appear like a bird's nest and even though these women all look gorgeous, really I'm a bit old for that look.'

Both Gita and the florist look up at my bun, which is already slipping, and I feel as if everyone is conspiring about my hair.

The next half an hour is a blur of flowers and ribbons, decisions on colours, and shapes: cascade, or hand-tied, crescent or round. My ears pricked up at the words *single stem*, but Gita dismissed the idea as too simple.

Somehow, by the end, I have a small bouquet of *Peach Avalanche roses, Memory Lane roses, Bouvardia* and *Limonium*. I'm truly none the wiser, but happy to be able to tell Leo what I've achieved.

We leave the shop, walk to the Pavilion Gardens Café and find a table with an umbrella. I order coffees and chocolate brownies, then we sit and look out over the park while we eat.

Sunbathers populate the grass with their picnic rugs and deckchairs. Some brave souls are full in the sun while others have, more sensibly, brought parasols to shade them. I look up to the Royal Pavilion and the domes and minarets along the roofline, glowing white in the sun. Sometimes I just want to be on the road and at other times, I adore living in this vibrant and beautiful town.

'So, is it just disorganisation with this wedding or

something more?' Gita asks, licking her finger and dabbing up every last crumb from her plate. 'It's just that I'm not sensing any excitement at all.'

I take a long sip of my latte and contemplate the best way to answer.

'It's not that I'm not excited, I'm just not terribly organised that's all.'

'Is that really all it is, Connie?'

I don't often have personal conversations with Gita, in truth I tend to steer clear of personal conversations full stop. Once you give people a little information about yourself they start to dig deeper, ask more questions. I'm not proud of some things I've done in my life, and there are other situations I've been in that I would rather no one knew about. How could I even begin to tell someone about the worst thing that ever happened to me, especially when it resulted in the best thing that ever happened to me? If I wasn't going to tell Simon the truth about his conception I certainly wasn't going to tell anyone else. I prefer to keep myself to myself generally, but recently, since I accepted Leo's proposal, I've been wondering if I ought to open up a bit more. How many secrets is it okay to keep from your husband? Right now, I have a sudden urge to let go a little of what's been rolling around my head.

'You and Farin are soulmates, yes?'

'I like to think so, but you have to remember that we met and married straight from uni. There's never been anyone else for me.'

'Well, there was someone else for me and I messed it up. Now I'm an old woman about to be married for the first time in my life and I'm still dwelling on what happened all those years ago.'

'You never forget your first love; that's what they say don't they. It doesn't mean you can't have many others. And, you know, being alone isn't easy as you get older. My mum will attest to that. Plus you'll have someone to do the bins, mow the lawn, reach those tins from the top shelves.' She's smiling now and I'm grateful to her for lightening the mood.

'God, ignore me! I'm being ridiculous. Leo is wonderful, and I'm lucky to have met him at this time in my life. I'm going to be a grandmother at the end of the year, too, and what could be better than sharing babysitting duties with my new husband. My son looks up to Leo like a father figure, so, when you really think about it, it's perfect, isn't it?'

'Only you can answer that, Connie, but it does sound lovely. Farin and I can't wait to be grandparents, but our lot don't seem to be bothered at the moment.'

I suddenly wish I hadn't said anything to Gita. It feels hugely disloyal to Leo, and also it rather proves my point that keeping myself to myself is the best way.

'Wedding jitters that's all. Thank you for helping me with the flowers. I've the wine and food to sort next.'

'Where are you having the reception?'

'It's an intimate register office service and then a meal with close friends and family in a restaurant. They have a function room at the back so we can have some dancing after. It's not a lot of razzmatazz; we're just keeping it simple.'

'Sounds perfect. What are you wearing?'

'I haven't bought anything yet,' I say avoiding Gita's eye.

'Better get on with that then – you've got quite the list.'

'I know, I know, I'm actually going shopping this afternoon. Thought I might get the train into London.'

'Perfect, wish I could come with you, but I've got to take

my cat to the vet for his jabs. In fact I really ought to go.' She drains her coffee and pushes her chair back. 'So, will I see you in the job centre?' she says with a grim smile, and I pull a face.

'Depressing isn't it, getting pushed from a job as a volunteer.'

'Yes, it is, and I'm furious with Sharon.'

'You wouldn't know it from your parting gesture,' I say, grinning, and Gita puts her hands over her eyes.

'I know, I couldn't help myself. Farin said I should ask her for a reference. What do you think?'

'I'd certainly be interested to see what she'd write,' I say with a laugh.

'I'm sure there's something else out there for us. Don't despair, Connie. Catch you later,' she says and then, pushing back her plastic chair, she steps over the low retaining fence onto the grass and walks away.

I'm not entirely convinced there is anything out there for me now, work wise. I trained as a bookkeeper many years ago. It was the sensible side to my life and one that worked well as I never used to travel that much in the winter months and could concentrate on my private clients, getting ready to submit their tax returns. I found more joy in the odd jobs I used to do on the road though: fruit picking in the French countryside, casual kitchen work in tucked-away restaurants, pulling pints at the Munich Beer Festival.

Now though, those days are over. I'll be a wife for the first time in my life and maybe I'll have to sell my van because Leo isn't keen on travelling. It's a new stage, a new path and one that I'm sure I can embrace if I try hard enough. I buy another latte and look up the train times on my phone.

4

John Lewis in Oxford Street is full of people making use of the free air con, and even the climate-change activists marching outside are occasionally dumping their placards to pop their heads through the doors for respite from the sweltering afternoon temperature. And who can blame them.

The changing rooms are not cool though. The assistant said that the unit had broken down on this level, and I stand in front of the mirror, knowing I'll have to buy this dress because I'm sweating into it. The cream and lavender silk is sticking to my skin and the matching jacket has the beginnings of wet patches under the arms. I pull it all off and hang it back up while still in just my underwear, then I take a tissue from my handbag and pat myself dry. It brings back unpleasant memories from my menopause years and I'm thankful that at least that's over.

I have quite the collection of shopping bags now and decide to treat myself to a cold drink in the roof café before I leave. Simon phones me as I take my first sip of the cloudy lemonade.

'Hi, Mum, where are you?' he says as soon as I pick up. It's always his first question and it's a fair one, because over the years, I could have been anywhere. The furthest I've travelled under my own steam is down to the beautiful city of Messina in Sicily after stopping in Reims, Strasbourg and Milan on the way. I took the car ferry across with the camper van I had at the time – a trusty old Bedford – but even that was struggling by the time I reached the island. I worked in an *enoteca*, a wine shop, for a week to pay for the repairs and then limped home. It was one of the most wonderful experiences of my life, but also one of the loneliest.

I've always been compelled to travel and ironically it was my parents who started it.

The summer of 1970 and I was in disgrace. Unable to articulate what had really happened the night of my parents' house party, I'd gone along with their assumption that I'd seduced a family friend, a married man, because they'd seen me flirting with him. The truth would have meant attention I really didn't want, and packing me off to Scotland sounded appealing. I'd have gone to the moon not to have to see his face again.

They sent me to my aunt's hotel in Inverness by train from our home in Kensington. I remember the look on my father's face as he drove me to the station in silence. Twenty minutes in the car with him was far worse than a week's worth of my mother's whiplash tongue. He made it perfectly clear that he thought I'd let him down. Then arriving in Scotland, somewhere I'd never been before, and lovely William meeting me at the station. He worked in my aunt's hotel gardens and had been sent to pick me up. He's the only person who really knows what happened that summer – that summer that shaped the rest of my life.

My thoughts return to my conversation with Gita and then I remember that Simon is on the other end of the phone I'm holding to my ear.

'I'm in the café in John Lewis in London.'

'That was not what I expected you to say,' he says.

'Is everything okay?'

'Yeah, all fine, it's just that you said you wanted me to come with you to the wedding venue to sort the wine and finalise a few things. I can finish early tomorrow and meet you there?' he says. 'It would be good to tick those last boxes and it will probably make Leo feel better. He's a bit out of the loop in Peterborough, not knowing how long he'll be there.'

'Sure, of course,' I say. 'If you can spare the time, that would be great.'

I'm exhausted. I can't remember the last time I hit the shops in such a big way, and as I head back to the station to catch the train home, bags swinging beside me, I feel the bite of a blister on my heel. I have a dress and jacket, shoes and underwear. There was something special, if a little embarrassing, about picking up a beautiful set of matching underwear at my age. For once it wasn't a quick purchase of an offer on three for two bras, and knickers that come in a multipack. It reminds me that perhaps I should make more of an effort. I'll be living with Leo soon and surely he deserves not to see my faded old pants.

We haven't really made a definitive plan about where we'll live. Originally, when Leo proposed, he said he wanted me to move in with him but he hasn't mentioned it since then. The sensible thing *is* to move into Leo's place in Pevensey Bay now I've lost my job and don't need to be in Brighton. His bungalow has a garden, which my flat doesn't. His bungalow has an open-plan kitchen-diner, which mine doesn't, but his bungalow also has more than a hint of his late wife about it. I won't speak ill of the dead, but goodness, the woman had a penchant for chintz. The whole house is stuffed full of Brenda's knick-knacks and dried flower arrangements. The curtains even have those swags and tails surrounding them in peach florals rather reminiscent of my wedding bouquet. I suddenly feel a bit nauseous and wonder if it's acceptable for married people to live in separate houses.

I have to run, but just make it on board before the train slides out of the station. Settling into a seat next to the window, I rest my head against the glass and silently congratulate myself on not being as decrepit as my years would suggest.

A couple sitting opposite have their fingers entwined and I watch as the man strokes his thumb across the woman's knuckles. They don't need to sit as close as they do – there's plenty of room – but her body moulds to his at every point from shoulder to ankle. They're young, maybe late twenties or early thirties, and I lose that spry feeling as something closer to nostalgia pricks at me. It isn't like that with me and Leo, of course it isn't – we're old, *older*. I look away, suddenly feeling every one of my seventy years.

I'm not a vain person. I'm not worried about people thinking I look old; I don't look in the mirror and panic about the lines around my eyes. I happen to be pretty fit and healthy. My face isn't sagging more than anyone else my age, and I still have a robust head of hair. I choose not to dye it and when I wear it down, it sits around my shoulders in a muted blonde-grey mane. But, this couple are in their prime, and mine – I have to admit – has evaporated into my history.

My phone vibrates in my pocket again and, as I pull it out, I see Leo's name on the screen. Moving away from the couple,

I walk through to an empty carriage. There's a magazine discarded on the seat next to me and I pull it onto my lap and pick at the corner of the cover while I call Leo back.

'Hi, you,' he says as he answers. 'Are you on your way back from the shop?'

'Actually I've been doing some wedding stuff.'

'That's great!' he says, his voice not as bright as his words. In fact, he sounds tired, or possibly resigned. Perhaps he's had a busy day in the café or maybe Fiona is draining him with her unhappiness.

'Flowers are sorted and I've bought my dress and extras.'

'Extras?' he says, and I find a ridiculous heat has appeared in my cheeks.

'Underwear,' I clarify and there's an audible gulp on the other end of the line.

'How's Fiona doing?' I ask, to change the subject.

'She's very upset, poor love, burying herself in work at the café. She's very glad I'm here to help now that Paul's gone. And, he's taken quite a lot of their shared possessions with him, the callous little shit.'

I find myself tuning out as Leo begins to list the items, my eyes moving over the cover of the magazine. *Art in Action*; the font dominates the front cover, each letter made up of tiny images of paintings and photographs, very eye-catching. I flip open the first page, then realise Leo has stopped talking.

'You sound distracted. Is everything okay with you?'

'I lost my job at the shop,' I say, and then wait for him to ask me to join him and Fiona, but he doesn't.

'Oh, that's a shame – what was the reason?'

'Age. They're bringing a new team in to give a younger vibe to the place.'

'Bit odd for a shop that sells second-hand stuff. I don't understand half of what goes on in the world today.'

'Leo, it does mean I could come to you and help support Fiona. I can lighten the load in the café and we could take her out for dinner. Perhaps go shopping to replace those things? What do you think? We could go off in the van for a little trip when she's settled too if you like.' I don't know why I add this last suggestion; I know he hates the van. Actually I do know why. I want to challenge him, because there is something going on in his head that I can't reach. I don't understand what's driving him at the moment. I'm not expecting such a quick response though.

'No, there's no need. She's got staff, you know, plenty of hands on deck here,' he says and there's a moment of silence as we both digest his words. Which is it? Does she really need his help or not?

'You know what Fiona's like,' he carries on. 'She's very sensitive, missing her mum, just needs her old dad around for a bit.'

I don't know what Fiona's like, because I've never met her, I want to say. He doesn't bother to mention the trip in the van.

'So, do you have any idea how long you'll be there?'

'I don't really know; it depends how the next few days go. See how she is. It's not that I don't appreciate your offer, you know, but there's nothing you could do here anyway,' Leo continues. 'I do miss you, Connie,' he says.

'Miss you too,' I say, automatically, and then I find I'm staring at a silent phone because he's hung up.

I rest my head back and uncross my legs. The magazine slips to the carriage floor, open in the middle with a double-page spread of artworks. I bend to retrieve it and am confronted with something that takes my breath away. All thoughts of Leo and his odd behaviour disappear instantly.

There's an image of a painting in the top left-hand corner of the page with some writing that I can't quite make out without my reading glasses. And even though the image isn't super clear, I recognise it immediately. It's so familiar to me, which of course it would be as I have the sister painting hanging on the wall in my living room.

Gripping the corner of the magazine, I draw it back onto my lap while rummaging in the front pocket of my handbag. My chest tightens and it's with trembling fingers that I slide my glasses onto my face and look again at the image.

The sun is setting over the loch, casting long reflections of iridescent gold light on the ripples of the water. I had always been amazed that they could have been produced with such a few touches of the paintbrush. In fact I wouldn't have believed it at all, if it hadn't been for the fact that I had witnessed those light touches at the time they were made. Reluctantly, I move my gaze from the painting and over to the words printed to one side.

Reclusive artist Alex Mackenzie is exhibiting for the first time in four decades.

In the beautiful setting of Linton Hall, Inverness, Highland Art Group are delighted to showcase this talented and hardly seen artist in a prestigious collection. Open to private guests on Friday 8th and Saturday 9th July, then to the public on Sunday 10th July.

Something gives in my chest, and for a moment I can't

breathe. I flip to the front cover to check the date, the year, but see it is current: 2022. Clutching the magazine to me, I stand up and then when I find my legs won't move and I have nowhere to go, I sit back down again.

'Alex Mackenzie,' I whisper, 'how could you do this to me now?'

Later, back at home, I take the cafetière from the kitchen windowsill and pile in my favourite coffee. The kettle boils and the sweet, nutty aroma begins to fill the air as I pour. My mind is whirring in a way that stops me from formulating a plan. After taking my coffee into the living room I stand in front of the painting I've looked at every day for the last fifty-two years. Tonight, it's as if I'm seeing it for the first time. A physical ache grips me as my eyes sweep the canvas, at the sun that rises over the loch with subtle shifts in paint tones to capture the light perfectly, so similar to its companion painting, while at the same time, vastly different. I still have the magazine from the train and I open it now, hold it up next to my painting. The two together again at last. Alex called them collectively, *Gold Was The Day* and when I take mine off the wall and turn it over I can see the name written in that familiar sloping hand across the back of the canvas along with its individual title: *Sunrise Over Loch Ness*. Alex, it appears, still has *Sunset*.

Thoughts crowd in on memories and just as I try to grab hold of one, to settle it, to decide, it's overtaken with another.

Because, the problem is, this article speaks to me like an invitation.

5

I pull my body through the water at a steady pace, a gentle breaststroke under the glare of the sun, the salt water in my eyes. I feel focused and very much like someone who hasn't spent a sleepless night with churning thoughts. It wouldn't surprise me, if I were to open my skull to find butter instead of brains.

Swimming has become something to centre me. From the local swimming baths I learned to swim in as a young adult, to lidos and open-water swimming when my confidence grew. No matter where I've lived over the years, if there has been a body of water, I have found it and got into it. Now in Brighton, I have the sea, but today, as my feet find the stones, I feel weary.

I turn to look out over the pier and the churning recommences. I've lost my job, a grandchild is coming, and after a lifetime as a single woman I have accepted a proposal of marriage. And if I can be honest with myself, I know that I said yes to Leo because of Simon. Not all those years ago when he was a child, when a father would have probably been a wonderful thing for him to have had, but now, ironically, as Simon is on the brink of fatherhood himself, when his dearest wish is to have his mother settled, a grounded granny. But, there is an exhibition in Inverness and it seems that Alex, who's been living under a rock for fifty-two years, has decided that *now* is a good time to climb out. I would laugh if I didn't have a such a huge lump in my stomach.

Turning back to the beach I can pick out the quick camp that I'd made with Victoria, a couple of hours ago. The rented, bright rainbow parasol is stuck into the stones, standing out amongst the many others on the beach today. Despite it being a Friday, people are taking advantage of the continued good weather. Not quite into the school summer holidays yet, it is surprising how many people, like me, are not at work.

'Cold?' Vic asks, as I approach, squeezing the salt water from my hair.

'Freezing! Invigorating though – you should get in there and see for yourself.'

'You know I would, but I only had my hair done yesterday and I'm not going to ruin Gail's masterpiece and my cash by getting it wet.'

I laugh and flop down onto my towel, closing my eyes against the blaze of the sun, but I can still feel my friend watching me.

'You look tired, Connie,' she says and I can feel the truth of those words, down in my bones.

'Simon and Diana are having a baby.' I stretch out, supine, a familiar position from my weekly yoga class. My palms are turned upwards, but the stones underneath my towel are poking me in the back.

'Wonderful! That's great news, isn't it?'

'They've been trying for a long while. This was their fifth IVF attempt, so yes, it is.'

'And you're going to be a grandmother at last! How do you feel about that?' Vic asks. 'Diana probably won't make it easy, but you never know, motherhood might soften her up a bit.' Sitting up, she pulls her linen shirt around her shoulders. 'God, this sun is too much.' She drags a floppy, wide-brimmed hat out of her bag and puts it on her head. She's recently become terrified of premature ageing, but I don't have the heart to tell her that, at nearly sixty, she's fighting a battle she should have given more attention to over thirty years ago. I can attest to that.

'I'm really happy for them, and of course it will be lovely to have a baby in the family.'

'But…?' Vic turns her piercing gaze on me again. Long divorced and childless, she has been able to please herself for most of her life, but she had wanted a child once. It hadn't happened though and she often talks about how she's going to miss out on being a grandmother.

'No buts at all – it's great news. Shall we go and find some better shade and get a drink? I'm parched.'

After stepping off the beach, I buy a bottle of water from the pop-up café by the entrance to the pier, and Vic a smoothie so green it has a hint of the neglected fish tank about it. We make our way along Marine Parade towards Edward Street and Queens Park, gulping noisily as we go, my flip-flops slapping against the hot pavement.

'I'm off in the van tomorrow,' I say as we settle on the grass underneath a tree near the pond.

'Oh really? You running away?' Vic means it as a joke, but it hits a nerve.

'I'm retired, haven't you heard? I can do anything I want.'

'Oh, that's what we're calling it now, are we?' she says with a smirk. 'So, where are you going?'

'I was thinking about going to an art exhibition in

Inverness,' I say, watching Vic's face for her reaction and she does look surprised.

'Bit of a trek to see some art. Anyone we know?'

'Alex Mackenzie: a landscape and portrait artist I used to know.' I keep my face still and my breathing steady so I don't betray myself. I can almost see the wheels of Victoria's mind turning the information over.

'Alex Mackenzie?' she repeats. 'No, I don't know that name. Any good?'

'The best,' I say quickly.

'Christ, Connie, are you blushing?' she asks, leaning closer and peering at my face – this doesn't help. 'Should I be worried? What does Alex mean to you?'

'Once upon a very long time ago... everything.'

I can see that all the cogs of her mind have slotted into place, and now I shall have to do some speedy back-pedalling, although it is a bit of a relief to say some of my thoughts out loud for once.

'I'm not actually going though; I was just thinking about it after I saw the advert for the exhibition. Just a silly blast from the past, that's all.'

'Okay,' she says slowly, regrouping her thoughts. 'So where are you going then?'

'I'm going to Peterborough to join Leo and see his daughter Fiona. Her husband left her and she's understandably upset about it. Leo is helping her out in her café. It's silly me not being there with them and I think it will be the perfect time to meet her, to get to know her.'

'Didn't you say she's a bit of a daddy's girl?' Vic asks.

'I don't think I used those exact words, but yes, Leo seems to think she's delicate. The thing is, though, if we're going to be married, I'll surely need to make an effort with her, whatever he thinks.'

'*If* you're going to be married? Connie, you *are* going to be married, in two months' time.' She laughs, her eyes wide and sparkling.

'Just a turn of phrase,' I say, shaking my head at her. 'In truth, Leo said I wasn't needed, but I think he's just trying to spare me the trouble. I should be by his side, shouldn't I? Otherwise, what's the point of it all?'

'I assume you're going to tell him you're going, or are you planning to surprise them both?'

'Perhaps a surprise, a test, I suppose.'

'Connie, the way I see it, Leo proposed without any pressure from you. It was out of the blue, wasn't it, so he must really want it – *you*. Are you concerned he's changing his mind?'

'No, it's not really that,' I say.

'Why do you feel the need to test your fiancé then? Turning up at his daughter's unannounced could be problematic.'

'But, don't you see, I should be able to do exactly that. Why *am* I being kept away? Why *am* I not needed?'

Vic smiles sympathetically, but I don't think she really understands how I feel. And anyway, the test isn't for Leo; the test is for me.

I pull into the car park and find Simon leaning on the door of his silver two-seater.

'You'll have to sell that and get something more middle-aged and child-friendly,' I say with a grin, as I step out of the van. 'Certainly something with some back seats.'

'And you'll have to promise not to turn up in *that* on your wedding day!' he replies, jabbing a thumb at Ruby. 'Diana's getting an SUV, anyway, so it won't be necessary.'

'I'm amazed that Diana's letting you keep that, whatever *she's* buying.'

'Mum, she's not that bad. She just cares, that's all. Actually, she said you didn't seem that supportive of our news the other night. Is that true?'

'Was my bone-crunching hug not enough to convince her? I'm very happy for you both. I promise,' I say, gently touching Simon's arm.

'Yeah, I know, maybe it's hormones,' he says with a shrug.

I think about Vic referring to Diana as a poisoned little witch. 'Yes, that's probably it: hormones. Right, shall we get on with this? I'm relying on you entirely for the wine choices. I'll deal with the menu.'

The restaurant is inside a beautifully restored Edwardian country house nestled in a cosy spot at the end of a windy lane off the A27. Leo had read out this information to me from the website when he booked it three months ago. In actual fact, it's a little dilapidated and perhaps only part-way through restoration. It has a hint of a chain pub about it and I'm a little disappointed to see plastic flowers in hanging baskets either side of the front door. The windy lane is a potholed track and we have to be thankful for how dry the summer has been so far. I have serious concerns about my tyres and Simon surely must be worried about his undercarriage.

We make our way through the oak front door. A woman called Barbara is due to meet us and she's standing inside, using her cream-coloured clipboard to fan the heat from her face. Her floral dress is ruched around a substantial cleavage and my eyes are drawn to the line of sweat disappearing into its depths.

'Hello, lovely people,' she says, with a rictus smile that belies her words. 'I'm Babs.' Her eyes flick between the two of us, her lips pursed.

'Hi,' Simon says, striding forward to shake her hand. 'I'm Simon and this is my mother, Connie.'

'Ah, not the groom then,' she says, looking relieved that she's not in charge of *that* sort of a wedding, although there is only just over eighteen years between us.

'Hi,' I say, taking her hand with a slippery shake.

'Gosh, it really is hot today,' Babs says, wiping her hand on the back of her dress. 'Welcome to Ashton Hall. Shall we have a seat and talk about your menu? I had rather hoped to have this sorted by now.'

'Sorry,' I say. 'Just been so busy.'

Babs tilts her head to one side. 'You can never be too busy to plan your wedding. It's the most important day of your life.'

I think she's joking for a moment, but she doesn't smile, so I have to assume she's deadly serious. She leads us through the bar area where people are enjoying afternoon pints of beer and goldfish-bowl-sized glasses of gin. There's a nice atmosphere, warm, inviting, but it doesn't seem to follow us through to the back of the building where the function room is. I think I'd been expecting a nicely decorated space, the sort of room you'd take a turn about. Perhaps some old masters filling the walls, an elaborate rug with a piano in the corner. Instead there's a fairly plain space with wooden floorboards badly in need of a good sanding, some limp curtains badly in need of a good washing and a bright green emergency exit sign above a door onto the garden. The tables are rectangular rather than the round that I would have preferred and the chairs look as if they've seen some action.

'Don't worry,' Babs says looking at my dismayed face. 'We cover the chairs in white and stick bows around them. You have a choice of pink or silver.'

I glance at Simon, but he's tapping on his phone. Turning back to Babs I muster up a smile. What does it matter? It's just a meal after the service and that's the important bit.

'I'll have a think about that one,' I say, knowing I'll be opting for no bows at all.

We sit down at one of the tables and my concerns about the chairs are founded as mine wobbles underneath me. Babs pulls papers from her clipboard and we begin to discuss the menu.

An hour later, we have agreed on a meal of tomato, mozzarella and basil salad to start; lamb shank for mains; and raspberry pavlova for dessert. Simon has chosen the wine and everything is starting to feel very formal and fixed. I'm beginning to feel faint at the effort to push Alex to the far recesses of my mind. It's not that I'm not a dab hand at exactly that – I've had to become one over the years – but it's this fresh news, fresh information. It means I've got to push all the harder. It's difficult to concentrate on decision-making with the thought of the art exhibition rolling around my head. It's also tricky to keep hearing Babs talking about my *very special day* without comparing it to all those very special days I shared with Alex.

'We find that for the *older* person's wedding,' Babs says with quotation mark fingers, 'we usually suggest we don't move too many chairs and keep the dance floor on the smaller side.'

'Why?' I ask, indignantly, bringing myself back into the room. Simon unsuccessfully turns a snort into a cough behind his hand.

'In my experience, there is usually less call for dancing,' Babs says with a bright smile and I take a deep breath.

'In my experience, as an older person, I find that everyone likes to have a dance and would appreciate the opportunity.'

'Well, of course, it's your special day, so it's your call. I just wouldn't want a lot of old people unable to sit down,' she says, un-clicking her pen with a finality that I find cheering.

'Are we done here?' I ask, standing up.

'I think so. If I have any further questions for you, I'll be in touch.'

Back in the car park I go to kiss Simon goodbye and he catches my hand.

'Where's your engagement ring, Mum? You haven't lost it have you?'

'No,' I say quickly. 'Of course not, I've been swimming today and left it at home.'

The truth is that my head was so full of Alex that I forgot to put it back on when I popped home after meeting Vic.

'Simon, I wanted to let you know that I'm going to Peterborough to be with Leo tomorrow.'

'Ah, sweet,' he says distractedly, pulling his phone back out of his pocket and reading a message. 'Diana wants me to pick up some chocolate on the way back. Is it okay that she's dropped her usual healthy diet and is eating a lot of crap?'

'I tell you what, why don't you tell your pregnant wife to eat better, see what she says.'

He looks up from his phone with wide eyes.

'I'll just get her the chocolate,' he says, quickly.

'Get her some crips too,' I suggest. 'And Diana will know what she wants and needs. A few fatty and sugary treats won't do her any harm in the long run.'

I'm suddenly reminded about the feasts that Alex and I would have. The things we'd pinch from the kitchen at the hotel, squirrel away until we could eat them together. Cakes and desserts, pies and quiches eaten with our fingers in snatched moments.

I wait for him to reply to Diana and then he tucks his phone away and pulls me into a hug.

'I'm so delighted for you,' he says. 'You're finally having your happy ever after.'

For a mad moment, I think he means Alex and I nearly choke, but I hold it together for long enough to realise that, of course, he means Leo.

'Leo is such a great guy and you'll be so content. He really wants this.'

It's only as I'm watching my son navigate the potholed lane in his car that I realise he's never asked me what I want; he's just assumed that my needs line up with Leo's. I shake off the disappointment in my son, because I love him and know that really he does want me to be happy. He just doesn't know what that would take, and perhaps I don't know either.

I climb into the van and start the engine, my thoughts now on my trip tomorrow – on the provisions in the cupboard behind me and the clean bedding rolled up right at the back. The truth is, I don't know if I'll be welcomed by Fiona, but I'm prepared to find out.

6

Fiona's café is called the *Cathedral Coffee House* aptly named for its location in Cathedral Square, Peterborough. I manage to get a parking space in Wentworth Street car park and pop a couple of hours on Ruby's dashboard. I think I'll know by then whether I'll be returning to add more time or heading home.

I'm beginning to lose my nerve as I cut between the shops and walk out into the square. I should have phoned; of course I should have phoned. Fiona might be furious at an unexpected house guest and who could blame her. I realise I wanted to put Leo on the spot, to really get to the bottom of what he expects from me and our up-and-coming marriage. Maybe driving here was not the best way to do it.

The square is bustling, unsurprisingly for a Saturday, and I pick my way through the shoppers until I find the café. The tables outside are full, and waiting staff hurry back and forth with steaming mugs of coffee, breakfasts, pastries and piles of pancakes. She's made a success of it for sure and she's in a prime location. I feel a moment of pride in the woman I've yet to meet.

The door is open and I glance around when I step through, hoping to see Leo before anyone else, but there's no sign of him. I see Fiona though, instantly recognisable, behind the counter, taking orders and chatting animatedly with the customers. Leo has lots of photos of her in his bungalow: on the mantelpiece, in sliver frames on side tables, holiday snaps stuck to his fridge. He even had a portrait of her painted and it takes pride of place on the wall above the fireplace. He adores his daughter and I honestly love him for that.

I queue up next to the counter and wait for my turn to be served. I feel ridiculously nervous and try to muster up a genuine smile for when we meet.

'Good morning,' she says, brightly. 'What can I get you?'

I find myself ordering an espresso that I don't really want and watch her as she makes it. This sunny, smiling woman is depressed and desperately missing her mother after the disappearance of her husband according to Leo. She is certainly putting a very brave face on for her customers. She turns back to offer me the cup and I fiddle in my purse for some money to pay.

'I'm actually looking for Leo,' I say, handing her a five-pound note.

'Oh, you know my dad?' she says with a smile.

'I'm Connie,' I say.

She hesitates with the note in her hand, a blank look on her face.

'I'm so sorry for turning up unannounced,' I continue. 'Incredibly rude of me, but I just wanted to…' What did I just want to do? I don't even know, now.

'Connie?' she says slowly and I can see her mind trying to work out who I am.

'Leo's Connie,' I clarify, but it sounds like ownership and I wish I hadn't used those words. She hands me back the five-pound note and turns to the woman serving next to her.

'Kath, can you hold the fort for a sec?' The woman nods and Fiona comes out from behind the counter. 'Let's have a seat; coffee is on the house,' she says to me and I follow her to a table in the corner by the window, but it's with reluctance, because it is suddenly very clear that Leo hasn't mentioned me at all.

I shove the fiver in my pocket and decide to leave my hand there so she doesn't see the engagement ring sparkling on my finger, a dead giveaway that we're more than just friends.

'You've just missed Dad. I sent him to the cash-and-carry to get some stuff. I'll be honest, he's getting underfoot a bit, bless him. He means well and wants to help, but I'm not sure him bumbling around the café is all that useful.'

There's a sachet of sugar on the side of my saucer and I open it one-handed, ripping the top with my teeth and pour a few grains into my coffee, just enough to take the bitter edge off the espresso. My mind is whirring with all that Leo has said about Fiona and now the reality of the woman before me. She is nice and friendly, not openly depressed and anxious. What was it Leo said? *You know what she's like; she just wants her old dad.* But I don't know what she's like because I've never been allowed to meet her and she hasn't made a conscious decision to reject me from their family dynamic because she clearly doesn't know who I am. I start to work the ring off my finger in my pocket, but it gets stuck on my knuckle. I think my fingers have swollen up in the heat.

'How do you know Dad?' she asks, and I find myself in easier territory.

'I met him last year at my son's barbecue. Simon has known him for ages; they used to work together at Quantum.'

'I've heard of Simon; Dad has definitely mentioned him. Connie, can I ask, are you and Dad an item?'

I contemplate lying but, really, why should I? It's not my fault Leo has kept his daughter in the dark, and why has he done that? She seems perfectly amiable. How on earth did he think we could get married without his daughter knowing?

'Yes, we are, certainly more than just friends,' I add and wait for some sort of outrage that doesn't come. 'I'm surprised he hasn't mentioned me.'

'I'm surprised too,' she says. 'He must know I'd be very happy for him, especially after his, well, you know, his terrible grief about Mum.'

'Cancer is such an awful thing and I'm so sorry for you.'

'Cancer? Is that what he told you?'

Fiona looks so troubled, I almost don't want to ask, but the truth has to be got at if we can ever move forward here.

'Not cancer then?' I ask as lightly as I can.

'Mum was hit by a drunk driver. Her head injury was catastrophic and Dad had to make the decision to turn off her life support. It was an unbearable level of grief that he suffered afterwards; he was desperately down.' She leans in closer and lowers her voice. 'He was suicidal.'

'Oh, my God, that's awful. Poor Leo, and you too. How terrible for you both.'

'It's why I'm a bit surprised to be honest.'

'That he didn't tell you about me?' I ask.

'That there even is a you. He'd always said he couldn't contemplate another relationship.'

Without thinking it through, I take my hand from my pocket and place it onto the table between us.

'He asked me to marry him,' I say. 'But now, I'm not sure if that's what he really wants.'

Fiona gasps and lifts my hand up to look closer at the ring.

'That's Mum's,' she says, a look of pure hurt on her face.

I begin to pull it from my finger as if it's going to burn me and there's an agonising few seconds where I think it won't come. With some painful twists and turns I do get it off and it sits on the table between us.

'What was he thinking?' Fiona says in a small voice.

'I'm so sorry, I had no idea,' I say, and she shakes her head.

'It's not your fault. How could you have known?' She looks at me then, properly looks at me. 'It's because you look a bit like her, I think.'

I cast my mind back to the photo I saw of Brenda, but can't really remember any similarities.

'I mean, if you had a haircut, you'd look very much like my mum.'

I feel a bit sick. The espresso sits nastily in my stomach with every chance I might be seeing it again.

'I think it's best if I go,' I say, suddenly very keen to vacate the café before Leo returns.

'Maybe it would be best to wait for Dad and talk to him. I'm not angry about him seeing you, or even about him proposing, really. I'm just a bit upset about the ring.'

'Understandably,' I say. 'And you've got your own upset to deal with too. I'm sorry to hear about your marriage. You must be devastated.'

'It's been a long time coming to be honest. Things haven't been right for a while.'

Rock solid, Leo had said.

'Paul wanted to have children and I didn't. He thought I'd change my mind, but I was never going to.'

'Your dad told me that *you* wanted children,' I say without thinking. It's really none of my business.

'Did he?' She looks surprised. 'Not true at all. *Dad* always wanted me to have kids; he likes the idea of being a grandad. It's just not for me and, anyway, I'm so busy with this place.'

'Leo said you were devastated about the break-up. I think he may have been over-egging the situation, because it looks like you have everything under control,' I say.

'You know what he's like; a worrywart, bit possessive of me, especially after Mum. He likes to be needed. Don't get me wrong, Connie, I am upset about the failure of my marriage, but it was inevitable and I'm very philosophical about it all.'

'It seems I don't know what he's like. He's been spinning me quite the yarn,' I say, feeling like I've had a cold slap across the face. I'm starting to wonder about Leo's motivations. I look like his dead wife; my son is having a baby and Leo desperately wants to be a grandfather. I start doing the maths. Simon and Diana may have only just told me about the pregnancy, but they have known for... I work back through the weeks. Simon and Leo are close and there's every chance my son could have told him back at Easter when he first found out. It was when the proposal happened. Surely, Leo isn't capable of such deceit. But Fiona said he was desperately depressed, suicidal, he could be capable of anything. I feel so sad for him, but also confused and honestly a bit stupid too.

I stand up and pull my bag onto my shoulder. Fiona stands too and slips Brenda's ring into her pocket.

'I suppose I should keep this?' she says, unsure.

'Of course you should,' I say. 'It really belongs to you.'

I take her hand across the table.

'Thank you for your honesty, and I'm sorry to have upset you. Of course, you know it was unintentional. I won't wait for Leo, but I will speak to him later, on the phone, when I've had a chance to digest everything.'

We walk to the door together and she pulls me in for a hug.

'I feel so sad now, because I think you'd actually be good for Dad. Please do talk to him and maybe you could find a way to get him to open up. Don't give up on him, Connie.'

I walk back through the square in a bit of a daze. I came here wanting to get to the heart of what Leo is thinking and what his intentions are. I don't think I would have guessed at how dark his thoughts were bent and how much pain he was hiding from me, though.

I get back to the car park and see that it's only taken forty-five minutes to turn my world upside down. Ruby is waiting where I've parked her in the shade and I climb inside, glad I closed the curtains, and take a bottle of water from the little fridge behind the driver's seat. I swallow it down in five large gulps and lean back in my seat, closing my eyes for a moment.

My mind is whirring again because I suddenly feel untethered. I angle the rear-view mirror down so I can see my reflection and I look a bit wired, perhaps from the espresso.

I pull my reading glasses down from where they're perched on the top of my head and take my phone from my bag and open Maps. There's Me, the blue flashing dot in a Peterborough car park and then I pan out to take in the whole of the UK. I haven't been on the road for a while. I thought I'd lost my nerve for long distances, but have I really? I was fine jumping in the van to come here without any problem. Didn't I feel a bit of a thrill when I joined the motorway? Since meeting Leo, I'd talked myself into putting Ruby to bed because he didn't really like travelling. But I do like it, actually, I think, as my eyes trace the network of roads on the map; I love it.

Without consciously thinking about it, I type Inverness into the search bar, but am I really going there? Surely I'm not driving away from my fiancé to pursue Alex in Scotland.

My fiancé – I glance at my finger, now bare of that beautiful emerald ring that belonged on the hand of his dead wife. *If you had a haircut, you'd look just like my mum.*

I shiver and click for directions. It's an eight-and-a-half-hour journey, so, ten in this van. I zoom in to check the route back to the main road out of the city centre, then turn the key and begin to drive out of the car park heading for the nearest petrol station to fill up.

I dither when I see the sign for the A1. I'm in the middle lane and need to choose. The sensible thing would be to go home, talk to Vic over a bottle of wine, give myself a hangover and feel sorry for myself for a couple of days. Of course, I need to talk to Leo, but I feel hurt that he hadn't confided in me about how he really felt losing Brenda. Then again, I'm just as guilty of that. I've spent most of my life brushing important situations under the carpet, not talking to my nearest and dearest, going through the motions of happiness without really feeling it.

I need to indicate left and I could easily slip in behind the lorry on the inside lane. I could be heading south with just a quick turn of the steering wheel. The thing is though, it's not just Leo who's been secretive and indecisive, because I've been having strange dreams about places and people imbedded in my past and that was before I saw the article for the exhibition. I'm not sure why I'm dithering, because I already know what I'm going to do. I indicate right, pull across the traffic and join the A1 heading north.

7

To begin with my driving is tentative. At every junction I feel the urge to turn around and head back home, but I keep going regardless, telling myself I'll just get a bit further and then decide. I don't feel the urge to go back to Peterborough though. That needs some space and time.

As the van eats up the miles, and the countryside opens up around me, I begin to relax. I allow myself to think about my destination for the first time since I stared into the depths of Loch Ness hanging on the wall in my living room. The last time I was in Inverness I was eighteen. I try to conjure an image of myself, the young woman I was, a child really, if I'm honest: Constance Fitzgerald. Unhappy and also terrified. But, that was before I met Alex. The person I became after was immeasurably different.

There's a blast from a car horn as a Volvo estate roars past me. I seem to have drifted across the carriageway and I'm straddling two lanes. Pulling the wheel sharply to the left, I move firmly into the slow lane and pick up one of the cans of energy drink I bought at the petrol station from the passenger seat. I also bought a sticky bun, which was probably a mistake. I open the lid and drink the viscous liquid down in one go. Vile stuff, but hopefully effective in keeping my mind focused on the road. It's been a while since I've driven so far and it will be good if I can get there in one piece.

By one-thirty, I've been driving for three hours and have consumed both energy drinks and the cake, fragments of which still cling to the steering wheel. My right foot seems to be welded to the accelerator and a nervous twitch is beginning in my left eye. I'm on the outskirts of Durham and decide to pull off the motorway and find somewhere to take a break. I drive into a multi-storey car park and finally remove my feet from the pedals. After turning off the engine I stretch out my arms to ease the stiffness. I'll allow myself a couple of hours before I get back on the road again.

I've missed this, just turning up wherever I feel like, no one really knowing where I am. I cut through a walkway of shops and come out onto a market square, surrounded by the most beautiful stone buildings. There's an information board next to a monument and I take a second to orientate myself. I've never been to Durham before, but I was supposed to go to uni here. I'd been offered a place to study law, but, of course, that didn't happen. All plans were turned on their head that summer.

I walk down the street past more shops and cafés making a note of where I can come back to eat in a while. But, for now I just want to sit down by the river for a bit and recharge my energy for the onward journey.

I find a bench on the banks of the River Wear and sit, gazing up at the cathedral, huge towers appearing from out of the trees. Alex had a cousin who lived in Durham, I remember. I wonder if that was the real reason it was calling to me from the motorway. It was one of the places that we said we would go, back then, when we had made our minds up to leave

Scotland, get on the road and disappear together, to get as far away as possible from all those judging eyes.

I pull the magazine from my bag to look at the article again, to see Alex's name written down, to make sure it's real and not just a weird dream. I stare at the picture of the painting while the river babbles away in front of me and it suddenly occurs to me that I should have brought my own painting: *Sunrise* and *Sunset over Loch Ness*. They should be hung together at the exhibition, but I can't go back for it now; it would take too long and besides, if I made it back home, I might change my mind, lose my nerve and stay in the safety of my Brighton flat.

I find a café with outside seating back up on the cobbled street. I go inside to order a sandwich and a cup of tea and then take a seat back outside, the sun beginning to burn the back of my neck. I pull the collar of my blouse up to cover it and then brave my mobile phone, buried deep in my handbag. Nothing from Leo yet, which is, perhaps, a good thing. I wonder what he thought when he got back to the café and found out I'd been there. Is the fact that the ring is back in his possession enough for him to think it's over? Is it over? Nothing can be properly decided until we have a much-needed conversation. I should have waited for him, given him the chance to explain, but instead I've done classic Connie; running away, leaving issues unresolved. I tell myself I need a bit of time to think, to process, but really I'm just putting off a difficult conversation. The truth is, I don't know what I want.

I contemplate sending Simon a message to let him know what I'm doing but decide against that as well. Instead I google campsites in Inverness as it occurs to me that I need somewhere to park myself and Ruby safely tonight – gone are the days of sleeping in lay-bys on my own. I find one near the leisure centre just a short stroll from the botanic gardens and the River Ness. I phone them and find out they have availability for a couple of nights. After a moment's hesitation, where I decide how committed I am to this mad plan, I give the man my credit card details, agree a late arrival and book myself in.

The chicken and avocado sandwich is delicious, the Earl Grey tea welcome, and I relax, enjoy the heat from the sun, the shade cast from the umbrella and the anonymity of being alone in a city far from home. I watch the passers-by: parents with a tight hold on their children's hands, couples with just as tight a hold on each other. I feel so removed from these people, as if I don't really belong to anyone, and that, I suddenly realise, is the most liberating feeling of all.

Eventually, I pay the bill and get up to leave. Walking back towards the car park, I notice a shop selling wool with the most beautiful baby's blanket displayed in the window. I push open the door and step inside. I haven't knitted or crocheted for years, but I have a sudden urge to make something for my grandchild. Inspired by the colour of the river, I choose a pale blue ball of wool that has soft green flecks in the strands. I buy a crochet hook because I remember finding it easier than knitting. When I get back to the van, I start a foundation chain and then crochet a few rows using a simple stitch I remember.

'This is for you, little one,' I say, stretching out the rows, admiring my progress so far. 'A woollen postcard, with love from Durham.'

I pass the border into Scotland at about five-thirty and it's an emotional experience. I wipe ridiculous tears with the back of my hand, but I don't stop the van. I keep ploughing up the A1, keen to take the North Berwick coast road while my van is still happy to do so. I have always kept my faithful old camper in top condition for the ten years I've had her. Before that, I had a more modern van, but the charm of this original VW was too much of a draw. Simon had told me it would be a mistake and I'd have to be towed out of every campsite. And, to be fair, I did have to be towed out of a few, but with careful driving and a couple of solicitous garages, I've kept her going.

I wind down the window and slow down as the fields flatten out and the North Sea stretches out in front of me. It's been too long since I've been on the road like this. A sharp stab of realisation hits me when I think about Leo and his lack of enthusiasm for travel. Not even just travel – he's never keen to spend more than a night or two in a strange bed. The only reason he's okay at his daughter's is because he's probably taken his pillow with him. I can barely get him in the van for a lift – he certainly wouldn't entertain sleeping in it.

I pull into a parking bay and get out. The wind is wild and I let my hair free from its clip, where it whips around my face as I drink in the sea air. Bright white gannets swoop overhead, looking for prey with their beady eyes, and I imagine myself swooping with them.

This is what it's all about, I think – being free.

I manage to limp as far as Perth before I stop again for fuel and use of the toilet. I've skirted the north of Edinburgh and navigated the Forth Bridge, but the sign for Perth was welcome. It's a long time since I've driven this far, and I still have a fair couple of hours to go. The knowledge that I'll be skirting the Cairngorms National Park is enough to push me onwards.

I arrive in Inverness at nine-thirty and head straight for the campsite.

I climb out and stretch my cramped limbs, Ruby seeming to sigh behind me.

'Well done, old girl,' I say, patting the bonnet. 'We've made it.'

The reception building is little more than a wooden hut and just as the man on the phone had promised me, there's an envelope stuck to the window with my name written on it. Inside is a map of the site and an arrow in pen showing me where my spot is. I glance through the window of the building and see they sell provisions when the shop is open during the day. There are bottles of wine lined up, just out of my reach and I sigh at my lack of foresight. Why I didn't think to pick one up when I stopped earlier I don't know. I shall have to content myself with a cup of tea and a bottle of water. And really, I might well be meeting someone I haven't seen for many years tomorrow. Already tired after my journey, I don't want to make myself look worse than I already do. I don't want to appear in front of Alex looking like a desiccated old woman.

I get back in and navigate the site to find my pitch, then park up and draw Ruby's curtains closed. I push up the pop top of the van so I have head space and smile at the new canvas I had fitted with its raspberry coloured roses. Not cheap, but worth every penny, I think. I decide to bypass both water and tea and instead I pull out my sleeping bag, lower the back bench seat into a bed, and climb on top.

I'm asleep in moments.

8

I fill the kettle from the water bottle, which I keep replenished and in the cupboard in the back of the van, and then light a flame under it. I rub the sleep from my eyes and try to shake off the vivid dream I was having just before I woke. These dreams are becoming a habit. I pull the cafetière from its box and pile in the ground coffee. Once I've poured in the water, I slide my feet into some sandals and pop a baseball cap on my head, then set off across the parched grass towards the toilet block.

Another hot cloudless day, the sun already doing its best or worst, depending on how you looked at it. I loved the heat when I was younger; I adored stretching out on a beach towel to catch some sun on my skin, always pleased with the golden glow I managed to achieve. Now though, as an older woman, I'm careful to wear a hat, cover my shoulders, no longer interested in how far I can toast my skin, but worried about the damaging effects of the sun, however much too late that may be.

The toilet block is not all that clean and I walk past three doors before I choose the least offensive cubicle. Still, I hover above the seat as I relieve myself, and use my own toilet paper that I've stashed in my pocket. I don't linger as I wash my hands, do no more than glance towards the mirror. I have no wish to see the missing fifty-two years on my face or begin to imagine what Alex will think of my appearance. I don't want to acknowledge that while I would always say that the least important thing about myself is what I look like, today, that might be further up my list of priorities. I think I'll apply some make-up later and think about what's best to do with my hair.

Back in the van I drink the coffee and consider what I might do today. I have eleven hours to amuse myself until the exhibition opens and a boat trip on Loch Ness seems a perfect way to kill a few, to occupy my mind. Maybe lunch afterwards. I turn my phone on to book something and prepare myself for missed calls and messages. There is just one, from Leo.

Connie, I'm so sorry. Please call me when you feel you can. I'd like to talk, to explain. This isn't the end of us. We can get back on track. Lots love, Leo

I stare at the message for a moment, letting the words sink in. We can get back on track, he's written, but can we? I hold the phone against my chest while I digest his words. I do understand how he feels, of course I do. He's trying to carve out a new life for himself while still grieving the life he had before. I can relate easily to that. I'm not angry with him; I just feel a bit sad.

I look up boat trips and restaurants and manage to get booked in, then I'm about to switch my phone off again when it pings and I'm expecting another message from Leo, but actually it's from Vic.

> Hope you're okay? Did Fiona allow you over the threshold
> of her café? Vic x

It occurs to me that nobody knows where I am and that
perhaps someone should, just in case, so I tap a quick message
back.

> I decided to go to the exhibition after all. I'm in Inverness!
> Only you know though, so can we keep it that way for now?
> Connie xx

I wait a few agonising minutes for a response and then it
explodes onto my screen.

> Bloody hell, Connie! Do you know what you're doing?
> Please be careful and don't get hurt. I hope he's worth it.
> Vic x

That makes me smile, of course, and then I reply:

> It's not like that. I just need to put old ghosts to rest. I'll be
> in touch. Cx

I switch the phone back off again and sit down on the
open doorway of the van, my hands under my chin, elbows
on knees. I think about Leo having to make that awful but
necessary decision to have his wife's life support removed and
a sob breaks free from my throat.

'Oh, God, Leo, life can be so cruel.'

For just a moment I feel as if I should be comforting him,

not running away, but then the memory of Fiona's face when she saw the ring, the fact he hadn't told her about me and my resemblance to Brenda pushes to the forefront of my mind. This is not simple, not clear or an easy fix. Fundamentally, though, if I'm going back to talk to him, to decide if we can work together, to make a life with him, he deserves all of me, not this regretful woman who hasn't let go of her past. Either way, I have a job to do here; that is clear.

It crosses my mind that I haven't decided what I'm going to wear tonight, so I pull out a few options from my bag and lay them across the back of the driver's seat. I've brought the cream cheesecloth dress I wore to my birthday dinner, but would it be ridiculous to turn up in something I wore the summer I met Alex? Or would it be a lovely thing for us to reminisce over? Maybe I should smarten up a bit; it could be quite a stylish occasion. Linton Hall does sound quite posh and didn't the article use the word *prestigious*? I rummage through the remainder of my clothes. The navy trousers are a possibility, perhaps with the one jacket I packed, but it's a rich shade of maroon and I don't want to look like an entertainer on a holiday park. It might have to be jeans with a blouse, but then I don't fancy sweating all evening; this heatwave is set to continue.

'Oh, for goodness' sake, will anyone care what I'm wearing? No, of course they won't,' I say, and elicit a response from someone outside the van.

'They might do, depends on the occasion.' A man's voice comes in through the open door and I poke my head out to see who's there. He's in his fifties, I guess, with shorts and flip-flops on and absolutely nothing else. He carries a towel over one hairy arm and a wash bag dangles from the other.

'It's an art exhibition,' I say, amused.

'Right then, you need something bohemian, unconventional. Basically, what you're wearing, but throw a scarf around your neck,' he says and then turns away towards the shower block. 'Have a nice time,' he says over his shoulder.

I am too surprised to answer and by the time I've gathered my wits, he's gone, off for his morning ablutions, although, that is as far as my thoughts will allow me to go. I glance down at my pale pink skirt skimming my ankles and the linen mix tunic top. Perhaps he's right.

The boat moves across the water at a fair pace. I've chosen a seat on the top deck, in the open, but the sun is burning down on me again like it did all those years ago. An unexpected lump arrives in my throat as my eyes wander over the gold ripples of water and across to the banks of the loch, up into the Scots pines. It's so odd to be back here on a boat on the loch. Of course this boat is much bigger than the one we used to chug up and down the water, finding secret places to moor and explore. We slept on the boat one night, the stars a blanket above us, the lapping of the water an encouragement to sleep, once the whispering had stopped.

'Do you mind if I sit here?' a woman asks, appearing in front of me and momentarily blocking the sun from my eyes.

'Not at all,' I reply. She's a welcome distraction from my thoughts.

The woman seems about the same age as me, little wisps of her grey hair escaping from under her large straw hat, heavy make-up sitting shiny in the lines around her eyes. I wonder why anyone would bother with make-up on such a hot day;

surely what doesn't get trapped by the wrinkles would just slide off your face in a sweaty mess. I reconsider making up my own face for tonight. She slips into the seat beside me, manoeuvring her bag between her legs.

'I thought it would be cooler out of the sun downstairs, but it's stifling inside. At least there's a breeze coming off the water up here. Is it your first time in Scotland, doll?' The woman has a Scottish accent, the voice of a storyteller, soft and melodic.

'Second time actually. First time was fifty-two years ago,' I say.

'What on earth did we do to frighten you away for that long then?'

'Nothing,' I say quickly, but the woman just laughs.

'Are you from Inverness?' I ask her. 'My aunt used to own a hotel over there.' I point in the general direction of the Lochside Hotel, but actually, that might be it, nestled in the trees. I can see the line of the roof and what looks like the tower, but it looks bigger than it used to. The woman is shaking her head.

'Right enough, it's the first time we've come to Inverness. Me and my husband Jim – he's downstairs with a pint – we live just south of Edinburgh, on a wee holiday.'

'I came here for the summer of 1970, when I was eighteen. I fell in love,' I blurt out.

'How wonderful,' she says. 'I fell in love with Jim in 1973 at the Edinburgh Reggae Festival. He spilt his pint over me when the Cimarons started playing. I was a bit stoned to be fair, but the care he took in cleaning me up was sweet. Nearly fifty years and three bairns later and nothing much has changed.' She looks wistful for a moment, then glances towards the stairs that lead down to the bar, to Jim, and her look hardens. 'Well, actually he doesn't clean up anymore – that's for sure. So, are you still with your chap?'

'No,' I say, quickly. 'I made a huge mistake that summer, a terrible decision that I've had to live with all these years.' I glance across at her and her face is warm as if inviting me to say more. And, isn't that why I'm here, after all? 'The thing is,' I begin, but the commentary has started up again because we've reached Urquhart Castle and the woman has looked away, towards the ruins.

'Ooh,' she says, jumping up. 'Let me just go and take some photos.'

The captain takes the boat in a wide arc and around into the bay where the castle sits. A photo opportunity that most people up on this top deck take advantage of. The woman joins them, snapping away on her mobile phone. I stand and walk down the steps to the back of the boat where's it's quiet and shaded. I take my phone out of my pocket with no intention of taking images of the ruins. I decide that this will be the last time I turn it on today, just check for messages and then off again until tomorrow. That way I can concentrate on what I need to do, although it occurs to me that I have no idea what I'm doing.

I've missed a call from Simon and he's left a voice message telling me how sorry Leo is, and that I need to give him some space to sort out his feelings, but not too much space because I don't want to lose him. I feel a bit sad about this message too. It's Simon who doesn't want to lose him really. I sigh, my finger hovering over the screen. I don't need to go to the exhibition; I could get back in the van and be home by the end of the day. I could talk to Leo, resolve our issues and get the wedding back on track. But, I know I won't. Nothing will get back on track until I resolve my issue, and my issue is, and always has been, Alex Mackenzie.

I switch off my phone and slip it into my handbag. We're heading back now and I stay down at the rear of the boat, not wishing to carry on that conversation. The moment has passed.

The boat is moving into the jetty next to the restaurant and I stand up, keen to get off now. The woman appears with her husband, Jim, who staggers around like he's had much more than the one pint. She's waving at me, and I have an awful feeling she's going to suggest we have lunch together. I raise my hand in response, a dismissive gesture, and then make my way to the stepping-off point. I walk down onto the landing and as quickly as I can up the slope and into the tunnel that cuts under the road. I'm up the steps and into the restaurant in no time and I find a tucked-away table with no view of the loch. I'm not bothered, I just want to eat quickly and quietly, then leave. I order salmon and new potatoes with salad then pull out the baby blanket and wait for my meal to arrive. The blue wool I bought in Durham will not make a full blanket and I decide to buy some more while I'm here in Scotland. Perhaps the colour of the sky or the green of Scots pines. It can be a travelling blanket, I decide: a postcard to my grandchild.

9

Alex's exhibition is being held in a private house just off the A82 heading out of Inverness, and I check the address again before I pull off the main road, away from the loch and up the driveway. I find a corner to tuck the van into, away from the main house and closer to a row of garages. As much as I love Ruby, she does not sit right in this environment.

The house isn't really a house, it's a property. A huge, lavish, probably listed property with stables and a large stone outbuilding, perhaps a studio. Alex obviously has friends in high places. I swallow down a lump of trepidation. This certainly isn't an intimate art gallery.

I lock the van and push the keys into my handbag, which hangs awkwardly from my shoulder. Everything about me now feels awkward.

Others are getting out of their cars and moving towards the main house and I hover, plucking up the courage to do the same. It's only when a small group gather at the entrance that I move forward and join the back, trying to appear part of them as they chatter about the exhibition and how wonderful it is to be here, how Alex seemed to have dropped off of everyone's radar and disappeared, but has now somehow reappeared.

'I wonder why Mackenzie decided to exhibit now, after all this time,' says a young woman with a pretty blue scarf artfully swathed around her neck and shoulders. I smile to myself, remembering the man at the campsite and his unsolicited fashion advice this morning. 'I suppose it's usually about money.'

'I very much doubt it. The artwork has always been sold under a veil, I've heard, not that I could afford anything of course. My son's boss commissioned a piece apparently, and it was thousands,' says one of the men wearing brown cords and a Fair Isle sleeveless sweater over a T-shirt. I glance down at my long skirt, wondering if I've made the right decision, but it's too late now; it will have to do.

I take in the information as we move forwards into the house. The thought of Alex being so revered and me never having bothered to try and reconnect... Then again, during the time when I would have wanted to, there hadn't been the means. In later years when information was only a click away, I'd been too scared to do it. Choices had been made, and they had to be stuck by. Which begs the question: why am I here now?

We shuffle along as a group, and the others don't seem to mind that I have tagged on to their party, the man even offers me a smile as we take a brochure each from a table positioned in the main entrance hall.

The room is vast with a grand piano right at the centre. Family portraits hang from the heavily wallpapered walls and tell of an estate that goes back some way in history. Fresh floral displays in vast vases sit on the tables showcased by three windows with views out over the grounds. There is nothing here that says Alex Mackenzie to me, but I have to remember, I don't know my old friend anymore.

I move away from the group as I experience a moment of something that could be fear or excitement. The two are so closely linked it's often hard to pick them apart. Beyond the doors in front of me is Alex, or certainly a record of Alex's life in paint. I take a calming breath and push the door open.

I'm met with a brightly lit room, no dark corners to hide in, despite my overwhelming urge to find one. The room has been stripped of anything resembling the decor of the entrance hall and has been transformed into an exhibition space. The area is cavernous and looks up to the galleried landing above. White screens have been placed along the lengths of the walls with Alex's paintings hanging perfectly. Of course they're Alex's – I would know them anywhere, that distinctive style.

I quickly scan the area, ignoring the artwork at first, in favour of the people. My eyes roam over the heads of everyone here, but not one face is familiar. Of course, it's quite possible that Alex only attended the opening or the private viewing. Maybe artists don't hang around for the last night. There's a crushing feeling in my chest, quickly followed by a huge sense of relief. There will be no grand meeting and I can just relax, enjoy the artwork, leave here with my pride intact and pretend this was just a silly idea all along. A waiter walks up to me with a tray loaded with glasses of champagne, so I take one and compose myself.

Beginning with some portraits, I immerse myself in the art, allow myself to remember watching the artist at work. How close I feel suddenly to Alex after all this time.

There are cards pinned to the wall next to each painting. Sometimes it's made clear who it is with their name, but others just say sitter #12 or sitter #13. Firstly I notice that every single painting has a red dot next to it, declaring it sold, and then I see sitter #1 and my breath leaves my body for a moment. Sitter one is me.

I am eighteen again with pink cheeks and bright eyes. My blonde hair falls in waves around my shoulders and my head is turned ever so slightly away as if I'm about to leave. Alex never had a photograph of me; this has been painted by memory. I raise my hand to touch the canvas, to trace my fingertips over the brush marks, but manage to stop myself in time. It's probably not the done thing.

There is no red sold sticker, I notice, and I very much want to buy it. I'm mesmerised, but eventually I pull myself away, determined to find the landscapes. For just a moment, I feel as if I'm being watched and I turn around, but everyone here is absorbed in the artwork. No one is looking at me.

Taking my glass I walk through to the next room: the library. I can see some of the books hiding behind the screens and peeping through the gaps. Here I find scenes of Scotland: lochs and rivers, mountains and forests, bleak landscapes and bright, sunlit glades. There isn't a building in sight; it is nature all the way.

As I make my way amid the maze of paintings I see it at last. The companion painting hanging alone on a large screen with a glaring space beside it. It looks odd on its own and the way it's been displayed makes it obvious that there's something missing. I take a couple of steps closer and then I notice the small plaque pinned next to it, declaring that it's not for sale. For the first time a chill runs through me and I try to take myself back to the time when I left with the painting. I didn't steal it; Alex as good as told me to take it, that it was for me, but still, all these years later the details are hazy, and why did Alex never sell this one? I open the brochure for the first time to look at the price list and gulp when I see the figures. There isn't a painting in here for less than three thousand pounds and this one in front of me is superior to all the others. I feel a presence behind me and I'm convinced someone is watching me now. I sidestep out of their way and then I glance back.

There's a woman wearing a black silk dress with gold trim on a plunging neckline. She has glorious golden, red hair, hanging in soft curls around her face. Her piercing blue eyes, not dulled with time, bore into my own. My legs feel like they may buckle.

Alexandra Mackenzie. Alex.

We stare at each other, my heart pounding so hard, she surely must be able to hear it.

'Lady Constance, what brings you here?' Alex says, without a flicker of emotion on her face. I open my mouth to speak, but nothing comes out. All thoughts of words vanish at the sight of my old friend. How beautiful she still is, how much I would have known her anywhere. All the years I have travelled and the cities and towns I've visited, always looking out for a glimpse of the woman I knew. I'd often thought that maybe she might have walked past me but I'd not recognised her, forgotten what she looked like, but now it is clear that in all that time of looking, I never once saw her.

'Alex,' I breathe, because that is all I can say, and still she stares unflinching. I force myself to speak. 'How lovely to see you,' I say, all mock smiles and fake cheerfulness, ridiculously over the top. Alex's eyes narrow and her lips remain in their thin, tight line.

'Where's my painting?' she says, and I shrink under her stare.

'I still have it,' I gabble. 'It's on the wall in my Brighton flat. I still love it,' I add and instantly wish I hadn't. Alex looks past me to the empty space on the wall. 'I should have thought to bring it with me; they always did look so good together.'

Her lips soften slightly at my words, but nothing close to a smile, and I plough on, hopeful. 'How are you? What have you been up to?' I ask, and her lips thin once more.

'What have I been up to? Do you mean for the last fifty-two years? I think it's probably more important to hear what you've been up to, don't you?'

I don't mean to and later I'll blame the glass of champagne I've consumed, but Alex's face is so severe that I snort out a bark of laughter. It does go some way to breaking the deadlock, because she looks surprised and for a moment it's as if the years have rolled back.

'Alex, your exhibition is wonderful and you look so well. You haven't changed a bit,' I gabble again, desperately trying to win my friend round, to see that smile I've missed so much, but she remains unmoved.

'You don't look the same,' she says. 'You look old.'

I laugh again and Alex's lips twitch. 'It was *our* seventieth birthday last week, remember? I am old – exactly as old as you.'

I managed to get invited to Alex's eighteenth birthday party, but only I knew it was my birthday too. Her friend had set it up in a secluded spot on the banks of the loch. There was music, a fire and a fair amount of booze. Alex and I weren't close at that point, but I was hanging off her every word, desperate for her to look in my direction. I would spend an embarrassing amount of time having imagined conversations with her in my head while I cleaned the rooms at the hotel. I'd come up with witty statements and clever jokes, but in reality, whenever I was face to face with her, I would hold back and keep my mouth shut, terrified of saying the wrong thing. The night of that party, though, everything changed.

A man approaches from the side now, dressed in grey wool trousers and a crisp white shirt. His silver hair is slicked back and flicks up on his collar. He's holding two glasses of champagne.

'Lex, darling,' he says, handing a glass to her. 'The Hislops want to see you. I think they're on the brink of buying something. Come and give them a nudge.' Alex takes the glass from him and knocks half of it back. 'Oh, I'm so sorry,' he continues, turning his attention to me. 'Please do introduce me.' He doesn't have the lilting Scottish voice that Alex has, but a surprising New York accent. Instead of rolling his Rs he's dropping them. I turn to Alex, waiting for an introduction that never comes.

'There's no need, Hank; she's no one,' she says, and with an expression that cuts to the bone, she walks away leaving me open-mouthed in her wake.

I rinse cold water on my wrists in the bathroom, swallowing down the sob that wants to erupt. What did I really expect? That Alex would run into my arms and declare that she'd spent the last fifty-two years missing me every single day? Yes, that's exactly what I'd been expecting because I'm a fool, an old fool. I dry my hands and reach into my bag for my hairbrush and lipstick, then – feeling ready to face the room again – I take a grounding breath and walk back out. I can't see Alex and that's fine because I don't want to see her. I skim the edges of the room, back round to the portraits and to the one of me. I glance again in the brochure at the price, think about my small savings account that holds only just over double that amount in it. But my need for that painting is acute. I can't explain why that should be; I just want it. I want badly to take something away from here. I move over to the desk in the entrance hall where the business side of things is occurring.

'I'd like to buy this,' I tell the woman at the desk, pointing to myself in the brochure. There isn't a flicker of recognition, but why should there be – I've changed.

'Great choice, such a beautiful face,' she says and then looks a bit closer at me. 'Could almost be you a few years ago.'

I smile. 'That's what I thought too,' I agree. 'Lady Constance Fitzgerald,' I say when the woman asks for my details, and she pauses with her pen on the page.

'Oh, aye, a lady no less.'

'So it would seem.'

Leaving the rest of my details, I walk out of the building a few thousand pounds lighter, but with a heaviness to my heart that is hard to quantify.

IO

The van is packed up and everything secure. I drive out of the space and stop at the reception hut to let them know I'm leaving early. Then I continue out of the site and up the lane until I find myself on the road to the Lochside Hotel. I just want to have a quick look before I leave.

My aunt, long dead now, obviously won't be there, and I have no idea who owns it, but I have such a yearning to visit one last time before I head back down south, to talk to Leo, to make some decisions about us, and start building a relationship with my daughter-in-law ready for when my grandchild comes. Because that is what I should be doing, not chasing this half-baked dream. Perhaps a box needed ticking and I've ticked it now. I didn't think I'd ever see Alex again and I have. Tick! I won't pretend I don't feel the humiliation and rejection though; that will accompany me all the way home.

I wind the window down as the air con seems to have packed up on me. I'm not surprised, I had it fitted by a hooky friend of Vic's and it's never run right. I lean my elbow on the opening, the burn of the sun instant.

The driveway still winds up to the hotel just as it always did and for a moment I'm back in 1970 in William's gardener's truck, driving up it for the first time, during that summer that changed my entire life.

He'd turned up at the station to pick me up and I'd liked him immediately – his gentle ribbing about my posh London accent and my stiff appearance. He'd been the friend I'd needed for those first painful days at the hotel, when it was made clear I wasn't going to be a guest, but was there to work. It turned out my aunt wasn't the kindly woman who appeared in the photograph my mother had of her. She was hard and cold, very much my mother's sister. And then there'd been Alexandra, Alex, Lex now perhaps, working on reception; the most beautiful girl I'd ever seen with her porcelain skin and flame-red hair, her cheekbones cut high, like those of a catwalk model. I longed for her to notice me, to befriend me, to offer me that smile I'd seen her give to others.

The hotel itself has grown in size considerably. Extended in every direction and now under the banner of a well-known chain, but still with the charm that it always had. I pull into a parking space away from the front of the hotel, then I get out and make my way to the front door. The woman on reception has her back to me, but her hair is red and falling around her shoulders and my stomach turns over as if I'm on a ride at a funfair. But she's not Alex, of course she's not.

'Good morning and welcome to the Lochside Hotel. How may I be of assistance?' She has an Australian accent and I calm myself, smile and step forward.

'Hello, I used to work here many years ago and thought I'd pop my head in while I was passing. Is it okay if I have a look around, maybe have some breakfast if the restaurant is open?'

'Of course,' she says handing me a menu and suggesting

I might like to sit on their terrace in the sun. She is professional, polite, efficient and I want to laugh as I remember how Alex was on reception. Her attitude was that guests were an inconvenience, that she'd always much rather be painting. If she hadn't been so beautiful I doubt my aunt would have put her in front of house.

I walk outside into the garden and find a table with a parasol. There's a huge decked area that wasn't there all those years ago. Aunt Agnes wouldn't have considered anything as continental as al fresco dining, and to be fair to her, the weather wasn't usually compliant. The summer I spent at the hotel had been unexpectedly warm, though. I remember everyone remarking on how unusual it was. Perhaps climate change has had an effect, but I do notice the covered patio heaters tucked down at the side of the decking.

The hedges are as beautifully clipped as they ever were and the borders are stocked with all manner of colourful delights. I think about William, wonder if he's still in Scotland, if he's still alive. I close my eyes for a moment and remember him with a spade or a rake, how he'd sometimes take his shirt off to weed around the back of the hotel where he thought no one could see him, his broad bare shoulders enjoying the rays of the sun. *I* could see him. I remember very clearly with my nose pressed against the glass for a good view. What a conflicting summer that was. He was only a couple of years older than me and Alex, so he could well be both here, and alive.

When the waiter comes I choose Lorne sausage, tattie scones, haggis and black pudding in what the hotel calls its ultimate Scottish fry-up, then I take my phone out to search for William Boyce in Inverness. I've missed a call and there's a voice message.

'*Hello, this is a message for Lady Constance Fitzgerald. I'm so sorry to have to tell you that a mistake has been made and the painting you were interested in is not for sale. No money has been taken at this stage. Our mistake entirely and I'm so sorry for any inconvenience. Good day to you.*'

I delete the message with a shake of my head. Alexandra Mackenzie, really sticking the boot in.

Funnily enough I find William in three easy clicks and cannot believe my luck. He owns a farm out near the airport. A family business the website tells me. Pig farmers, now turned to arable. As soon as I've devoured my breakfast and paid, I'm in the van and on my way. Surely one friend from my past will be pleased to see me.

I knock on the door of the farmhouse, wondering what on earth I'm going to say to whoever answers it. Coming back here to Scotland has not proved fruitful so far, and William probably won't even remember me after all this time. I prepare myself for another embarrassing encounter.

It's a man who answers, a William of about thirty, which throws me for a minute. He has the same dark eyes, but is a little shorter than the twenty-year-old man I remember and I assume he must be his son. He runs a hand through his wet hair.

'Hello?' he says. 'What can I do you for?'

His voice is just like his dad's and I can't help the smile spreading across my face.

'Hello,' I say brightly. 'I was looking for Will, William I mean. Your dad? Have I got the right place? Is he here at all? My name is Connie Fitzgerald.'

He opens his mouth to speak, but stops before any words come out when something seems to catch his eye over my shoulder.

'Lady Constance!' A voice booms behind me on the front path, and I spin round to see a tower of a man with a thick white and ginger beard and wild curls trying to escape the hat he has pushed down onto them. 'What on earth are you doing here?' He steps forward and pulls me into a tight hug, as if this is a usual occurrence for us. I sigh.

'Please don't call me that.'

Morag, William's wife, pours us glasses of lemonade loaded with ice as we take seats outside on the sunken patio. The sun is still rising overhead, but the trellis that surrounds us, covered in trailing and climbing flowers and foliage, offers some shade. Morag is a tiny woman with cropped silver hair, a warm expression and a comfortable smile. Despite her slight frame, she looks strong. Her arms are defined in a way that mine are not. Yoga has helped me to keep fairly fit over the years, but Morag has spent her life working outside. Her skin is tanned and her hands are weathered.

'You're a farmer now, Will. How long have you been farming?' I ask.

'So, it was my father's brother's business and him and his wife had no children, so I took over when they passed on. It's been 'bout thirty years, but mostly my lads run things now. I still can't believe it's you,' he says. 'So, what *does* bring you back here after all this time?' William slurps his drink, the ice cubes clattering against the sides of the tall glass.

'I was just travelling around in my van and saw that Alex

had an exhibition on and thought I'd drop in,' I say as casually as I can while lifting my own glass to my lips to hide the burn in my cheeks.

'Oh aye? Just happened to be passing by after all these years?' He smirks. 'And how did that go down?'

I lower my glass back onto the table and my shoulders slump. 'It went down really badly.'

'You broke her heart, Constance. You do realise that don't you?'

'Connie,' I remind him. 'It was a long time ago; we were just kids.'

'She came to see me; we had an argument. She accused me of… well to be honest I don't really know what she accused me of. Said I was supposed to be your friend, and what sort of friend was I? She was right mad wi' me. I guess she didn't like me taking you back to the station to catch your train. She thought I was helping you run away. Seems a bit mad now, but she's not really spoken to me since.'

'You see her though?'

'From time to time, but she's always kept to herself like. We all just went off in different directions. But, Connie, that summer, it was good times wasn't it.'

'It was, it was the best time.' And I do mean this. I sometimes think what my life would have been like if I'd never had those six weeks in Scotland. My parents had a plan for university; they also had their eyes on Jonathan Highcliffe if the uni place didn't come off. Me, settled in a career or reputably married with children. What they didn't factor in was my pregnancy. What a huge disappointment I was to them. Who am I kidding…already pregnant, Scotland or not, my life would have been exactly the same. I just wouldn't have been able to carry that bittersweet memory of Alex through it.

'You and Alexandra were a couple?' Morag asks me.

'No, we were never that. We were just eighteen,' I say, as if that explains it all. I look over at William who's rolling his eyes.

'I'm leaving anyway, just popped in to say hello, and then I'm heading home.'

'You can't just go again now. Go and see her, tell her why you left, make amends.'

'I doubt she'll talk to me. I don't really want to put myself through it to be honest.'

'She might if you give her another chance.'

'When was the last time she spoke to *you*? She's a holder of grudges. It was a mistake to come; it's been too long.'

'She's ill. Did you know that?' Morag says and we both turn to her, our heads snapping around at her words.

'What's wrong with her?' I ask, but Morag just shrugs.

'I don't rightly know. I have to say it was just something that Hilda told me. Said she'd seen her going into the doctors a fair bit. And one time in the car park she told someone she'd had devastating news. But Hilda had none of the particulars. She hobbles,' she adds, as if that explains it.

I don't remember her hobbling last night, but then I'd been a little in shock.

'No one knows much about her. She keeps herself to herself and always has.'

'But she told someone she'd had devastating news?' I say, dubiously.

'Aye,' Morag says.

'You did no' tell me that,' William says, visibly shocked. 'Why did you no' tell me that?'

'Well, it's nobody's business and I don't think it's supposed to be common knowledge. But if this lass means something to her, perhaps she should know.'

'Lass? I'm seventy.' I laugh.

'Aye, well, you know what I mean. You were a lass to her back then I dare say, and would probably still be a lass to her now.'

'She said I was no one.' My voice comes out as a strange strangled sound and for a horrible moment I think I'm going to cry.

'I doubt she meant it,' says William, kindly. 'She'll just be sore on account of you upping and leaving like you did. Why did you do that, anyway?'

'It was a family matter; I had to go home. I did mean to come back, but it was impossible to start with.'

'Impossible?' William asks, but Morag shuts him down quickly.

'You're no' but a man; you know nothing,' she says and he rolls his eyes again.

I think about the American: Hank. 'But she's married though? The American?'

'No, that's her business partner. Her husband died last year.'

'She did marry then?'

'Oh aye, she married a very rich man. Lord Sebastian Linton, no less.'

'Bloody hell!' I say, imagining the Alex I knew: the skinny, fearless girl she was, marrying a lord of all people. 'And she calls me Lady Constance! What a cheek... So the house where she had her exhibition – that's her house?' I ask, as it all slots together in my mind.

'Yep, that great big monster is where she lives. No one had really seen her for ages. I'd kind of forgotten all about her, then the house was opened back up after being empty for a long time and they both turn up, married.'

'She only got married a couple of years ago,' William says, with a knowing look I don't really understand. 'A marriage of convenience we all thought. She never got over you,' he clarifies.

'And what do you know of it?' Morag chips in.

'I just know,' says William. 'I just know.'

11

The road back to Linton Hall winds its way around Loch Ness, and I keep glancing out of the window at the vista. Alex's painting is everywhere: gold rippled water, the dappled reflections of the surrounding trees, the loch seemingly endless, disappearing into the distant haze.

Morag's words are spinning through my mind. Alex is ill. How ill is ill? Is it terminal? She didn't use that exact word, but she hinted, didn't she? Devastating news? I have thought of every dreadful possibility, the terrible options flying through my head in a grisly list. The exhibition was her last then, I think, as I take a turning at speed, the van wobbling violently before I have it under control. I ease my foot from the accelerator and take a deep yogic breath to calm me, to slow my breathing, but my wish to get to Alex is acute. After all this time though, I probably need to slow down. I can hardly go marching in there talking about imminent death. And anyway, I remind myself, Alex was not happy to see me last night, and is not likely to have changed her mind now.

I turn off the main road and back onto Alex's driveway. I park again by the detached garages off to the side with their three large oak doors. I wonder, absentmindedly, how many cars Alex actually has. Perhaps her late husband, the lord, had a fleet. I roll to a stop and pull on the handbrake, the van deciding that now is a good time to backfire. I cringe and glance at the house, imagining Alex looking out with her narrow eyes. There's no one there, and I allow myself a moment longer to take in the property.

Alex lived in a tiny house with her family when I knew her. She shared a bedroom with her younger sister, and one bathroom with her parents and three other siblings. It was chaotic and warm; the family were kind and lovely. I remember her mother always with an apron on, flour down the front, the makings of a cake on the go. I never saw my own mother with a floury apron, but then she never baked. The closest she would get was to slip a silk wrap around her shoulders to protect her clothes when she applied her make-up before guests arrived.

Alex has done very well for herself. I bite my lip as the thought occurs. Faced with her imminent demise, all of this really means nothing at all.

I climb out of the van and walk up to the front door with a renewed sense of confidence, but when I ring the doorbell, there is no response at all. I decide to go for a snoop around the back.

Between the house and the boundary hedge is an iron gate and a pathway winding round behind the building. I push it open and follow the path until I'm in the most beautiful garden. The borders are stacked full of summer plants in a riot of colour. An impeccably clipped lawn stretches towards the cedar trees beyond as if a carpet has been rolled out. And, in the middle, is possibly the most stunning willow I have ever seen. There is a stone patio with perfectly placed rattan furniture and a hammock swinging in the shade. A canopy is strung between the edge of the house to a garden room like a sail. The whole place is utterly idyllic.

I can hear animated voices and duck back to the path while I try to see where they're coming from, but after only a few moments I realise that it's an audiobook or a podcast I can hear – some sort of recording – and it's coming from where the hammock is swinging gently. I hesitate, suddenly unsure about creeping around Alex's garden, invading her privacy. I can't get an image of her narrow eyes and unsmiling mouth from last night out of my mind. She called me a nobody. There was no tearful reunion. My confidence leaves me. I go to take another step back the way I've come, deciding that leaving is probably the best option, when Alex's arm suddenly flops down from the hammock and hangs limply to one side.

She's dead. I'm too late! The thought is like a stab to my heart and I take a step closer. I take another step, swallowing down a sob that threatens in my throat. I can see her now, stretched out, one arm above her head; the other, dead and hanging. She looks so peaceful lying there, no more worries about her illness. Whatever that illness was.

The audiobook is still playing from the phone resting on her chest and I lean over to turn it off. It doesn't seem right to have that still babbling on, while Alex lies there. I take in her face, her beautiful alabaster skin, lined with time and still with that lovely sprinkling of freckles high up on her cheeks. For a mad moment I want to lean down and kiss her, a gentle goodbye, but instead I pick up the phone and press for silence.

Alex's eyes flick open and she looks shocked for a moment, taking in the scene before her. Me leaning over her, phone in my hand, a tear winding its way down my face.

'What the absolute hell are you doing?' she demands, as I stumble backwards.

'I, I... I thought you were...' I can't get the last word out. It seems ridiculous now that Alex is breathing again, alive again.

'Asleep, you thought I was asleep, because I was asleep?'

'No, actually I thought you were dead,' I say, because really, what else is there to say? Alex is trying to sit up, but she must have forgotten she's in a hammock, because she sways for a second as she tries to get purchase, and then the whole thing moves in one fluid motion and she is unceremoniously dumped onto the patio. I move to help her but she hastily lifts a hand up into the air.

'Don't you dare, Connie Fitzgerald; don't you bloody dare.' And with nothing much holding me back now and because, for the second time in two days I have heard my name on Alex's lips, I laugh loudly to disguise the huge grin that threatens to overwhelm my entire face. We stare at each other and finally Alex smiles.

'What the hell are you doing here, Connie?'

Alex walks out of the French doors carrying two mugs of coffee, but she struggles with each step. I begin to get up from my seat to help, but change my mind when I take in the grim determination on her face. She always was a single-minded woman and didn't take well to offers of help. I stay in my seat and take the opportunity to really look at her, to see what the intervening years have done to my friend.

She has a softness to her now. Not just in her body, but in her face too. Those angular cheekbones have rounded, giving the impression of a person more likely to smile. The lines radiating out from the corners of her eyes say the same. Her hair is shorter, but still with the same brilliant golden auburn hue. Well, not exactly the same; it now smacks of a trip to the salon to achieve it and has lost some of its depth, but it's similar. She's wearing dark-blue jeans and a white blouse just open at the top to reveal a gold pendant around her neck. She has a wedding band that looks platinum and an engagement ring with three large diamonds dazzling in the sunlight. Alex is beautiful and she looks chic too. I suddenly feel just as I did when we first met: gauche.

'So, how did your exhibition go?' I ask before taking a sip of my coffee.

'We're making small talk are we? Connie, why are you here?'

'Hardly small talk – it was quite the exhibition. And that *is* why I'm here.'

'How did you even know about my exhibition?'

'I saw an advertisement in a magazine that I picked up off the seat on a train in London and recognised the painting.'

Alex lowers her mug to reveal the look of surprise on her face.

'You found a discarded magazine and that's why you're here? You've got to be joking, right?'

'No.' I laugh. 'It's true.'

'You're a piece of work, Constance,' Alex says, but she's not laughing with me; she's not even smiling now. She reaches into her pocket then and pulls out her phone which is silently vibrating. 'Hank, darling,' she drawls, almost mimicking the accent I remember from him last night. 'What? But my appointment is at eleven-forty-five. Well, I suppose I could do that, but...' Alex looks across at me suddenly, seeming to take me in properly for the first time. Her eyes roam over my face and across my shoulders, and I try very hard not to squirm in my seat. Her gaze is just as penetrating as it was all those years ago. 'Okay, well, I guess I'll have to,' she says and hangs up.

I finish my drink slowly, waiting for Alex to say something and hoping it isn't a swift goodbye. She doesn't say anything for a moment, but seems to be weighing up her options.

'Hank has buggered up his ankle on the squash court this morning and can't drive me to my doctor's appointment. I could phone for a taxi, but – as you're here – could you make yourself useful and take me?'

She doesn't ask nicely; she doesn't say please, but I'm already fishing in my handbag for my keys.

'Of course I can. It will be my pleasure,' I say.

'I doubt that,' Alex replies with a short sigh.

12

I edge the van away from the house slowly, as if I have the most precious cargo on board and in a way, I have. Alex Mackenzie is sitting in the passenger seat looking apprehensive, and very much as if she might change her mind and leap out. I put my foot down; that's the last thing I want to happen.

She's tense on the seat beside me, and I knew this wouldn't be easy, but hoped it wouldn't be this much of a challenge.

'So, you're a hippy these days,' she says glancing at my skirt.

'Is that what it looks like? You're not the only one to say that, to be honest. I just like buying charity shop clothes because I can't bear the waste and I like to be comfortable.'

Alex turns her head to look out of the window, but I catch the smirk on her face before she does.

'You've changed from that Kensington chick who turned up in my home town,' she says.

'It's been fifty-two years since I turned up,' I retort, but realise a little too late what I've said. Alex turns back to look at me, and even though I have my eyes firmly on the road I can feel her gaze hot on my face.

'Yes, it has been fifty-two years. You're quite right, Connie.' She breathes out a long low breath and then in almost a whisper she says again, 'Fifty-two years.'

I grip the steering wheel, my emotions mixed. She hasn't forgiven me for leaving – that is clear – but to know she is still so affected by me is heartening. This is not going to be easy.

We pull up outside the doctor's surgery and Alex has gone back to being uncomfortable. She's gritting her teeth and steadfastly not looking at me.

'Shall I come round and help you?' I ask and she shoots me a look.

'No,' she says simply, before shifting in her seat to face the door. She pulls the handle and pushes it open as wide as she can, then begins to shuffle her bottom round until her legs are dangling down. Then she seems to slump in her seat. 'For Christ's sake Connie, why do you drive this ridiculous vehicle? You're going to have to help me down.'

I leap out from my side and straight round to help her. Alex's face is thunderous as I slip an arm around her to take as much weight as I can, then she seems to slither to the ground with a sound that speaks of pain escaping from her lips. She begins to hobble towards the surgery building.

'Do you want me to come with you?' I call out, already knowing the answer. Alex doesn't respond and I climb back into the van, sensibly deciding that what she meant with her silence was: absolutely not.

As I wait, I deliberate what to do next. What I should do is drive Alex home and then leave, but now I'm here, now I've seen her, I know *that* is going to be nearly impossible. Hasn't she let me into her world a little, a very little? It would be a shame to leave now and not get to say all that I want to, all that I've waited these years to say. It's a sad state of affairs to think that I'd rather be here with someone who doesn't seem to want me, than to go home and see my family. For the first time since I drove over the border I feel a bit bereft. Haven't I left my family? Haven't I done exactly the opposite of what I did in 1970?

This time, I've chosen Alex.

The door to the surgery opens and she reappears. I fight the urge to go and help her as she limps back across the car park, but I do climb out and aid her back into the van, touching her as little as possible and ignoring the murderous vibes radiating from her body.

'How did you get on?' I ask cheerfully as I start the engine.

'I don't want to talk about it; it is what it is,' she says, shutting down that conversation before it can go any further. I decide to persist, though. I want to know what it is that's wrong with her.

'Maybe it would be good to talk about it, don't you think?' I ask, as I pull out of the car park. I catch the look on Alex's face as I glance left and turn onto the main road. I can't make out her expression. It swings between annoyance and confusion and settles somewhere in the middle. 'Shall we go and get some lunch, or do you want me to drop you back home?' I brace myself for the answer, fully expecting a big, fat no.

'Aye, go on then,' Alex says. 'This whole thing couldn't really get any weirder could it?'

I can't help the smile twitching on my lips.

★

The pub I've chosen is quiet and we take our drinks into the garden after ordering food at the bar. I find a spot in the shade and move a dirty ashtray onto a neighbouring table, then brush some crumbs onto the ground. Perhaps not what Alex is used to these days, although she doesn't seem bothered.

We sit and then stare at each other for a moment. I can't think of the best way to begin with all that I have to say, so I sip at my Diet Coke and hope that Alex has something.

'Did you say you live in Brighton? I thought you said, last night, that you had a flat there,' she asks.

'Yes, I do, been there for five years. North Wales before that and lots of other places in my time.'

'So, what made you move to Brighton?' she asks, her large Rioja disappearing fast.

I think about this for a moment, because the truth is that being closer to Simon is the reason I moved, or rather, Simon thinking I should be closer to him. Is this the time for revelations? But, there is no other time; once I drop Alex home I might never see her again.

'My son, Simon, he wanted me to be closer to him.'

Alex just nods as if it's of no consequence whatsoever, when the truth is quite the opposite. Simon was the reason for everything.

'What about you?' I ask quickly. 'Do you have any children?'

'God no!' Alex shudders as if I've asked her if she eats mud for breakfast. 'I once heard Tracey Emin talking about having children and how her creative yearning and her want to be an artist far overrode the physical feelings of wanting to be a mother. That's exactly how I feel.'

And there it is: the other reason for everything. I sit back in my chair, winded.

'Goat's cheese salad, and a dirty burger?' A waiter appears with our food and we begin to eat. I pick at my salad leaves while Alex pours ketchup over her chips.

'I heard your husband died. I'm sorry,' I say. 'You must miss him – the lord.'

Alex raises both her eyebrows and reaches for her wine.

'That's quite the assumption,' she says. 'I sense judgement too.'

'No, not at all. I was perhaps a little surprised that you'd married though.'

'Connie,' she says leaning forwards with her elbows on the table as if she's about to impart some great wisdom. 'You knew me for, what, six weeks, over fifty years ago? And let's be honest, you barely knew me then,' she says, picking up her burger and taking a huge bite. I watch as a dribble of fat slips down her chin. Even though I know that she's lying it still hurts.

The drive back to her house is over too quickly. I haven't said the right things and now I'm running out of time. I know now that Alex only agreed to lunch for the opportunity to dig at me, remind me that she's still hurt by the manner of our parting all those years ago, make me feel as if I mean nothing to her. If this is her dying wish, then I have come a long way to have my backside kicked. Alex has spent the journey on her phone, sending messages and ignoring me, and now we're back on her driveway.

There's a large white van parked outside the front of the house; her door is open and there's activity going on inside.

'It's looks like you're being burgled,' I say, guessing by her reaction that she isn't. Alex looks annoyed, inconvenienced, not scared or worried.

'They're taking down the exhibition, but really, it amounts to the same bloody thing,' she says with a cold voice.

'I gathered,' I say.

I pull up behind the white van, but don't switch off the engine. Alex tucks her phone back in her pocket at last and turns to me.

'I have something to ask of you,' she says, immediately piquing my interest. 'I've got a bit of a problem because of Hank. We were supposed to be delivering some of my work over the next couple of days, but he can't drive, and neither can I at the moment, so I'm a bit stuck.'

'Oh, you want me to do it?'

'I don't trust couriers and some of my clients expect a level of personal involvement,' she says.

'Not sure that me rocking up in my camper van is going to be much of a personal service, but yes, I'll do it if you're stuck. Where do they need to go?'

Alex takes a breath. 'Two are up here in the highlands, then one is in York, one near Preston, then a couple in Wales, Bristol, one more *en route* to Truro and then...' She trails off.

I take an even bigger breath and switch off the engine. That's not just popping a couple of paintings to their new owners, that's a full-on road trip. I need to get back home, don't I? Sort out my situation? Talk to Leo? Alex watches me as I weigh it up. I have to ask myself why I really came up here. Yes, to see Alex, of course – after all this time I was curious about what she was doing and had done with her life – but, didn't I want to explain and apologise too? Don't I owe her something? If I do this for her, then maybe it will go some way to making amends. Isn't that what my coming here is all about? I can deliver them on my way back home. It will take a few days at least, but I can do it. I turn to Alex.

'Okay, I'll do it for you. Just load me up and I'll be on my way,' I say.

'What – you think I'm just going to let you take off on your own with my paintings? No way, Connie, you've got previous!'

I look at her, surprised. Surely she can't think I'm going to steal her work. I begin to protest, but she has her hand raised to stop me.

'No – I'm coming with you.'

13

I spend the night in Alex's spare room – one of her many spare rooms, but I barely sleep. I stare into the darkness, contemplating what I'm doing. It scares me how easy it was for me to leave Peterborough without speaking to Leo. A man I was planning on spending the rest of my life with became a figure in my rearview mirror at the thought of seeing Alex again. Have I made a conscious decision to break things off with Leo without actually telling him? Am I leaving that option open-ended to see what happens with Alex? The reason I don't sleep, I realise, is because I don't think much of myself at the moment.

In the morning I phone Simon to say I'm helping an old friend deliver some paintings, but he's so full of news that Diana had felt the baby kick, that he brushes away my words. Of course, this is far more exciting than a conversation about artwork. He doesn't mention Leo, so they probably haven't been in contact since last time. Even though I've finally been honest with my son about where I am and what I'm doing, I still manage to feel dreadful when I hang up.

I bite the bullet and compose a message to Leo. It isn't fair to leave him waiting for me to be in contact. And, now that I've committed to a few days delivering Alex's paintings, it could be a while before I see him. I stare at the screen for ages contemplating what to write. I know he deserves more than a text message. Once I start typing it all comes flooding out.

I tell him how sad I am for him and his grief about Brenda. I say that I'm hurt he wasn't able to tell Fiona about me, but projecting his own deep-seated grief onto his daughter isn't healthy. Fiona is a lovely woman, I type, and is living a happy and fulfilling life. No one can ever be Brenda, I continue, and if he ever wishes to have a meaningful relationship with someone else he would need to love them for who they are and not as a replacement. I tell him that it isn't all on him, though, and that I have unresolved issues to deal with too. Then I run out of steam and decide that I'm rambling.

I read it back and then begin to delete the words. Finally when the screen is blank I begin again.

Leo, I'm sorry I didn't wait for you on Saturday. I should have given you time to explain how you feel. I realise that we both need time to think about what it is that we really want. I've met up with an old friend and I'm going away for a few days with her. If you still want to talk to me when I get back then I would love to meet up with you. Connie x

I shower and dress, then make my way downstairs. The team of people have stripped the exhibition from the house and carefully wrapped all of the paintings, which are now labelled and stacked in the main entrance hall.

I find Alex eating toast and drinking coffee at the kitchen table. It's another vast room, but distinctly more modern than the oak panelling of the rest of the house. The white granite worktops are startling in the morning sun, flooding through the arched window above the sink. Banks of handleless cupboard doors in a soft elephant grey stretch around the space, but it isn't as stark as you'd expect. Alex's artwork warms the walls and her collections of sculptures and *objets d'art* bring character to her shelves and spaces. This is *her* domain – not the dark and austere library or the cold and soulless living room, but here in the warmth and light.

I help myself from the coffee pot and pick at a croissant Alex offers me. We hadn't spent the evening together. I said I had some things to sort in the van and when I'd come in, Alex had been dozing in front of the television, a half-finished glass of whisky on the table beside her. I had turned the television off and covered her in the blanket that was folded over the back of the armchair.

'Are you sure your van is up to this trip?' she asks me now.

'I'll need to refuel and check the water before we leave, but yes, she's more than capable.' I cross my fingers under the table and hope I'm right.

'She?' Alex smirks. 'What's her name?'

'Ruby.' I bristle.

'Apt,' she replies, brushing toast crumbs from her top. 'We'll need to stay overnight *en route*. I'll book a hotel for York and then we'll see how we go from there.'

I'm not sure if she means to book for us both, but don't like to ask. I can easily sleep in the van anyway.

'So, the local deliveries can wait. I think it's best if we get on the road for York today. Does that work for you? I reckon if we leave soonish, we can be there by five, six, with breaks of course.' Alex is animated now, almost excited, and I swallow down the last of my coffee. To know I have hours ahead of me, side by side with her is something a couple of days ago I would have only dreamed about, but now it's actually happening, I'm beginning to lose my nerve. Will we be making stilted small talk the whole way? Will Alex continue to be this cheerful or slip back to the unimpressed grudge-bearer of only yesterday? It's a lot for me to get my head around, and a lot of miles for me to cover.

'That sounds fine,' I say brightly, shoving the last of the croissant into my mouth and swallowing down some coffee. 'Exactly how many paintings are we taking? I can't possibly fit them *all* in. What's the plan?' There must be ten times the number I can take stacked in the front hallway.

'It's not all of them; there are eight that I need to deliver. Those ones are particularly special and need my personal touch, but the rest can, well, it doesn't matter about them. They can wait until I get back.'

She turns away to rinse her mug in the sink and seems twitchy all of a sudden.

'It's fine, Alex,' I say, keen to reassure her. 'It will all be fine.'

She turns back to me with a look that could be gratitude – it's hard to tell – but there's a vulnerability about her too. We both watch as the kitchen suddenly darkens and the worktops lose their glare as a dark bank of cloud works its way across the face of the sun.

Alex stands on the driveway and watches me load the paintings into the back of the van. Actually, watching would be preferable. In reality, what she's doing is dictating and directing. I do my best to stack them carefully – there's limited space – but she just keeps barking orders.

'Not like that! You'll damage the frame! No, Connie, you can't lay it flat! Does it look as if that's the best place for it!'

It's a testament to my inner strength and also to my desperation to please her that I don't lose my temper.

When I'm done and about to climb into the driver's seat ready to go, Alex drags out a huge suitcase onto the doorstep.

'Oh, and there's this,' she says, 'my case.'

I'd assumed that the holdall and the tote bag she had on the passenger seat was her luggage, but it seems I was wrong. She's packed enough for weeks away it appears. She locks up the front door and I notice her shove the keys back through the letter-box. Then she turns and looks at me expectantly. I know she can't manage the suitcase across the driveway, so I go to help, and between us and a large groove through the gravel we get it to the van. I pull it up inside and wedge it between a storage cupboard and the back seat. The paintings I've secured with bungee cords and everything now seems ready to go.

Alex puts two fingers into her mouth and lets out an almighty whistle. I'm surprised for a moment, until a golden-coloured dog comes running around from the back of the house in a flurry of fur and flapping ears. It jumps up into the passenger footwell and Alex climbs in beside it, then closes her door.

'Who is this?' I ask, wondering where its lead is and if it's friendly. I'm not going to ask Alex. I imagine it's a case of, love me, love my dog. To be fair, two sweet brown eyes look at me intently while a tail swishes back and forth across the carpet.

'Bardo,' she says, 'my dog.'

'You didn't say anything about a dog. I didn't even know you had one, to be honest. Where have you been hiding it?'

'He was with a friend while the exhibition was going on. He's back now. Is that a problem?'

'As long as he's a good traveller then, no, not at all.'

'He's loyal, dependable, trustworthy and has never run away from me, not ever.'

I ignore the jibe and start the engine.

'Well, looks like it's going to be the three of us then,' I say and pull off of her driveway, wondering what the hell I've got myself into.

We're on the A9 heading south when the first drops of rain hit the windscreen and the inadequate wipers do their best to clear them. The noise of the squeak and scrape as they edge their way across the glass is irritating at the best of times, but with Alex beside me, I begin to feel tense. Her dog is actually very sweet, though, and curled up in the footwell no trouble at all.

There's been little conversation so far. I have occasionally punctuated the silence with inane comments about the scenery, but I'm not getting much back. We need something to break the ice. Alex has brought a sketchbook with her. She has it open on her lap and her pencil is moving quickly across the paper. She spends most of her time looking out of the window and only occasionally glances down at what she's doing. What she's producing though, is a beautifully detailed little study of what she can see outside: the heather and gorse on the verges that flank this stretch of road, the peeling bark of the birches and the parched grasses.

I'm as humbled by her talent now as I ever was, and I'm transported to a time when I would sit and watch her paint in the old shed in her parents' garden. They were keen for her to keep all that mess out of their way. We balanced her brother's record player out there on an upturned flowerpot and would listen to Aretha Franklin's new album, *This Girl's in Love with You*, time after time, after time. I'd sit cross-legged on the garden-chair cushions that no one had bothered to put outside and watch her work. That heady mix of a hot summer, a confined space and my budding infatuation with her and her talent, and it was never going to be long before something boiled over.

When Alex notices me glancing at her work, she closes her sketchbook and drops it into her bag. She takes in her surroundings for the first time, touching the dashboard, unwinding the window a little, looking over her shoulder into the back.

'It's actually quite sweet,' she says.

I'm warmed by her words; anyone who likes Ruby is okay by me.

'I mean, it's a wee bit twee, all matchy-matchy, but sort of sweet too.'

I suppress a sigh and decide to accept her backhanded compliment.

'Tell me about your son,' Alex says. 'Simon, is it?'

Alex always did have the most impressive memory. I have my eyes on the road, but can feel hers on me.

'Yes – Simon. He's married for the third time and has a baby on the way with his wife, Diana, who's fifteen years younger than him and hates me.'

'Really, do you like *her*?'

'I want to, I absolutely do, but she's so cold.'

'Well, perhaps you did something to piss her off. It happens you know.'

I ignore the barbed comment. 'I think, what I did and still do that pisses her off is have a good relationship with my son.'

'Oh, she's pure jealous then.'

'I don't think it's that, but she does seem insecure.'

'Does she have a good relationship with her own parents?'

'No, not that I can see. Her mother openly calls her a mistake.'

'She's jealous all right, then. But it's an easy fix. Just make her feel like she's the daughter you never had.'

I glance round at Alex, surprised at her words. A woman not only with no children, but never with a desire to have them either.

'But she says such horrible things. Do you think it's that easy?' I ask.

'Aye, I do, and before you say it, I've got loads of nieces and nephews; I know how people tick. You're the grown-up; it's up to you to reach out. And don't take no for an answer.'

I contemplate this and how obvious it seems. All the times I've kept out of Diana's way, or bitten my tongue to avoid an atmosphere. Should I have ploughed on regardless? Should I have been the grown-up despite her age?

'I *am* crocheting her a baby blanket. That could be a peace offering,' I say, but Alex doesn't respond. It reminds me that I meant to pick up some wool in Inverness. Too late to turn back now.

I have an overwhelming and sudden desire to contact Diana, let her know that I want us to be friends. I don't think I've ever done that. I mostly try and keep out of her way. Perhaps I could send her a message, tell her about the blanket. It could be a present as much for her as her baby. We could begin to build some bridges.

I glance at Alex, sitting cross-armed in the seat beside me, her face relaxed but not quite smiling. Perhaps we have broken the ice here. We're having a normal conversation, not about the weather, but about real family issues. While Alex hasn't exactly thawed she is at least talking.

'There's a service station just up ahead. I need a pee and Bardo does too. This will be a recurring theme throughout this trip,' she says with a grim smile.

I think about that and what it may mean for her mystery illness. Bladder problems – could be cancer? Then again, I need a wee too. So, possibly just our age. I pull the van off the main road and into a parking space.

'And, about your daughter-in-law,' Alex says, turning in her seat to face me. 'There's every possibility you may be a terrible mother-in-law and Diana has every reason to dislike you. Don't forget, Connie, you chose to have a family; the very least you can do is to care for them.'

Alex hasn't thawed at all.

We're on the outskirts of Edinburgh by two and I suggest we stop for lunch. Alex directs me into the city.

'There's an NCP car park behind the castle,' she says. 'We can walk up from there.'

'Do you have somewhere in mind to eat then?' I ask.

'Yes, The Witchery, by the castle; it was a favourite of mine and Sebastian's.'

It's the first time she has mentioned her husband, and I want to capitalise on it and dig in a bit deeper, but navigating the busy Edinburgh streets is tricky, so I keep my mouth shut for now and my eyes on the road. We pull into the car park and I get a ticket for a couple of hours, gulping at the cost: nearly ten pounds!

'How far is the restaurant? Are you going to be okay to walk it?' I ask, but Alex is swallowing some tablets from her handbag.

'I'll be fine,' she says, with that same look of grim determination. We leave the car park and walk up the steps bedside it until we're onto the road at the foot of the castle, built high on volcanic rocks. I don't tell Alex that I've been here before. It's clear she wants to be the guide, as she begins to give me some of the history, and I'm happy to let her.

We walk slowly up the hill, past the coaches parked up waiting for their tourists. Bardo is happy trotting along between us and it gives me such hope seeing Alex with a dog. It does take the edge off her, watching her with her floppy-eared spaniel. She's wearing black jeans today and there are a few of Bardo's hairs stuck to them. For all her make-up and blingy jewellery, her severe expression and stiff posture, those few stray dog hairs make her very human.

We pass a restricted parking bay and Alex stops to take a breath. I wish for a moment I could have got my hands on a permit, but she rallies and we turn onto The Royal Mile along with so many others.

'I forget what a beautiful city this is,' I say, staring up at the Gothic spire towering above us.

'It's the tallest point in central Edinburgh,' Alex says. 'And every August the building becomes the central hub for the Edinburgh Festival.'

Alex is trying to sound as if she knows this, but I catch her glancing at her phone, no doubt on Wikipedia.

'They're serving fish and chips. We could just grab some here, save walking any further,' I say, pointing at the blue van parked up out the front. In answer, Alex keeps walking and I trail on behind her.

Not far up the cobbles we arrive at the restaurant. It looks expensive, and I wonder who's paying and whether dogs are allowed.

'Should we have booked? It's so busy today,' I say, just as someone pushes past me, knocking my handbag off my shoulder. I pull it back up and over my head for extra security, check the zip is pulled tight and is on the front of the bag. It's one of the many things I've caught myself doing as I get older. Would I have worried about securing my bag when I was younger? No, I'd have shoved my stuff into pockets and not given them further thought. 'What about the dog; surely we can't take him in.' I glance down and see him sitting and looking from one of us to the other, patiently waiting for us to make a move. I bend down and stroke his soft head.

'I know the owner,' Alex says. 'It won't be a problem.'

Bardo cocks his leg and relieves himself noisily on the iron railings to the left of the door and then follows Alex inside. I glance up at the royal-looking flag hanging above the door, smooth the top of my hair with my hands and then tag along behind them.

We're offered a table even though the owner isn't there. Alex's name seems to carry some weight. The seats are high-backed red leather, candles sit tall in sliver holders and the napkins are tied with red velvet ribbon. I have my chair pulled out for me and as I sit down I take in the scent of the pretty floral arrangement on the table: roses, heather and tiny fern fronds.

'Lunch is on me,' Alex says, picking up a menu and ordering a large glass of wine. Despite the beauty of the place, my heart sinks a little at the thought of the cost.

'I'll just have a sparkling water, please,' I say to the waiter. 'We've got four and a half hours of driving ahead of us.'

I order lemon sole and Alex orders a seafood platter. When it comes it's a tangle of Scottish langoustines, oysters, mussels, clams and crab with half a lobster sitting on a bed of ice staring at me. I glance at my watch and contemplate the possibility of not reaching York before bedtime.

Alex tucks in happily, only stopping to wipe her mouth and offer titbits to Bardo, who sits under the table, quietly waiting. She's enjoying her second glass of wine. I see she is a woman keen to embrace everything life has to offer while she still can. I'm about to be brave and ask her about her health when she speaks.

'There's a lot of history here,' she says, waving an oyster shell in the air. I know she means the building, but it could so easily be a statement about ourselves and I suppress a smile.

'It looks just like the inside of your home,' I say, and Alex laughs.

'My home,' she says, wryly. 'Yes, I suppose it does a bit.'

I begin to relax. Alex seems in good spirits, literally, and the lemon sole is delicious. I decide not to spoil the atmosphere with awkward questions.

She is unsteady on the way out of the restaurant and twice I offer up my arm for support. Twice she declines.

'Do you mind if I get some wool while I'm here?' I ask her.

'Sure, whatever you want,' she responds with a shrug.

'There's a shop just off the High Street,' I say, making my way back down the hill. 'Will you be okay with the walk?'

'Of course I will be,' she says, and marches ahead for a few paces before sliding back beside me. We wander past the huge body of St Giles' Cathedral and slip into its shadow before the heat of the afternoon sun finds us again on the other side. I take my baseball cap from my bag and stuff it onto my head. The shop is further than I remember, and I'm concerned about the combination of wine and heat on Alex, but she accepts the bottle of water I offer from my bag and eventually we arrive. She waits outside with Bardo, while I pop in and pick up a ball of cream wool with grey and warm stone-coloured flecks. It reminds me of the walls of Edinburgh Castle. I show Alex when I walk back out of the shop, pleased with my purchase, but she looks surprised.

'For a baby's blanket?' she says. 'Odd choice.'

I drop it into my bag and begin the walk back to the van.

The sun is warm on our faces as we make our way back past the castle. I'm squinting into it because I left my sunglasses on my seat in the van, but Alex has hers and she is the epitome of a chic older woman. For a mad moment I want to take a photograph of her or suggest a selfie of the two of us, the castle as a backdrop, but I hold my tongue.

'Ah, the wool,' she says, pointing up past the craggy rock face to the castle above. 'That's canny.'

We leave Edinburgh, replete, and only make it as far as the A68 before Alex falls asleep. She's reclined her seat and balled up her cardigan as a neck support, Bardo on her lap. I keep going, occasionally glancing at my sleeping friend. It is so hard for me to believe that after all this time wondering about her, she is right here next to me, content and comfortable. I turn the dial for the radio and find some gentle music, making sure the volume is down low. I tap my thumbs on the steering wheel in time to the beat and let out a soft sigh of contentment. For now, all is well.

14

We arrive in York at seven and head straight for the place Alex has booked in the city centre. The Elm House is a pretty stone building, a holiday home with private parking and I'm grateful for that. York Minster cathedral looms overhead as I reverse into the tight space, and I wonder why Alex hasn't booked into a hotel.

'I like to be self-sufficient when I'm away,' she says as if I've spoken aloud. 'I don't mind a good hotel if the service is excellent, but I'd rather do my own thing if I can. Plus, I will sneak Bardo into a hotel, but it's easier if I don't have to.'

I turn off the engine and watch her as she applies some lipstick in the visor mirror. She doesn't seem like the sort of person who is self-sufficient anymore. She used to be, though.

Alex could cook up a meal from next to nothing for her family. She would peg washing on the line in the garden with her little brother hanging from her back like a monkey. She once fixed the engine on her uncle's boat so we could take it out on the loch. I was in awe of her and her limitless attributes. I was just a posh London girl with a good education under my belt. Lady Constance Fitzgerald, Alex called me when she first met me. I wasn't a lady, not really, although my mother certainly thought herself of noble stock with the circles she and my father moved in. My parents both coddled and neglected me at the same time, and then rejected me when I returned from Scotland six weeks later in even more disgrace than when I'd left.

'This looks expensive,' I say, feeling again that inadequacy. Alex wafts her hand about as if the cost is of no consequence and I'll just have to assume she's paying.

'Don't worry about it, Connie, just relax.'

Alex walks the dog over to a patch of grass so he can relieve himself and digs in her pocket for a plastic bag to clear up. Then he disappears towards the minster at a sprint.

'Alex! He's running away,' I say, beginning to chase after him, but Alex puts her hand out to stop me.

'He's just gone for a run; he'll be fine,' she says.

'But, what about the road? He could be killed.'

'Honestly, he's fine and has excellent road sense.'

I want to protest, but then he reappears from round the corner and trots up to us. Alex looks smugly at me, although I think she's being irresponsible. But then, Alex has never liked rules.

We open the door with a keypad and after Alex has pressed the numbers, we drag our bags inside and she closes the door. I take a breath and step away from her as the atmosphere suddenly becomes quite intimate in this small private hallway.

'Pick whichever room you want and I'll get some wine open and feed the dog,' she says, also moving away. 'I asked them to leave a couple of bottles in the kitchen for us.'

I walk up the windy staircase to check the bedrooms, already deciding to take the smallest, and I hear the pop of a cork behind me. What must it be like to live the way she does?

I quit that world many years ago and it seems that I have vacated it and Alex has taken up residence in it now.

Both rooms are beautifully decorated and furnished with velvet curtains and rich, dark floral bedding, and I take the one without the en suite. I drop my bag onto the bed and use the bathroom on the landing. Downstairs, Alex is in the living room with her feet up on an oak coffee table, her shoes thrown down beside her. Bardo is asleep in the soft bed Alex has brought for him. She's cradling a large glass of wine and I see there's one on the table for me too. No more driving until tomorrow – I swoop down and lift it up, swallow a large mouthful, then I sink into the chair opposite her and we relax into a comfortable silence.

My eyes feel heavy and it would be so easy to fall asleep here, but the wine has already hit me and I need to eat. The thought of going out again is more than my tired body can cope with.

'Do you fancy a takeaway?' I ask and Alex smiles.

'A woman after my own heart,' she says, and then quickly looks away, but I keep my eyes on her while she studies the painting above the fireplace.

I get my phone out and look up places nearby that deliver and within half an hour we have plates of Goan fish curry, tarka daal, cauliflower bhaji and fluffy naan bread. It's all delicious and despite our large lunch, we manage to finish the lot. And then we stay at the kitchen table, even though we should probably go to bed, and I tentatively ask Alex about her career.

She sits back in her chair and contemplates. Whether it's what to tell me or how to say it I'm not sure, but eventually she begins.

'I studied art in Aberdeen, travelled, came back, travelled

again, came back and then settled in Inverness,' she says, which really only makes me want to ask more questions. Her parents didn't encourage her painting. As loving a family as they were, they were practical, and would have promoted her getting a 'proper job'. I remember her dad was always complimentary about whatever she produced, but then he'd move the conversation on to work. I'm so happy that she made it to university, but I wonder how she managed it. How did she go from that tumbledown little house with her quirky and loving, but potless family to being able to study art? Someone must have helped her. Even though there wouldn't have been tuition fees at the time, there would have been living costs.

'Where did you travel?'

'I won a scholarship and studied in Italy, then worked and travelled in Spain and France. It was wonderful, but my yearning for home was always greater than my wish to be away.'

'I overheard someone at your exhibition saying you were a reclusive artist; in fact, the article I read said the same. How do you produce such...' I falter for a moment on the word, but I've had enough wine to aid me '...expensive pieces and stay reclusive?'

She looks surprised at my question, but then her eyes narrow and it looks like I've annoyed her again.

'It's quite simple, Connie, I paint damn good paintings and don't shoot my mouth off about it.' She reaches for her wine and finishes the glass.

'I've travelled,' I say, but she just shrugs. I know she's dying to know though, because I can see the questions burning in her eyes. 'I didn't get to *all* the places we talked about going to though.' I foolishly throw this out there and I now know I've had too much wine and should probably go to bed.

'You've got a bloody nerve; you really have, Connie. Glad you got to some of the places that *we* talked about going to.'

'I'm sorry; I truly am. I'm sorry I left. I'm sorry you weren't there when I came back.'

Her eyes snap up at that, but she pushes her chair back and stands up.

'It doesn't matter now does it and, let's be honest, it probably didn't matter much then, either. I'm going to bed.'

She fills her glass again and then walks out of the kitchen, leaving me with the plates to clear away.

It's raining properly when I wake in the morning. I can hear it bouncing off the roof of my van, parked below my bedroom window. Alex is in the kitchen with a cup of tea and she's making her way through the packet of biscuits that were left for us along with a small fruit cake and a bottle of cloudy lemonade. She drank twice as much as I did last night, but she looks fresh-faced and seems much more awake than me. I brace myself for silence or the cold shoulder, but she smiles and makes me a tea. Bardo ignores me, his head in a bowl of his own biscuits.

'I thought we could take a walk through the museum gardens and have breakfast at Bettys before we drop the painting off, if that sounds all right with you?' She opens a plastic pot with a selection of pills inside and throws them into her mouth before finishing her drink.

'Betty? A friend of yours?' I ask.

'A famous tea room,' she says, rolling her eyes.

'Oh, right, of course,' I say, remembering the one in

Harrogate. 'But it's pouring down out there.' I take a mug from the counter and also grab a biscuit to see if it'll help to mop up last night's overindulgence.

'Bit of rain never killed anyone,' she says. 'Do you have an umbrella in the van? You seem to have everything else.'

'I do actually – I have three. Will you be okay with the walk?' I ask, but she just frowns.

'Of course. Why wouldn't I be? I'm not at death's door yet, you know,' she snaps, but then her face softens and for a moment she seems to be deciding whether to be nice or not. Luckily she seems to choose the former.

We pack up our things and put them in the van ready for when we get back. Alex lets Bardo out for a bit, but then we leave him in the apartment and set off at a sedate pace down the street and towards the museum. The rain has eased a bit and is now more of a drizzle. I've given Alex my favourite rainbow umbrella – although I don't tell her that – and she rests it on her shoulder as she walks.

I've done this walk before, the last time I was in York, some years ago, and the gardens are just as pretty as they were then, with their Roman ruins and tended borders. We wander down past the museum towards the river, where we leave the gardens and begin walking up the steps of Lendal Bridge towards the shops. We pass a McDonald's and even that looks fancy within the stunning York architecture. And then I see Bettys on the corner and understand why Alex wanted to come here. It looks totally up her street. I do remember it from being here before, but the queue to get in and the price list had put me off. Neither of these things faze Alex. We are greeted and seated at a table by the window after leaving our dripping umbrellas at the door. I pick up the menu, and am about to untangle my glasses from my hair, but Alex takes it off me.

'I'll order, trust me,' she says. 'Can we have the imperial breakfast for two please?' she asks the young man serving us. 'Connie, shall we go for avocado and poached egg?' she asks me, and I breathe a sigh of relief. I was expecting something more than that, but poached egg and avocado I can handle.

'Tea or coffee?' he asks. 'And orange juice or perhaps a glass of mimosa?'

I'm beginning to feel this may be just as extravagant as I originally thought.

'Do you mean a cocktail for breakfast?' I ask.

'Yes, madam, it's orange juice and champagne, but we add a splash of Grand Marnier.'

'Just the orange juice, thanks,' I say, but am not remotely surprised when Alex orders the cocktail. I imagine she'll be asleep as soon we set off again. When the food comes, it arrives like an afternoon tea. My eyes are wide as I take it all in. A plate is put in front of me with a rösti and poached egg and avocado. This would be sufficient, but then a three-tier plate stack is placed down in the middle of the table.

'Miniature Bircher muesli,' he says pointing to two glasses on the top. 'Spiced fruit loaf with cinnamon sugar, served with crème fraîche and berries,' he continues, pointing at the middle layer. 'And pain au chocolat,' he finishes with a flurry.

'Thank goodness,' I say. 'We may well have faded away from hunger without those pains au chocolat.'

He dutifully laughs as if he's never heard that before, and then he leaves us with our breakfast – a breakfast that could easily feed several people. Alex tucks straight into her cocktail.

'How are we going to eat all of this?' I say to her as she puts her drink down.

'Eat what you can and then they'll box the rest up and we can eat it on the way or give it to the dog. Looks great doesn't it?' she says, pushing a forkful of egg into her mouth.

Alex may well have rounded her edges a little now she's older, but she's still very much a slim woman. I have no idea where she puts all the food she eats. I think about her mystery illness again and then try and push that thought away.

'I've eaten little over the last few months, getting my exhibition together. I can finally relax and enjoy myself,' she says, but as she takes another sip of her drink, I see a trepidation in her eyes. 'Well,' she says, 'I certainly don't have to worry about the paintings now, that's for sure.'

'You can admit to enjoying yourself in my company then?' I ask her and watch as she tries very hard to suppress a smile.

'Tolerate, perhaps.'

I decide not to push her any further and tuck into my breakfast, but I can't suppress my own smile. I might be winning her over.

We leave Bettys with a fair amount of our breakfast tucked into little boxes. I pick up our umbrellas on the way out and have a feeling that if I hadn't, then Alex would never have remembered. It probably wouldn't have bothered her that my favourite umbrella would be left languishing in a York tea room. I turn to head back to the apartment, but Alex stops me.

'Don't you want to get some wool?' she asks.

'Oh, yes, I do if that's all right.'

She doesn't reply, but begins to tap on her phone and directs us away from the tea rooms. We walk past a row of high street shops until we arrive outside *Duttons for Buttons*. The little shop is stacked top to bottom with boxes of buttons. They make for a lovely display and even Alex can't help herself but look. I find some wool tucked away at the back of the shop and choose an apricot colour that reminds me of the glow last night coming from York Minster's floodlights. I pay and then we head back to the apartment.

15

We're back on the road and leaving the city centre. I am stuffed and almost had to roll myself back to the van. Alex is navigating, which at least will keep her awake. She's good at navigating, giving me plenty of warning for turnings and exits off roundabouts. She also keeps up a running commentary on what she can see and what she knows about where we are, which she reads from the screen of her phone, but makes it sound as if the information is plucked straight from her head. She's a born storyteller, I remind myself.

The windows are down and the breeze is warm but pleasant enough, now that the air con has died. The drizzle has stopped, but there's still a summer mugginess about the air. Bardo is in the back, curled up in his bed after another run around the minster. I feel that Alex is not the strictest of dog owners, even though it's clear she loves him. In fact everyone loved him as he ran among the tourists. I'm not used to animals, having never been around long enough to sensibly own one. I wisely decide to keep my mouth shut about it. Bardo is clearly a smart dog.

We are comfortable with each other for now, and I don't want to say or do anything to change that. If someone had told me last week I'd be on the road with Alex today, I'd never have believed them, and I feel a little joyous.

'So where is this place we're going to?' I ask. I know it's not a long drive from York, but Alex never said exactly where it was. Now we pull into a village called Bishopthorpe, which I've never heard of, and I ease off the accelerator.

'It's just around the next corner on the left, so go slow and, oh, we're here. Just in here, Connie.'

I indicate and pull into an expansive driveway. There's a stone archway with a clock tower in front of us and perfectly green lawns either side with precision stripes.

'Don't go through the arch,' she says. 'Can you pull into this little car park on the left?'

I do as she tells me and find a space next to some rather austere-looking white portcullis-style doors.

'Not sure how long I'll be. Will you be okay here waiting for me, with the dog?'

'Sure,' I say, although I'd rather go with her for a nose around. I did see the sign that read *Bishopthorpe Palace* and now my mind is whirring with who she's delivering the painting to. She moves round into the back of the van and selects the right painting – one of the smaller pieces that she can easily carry herself. I get out to help her though, because she is still a bit wobbly.

She takes the painting and I watch her as she disappears through the archway, her gait just slightly off. Once she's gone I make a cup of tea from the gas stove and drag out a folding chair to sit on the grass while I wait. I take my crochet with me and whistle for Bardo, who ignores me. I can't make anything like the sound that Alex can. I pop my head around the door.

'Are you coming out?' I ask him, and he lifts his head and

sniffs the air. Something makes his mind up and he jumps down onto the ground and sets off for a snuffle in the hedges. I settle with my blanket and catch up on a few rows with the Edinburgh wool before switching to the apricot colour from York.

The rain has eased and now there's just a murderous-looking black cloud disappearing towards the east, which is perfect, as we are heading west, to Wales.

Someone comes out from a side door and walks towards their car: a middle-aged woman wearing a smart navy trouser suit. Her heels click on the surface of the driveway and her leather bag swings from her shoulder. When she catches sight of me she stops altogether and stares. Then she changes direction and begins to head my way. I think for a moment what I must look like to her – an ageing hippy with a camper van, stopping for tea on this strip of grass in the grounds of Bishopthorpe Palace with my dog.

'You can't camp here,' she says sharply, and I immediately begin to acquiesce like I always do. But then I change my mind and take another sip of my tea. We'll be gone shortly, and I'm hardly causing a big problem.

'I'm not camping,' I say in my best Waitrose voice. 'I'm waiting for my friend who has business with the owner. She won't be long and then we'll be gone.'

She begins to say something and then seems to decide otherwise. She nods briefly and then turns back towards her car, but Bardo has chosen that exact spot to defecate and I leap out of my chair to clear it up. I can hear her hissing something all the way across the car park. I take my phone out and look up Bishopthorpe Palace, to find out who the owner actually is.

I read from the site that it's a multi-functional building,

hosting working offices, meeting rooms, worship areas and living quarters. The house and its grounds are also used for charity open days, retreats, evening receptions, village fetes and more. Wow, what a place and what an unusual mix of uses. The photo of the building is stunning and I quickly tap on the history to read more. My mouth dries instantly when I see what it really is: the home of the Archbishop of York. It's only then that I really see all the tabs around the edges of the screen and how often the word *archbishop* is actually used. The website is even called archbishopofyork.org for goodness' sake. I am very much going to vacate this patch of grass. I tip the remains of my tea into a flower bed and fold up my chair as quickly as I can. I shuffle Bardo back into the van and even consider parking up the road a bit, but then, Alex reappears *sans* painting and with a large smile across her lips. My heart leaps a little at the sight of her.

'All done,' she says, and I give her a hand back into the passenger seat. She seems to have stopped worrying about my help, but I'm still cautious. Alex can turn on the sharpest of edges.

'What do we do with this?' I say, the bag of dog poo swinging from my fingers.

'We take it with us and pop it in the first bin we come across.'

Bardo wags his tail as I drop his bag of waste into the back of the van. He seems very pleased with himself.

'Quite the place,' I say, stepping up into my seat. I should have had coffee, not tea. I feel a bit weary and there's miles to go. 'Who bought your painting?' I ask, but Alex presses her lips together tightly. 'I looked up who lives here,' I say. 'And your dog crapped on his grass.'

'I cannot betray my client confidentiality,' she says, with a smirk.

'Amen to that, then,' I say, and we both giggle as I turn the key to start the engine. For a moment I think it's not going to happen. There's a splutter and I can feel Alex's hot gaze boring into the side of my head. Then it does start up and I breath an inward sigh of relief. She turns to her phone while I listen to the sounds coming from the engine. I'm not sure how happy it is. I'm pushing it, really.

'Right, next painting stop is Preston or near enough. It's a good couple of hours. Do you think that will be all right? Do you think she'll make it?' she says, giving me a sideways look. She's listening to the engine too. 'If we stick to the A59 it does take a little longer than if we head south and skim Leeds on the motorway, but I know people in Harrogate and Skipton. We could stop there.'

'You want to visit friends?' I ask, but she laughs.

'No, Connie, I don't want to visit friends, but if we need a garage, I do know people who can help.'

'Right, of course, but I think it'll be fine. I promised you it would be, and I keep my promises.' I say this with a light touch, but no sooner are the words out of my mouth than I want to shovel them back in.

'Aye, well, that's why we might need a garage,' she says grimly.

I pull out of the archbishop's front garden and back onto the main road. Alex begins her navigation again, but she's lost her touch and I don't get any commentary this time as I head away from Bishopthorpe a long-lost friend, her dog and a bag of his poo on board.

*

For the next few miles the road is flat and the fields either side stretch out like parched blankets. It's been weeks since we had substantial rain and the countryside is showing how it's feeling the full effects. Everything has a golden, dehydrated tinge to it and even the hardy grasses swaying on the verges look as if they're praying for a few more drops of water. What we've had recently just isn't enough.

We are quiet inside the van and Alex has her face turned to the window. I'd dearly love to know what she's thinking about. Is she remembering the past like I am? Is she thinking about how close we were back then and how we could be again if we could only just talk? Or is she focused on her paintings and getting them safely to their new owners?

I want to remind her of all the good times. How we'd hike up into the forest and hold hands while we walked, away from prying and judging eyes. How we'd swim and run and dance and what it felt like to kiss, how wonderful it was to touch. I won't though, of course I won't. It would probably be the last I'd see of her.

I sigh and turn on the radio. We haven't had much music since we've been in the van. It's mostly been Alex and her commentary, but the silence is too much now and I'd like to lighten the mood. I scroll through the stations of chat until I hear music, but as I return my hand to the steering wheel the voice of Kate Bush comes through. *This Woman's Work* is playing. I nearly turn it off. The lyrics, although written from a man's point of view, cut close to the bone. Alex continues to stare out of the window as the song fills the van. Kate singing about words left unsaid and things left undone. It could be the soundtrack to our lives.

I feel tears pricking at the corners of my eyes, but I blink them away and try to stay focused on the road. Alex suddenly turns to me, her eyes shining too, but she's smiling; no, she's laughing.

'For Christ's sake, Connie, you were always good at killing the mood.' She turns the dial and finds something with a heavy bass and winds down her window. The breeze blows her hair around her face, but she's still smiling. My breath catches in my throat. 'There's a petrol station just up ahead. Can you pull in? I need some chocolate and a pee,' she says.

We're on the outskirts of Knaresborough and Alex directs me to a garage with a Co-op attached to it. I pull in reluctantly. The van is going for now and I want to keep it that way.

I take the opportunity to fill up with fuel and use the toilet too. Alex buys a tonne of chocolate, which she throws into the pocket on the back of her seat before grabbing a ball from her bag. She whistles to Bardo and he trots across the road with her. I back out of the garage and pull up to wait. There's a sign for Knaresborough Town Football Club. Surely she's not going to exercise her dog on the pitch! I get out to tell her, but can already see her throwing the ball and Bardo sprinting after it. I get back in and sink in my seat, disassociate myself from the situation.

She's back after ten minutes with a happy dog who laps at a bowl of water she puts down for him. Now with three empty bladders and a van full of snacks we're back on our way, the van cooperating for now.

16

We cross the River Ribble into Preston at three o'clock. Alex has returned to her navigational chatter while adding in her potted history of the city.

She starts with Preston being mentioned in the 1086 Domesday Book, moves through the Roman period to the English Civil War and the Battle of Preston in 1648, and then on to a visit by Charles Dickens during a strike by cotton workers in 1854. Before we reach the city centre, Alex is telling me to turn right and head north while informing me about the opening of St George's shopping centre in 1966, and my head is swimming.

'Are we stopping soon, Alex? I'm quite tired, to be honest,' I say, feeling that an afternoon nap is just what I need, and I'm more than happy to pull over and do that in the back of the van if I can shift the dog. He's abandoned his bed on the floor, because it's too cramped with the paintings and Alex's suitcase, and he's taken up residence on the seats.

'We are, Con,' she says and then seems to catch herself at shortening my name. She used to call me Con when she was being affectionate, Connie the rest of the time and Lady Constance right back at the start, when we first met. I hold on to that thought. 'My friends have said we can use their house for a night or even two if we need it. They're in Spain for a month and it's empty. It's a couple of miles up the road.'

'That's so kind of them,' I say. She seems to have friends everywhere. This reclusive artist with a hoard of mates.

She directs me up the A6 and then off into a leafy residential road with an eclectic mix of properties. Some are pretty bay-windowed 1930s semi-detached houses, some are bungalows and others are mock Tudor modern properties. One thing they all have in common, though is money. I think we must be in one of the more salubrious areas of Preston.

'Just here, on the left,' Alex says pointing to a substantial bungalow behind clipped hedges. I pull onto the driveway and come to a stop outside the front door. The place is vast, a single-storey long beige building, with no character at all. The windows reach down to the ground and whatever lies beyond is shrouded by vertical blinds drawn to an angle that makes voyeurism impossible.

'I know what you're thinking,' Alex says, opening her door. 'But wait until you see inside. Leave your sense of taste for the traditional at the front door.' She laughs.

Bardo jumps down from the van when I open the side door and immediately cocks his leg on one of the potted bay trees that stand sentry to the front door. I wonder if we should wash it away, but Alex is fiddling with the key in the lock.

'There's a key safe for the cleaners,' she explains, as she swings the door open.

Footballers' homes is the first thought I have when I take in the crystal chandelier hanging in the hallway. There's no second floor to this bungalow, but they have made a space into the roof with a glass skylight above and the hallway is flooded with sparkly, fractured light shining from an ornate fitting. The walls are covered in rich, dark wallpaper decorated with tropical birds sitting in golden trees. Paintings, ornaments, plants – the place is festooned with expensive-looking *stuff*.

Alex leads the way into the kitchen at the back of the house, which unsurprisingly is vast and gleaming. Dark blue and gold is the theme in here and the whole room sings with its particular style. My thoughts go to my tiny kitchen and its fairly basic cream, shaker-style doors and standard black Formica worktops. These tops are granite, sliced through with gold, blue and black, and they cover a huge island in the middle and a long breakfast bar that separates the kitchen from an orangery. I might call it a conservatory with its vaulted glass roof and sides, but the oak struts that support it make it look far grander than that. The area is covered in well-tended plants that hang, climb and creep. My eye, though, is on the large sofa by the doors to the garden. That nap is still forefront in my mind.

Alex steers me away, much to my disappointment, and off to the right, out into another brightly lit space, but she's taken my hand and I'm so surprised at her touch, I follow without a word, her warm skin wrapped around mine.

We're in an indoor swimming pool room with a jacuzzi. And is that an actual palm in the corner?

'Goodness!' I say.

'I know, it's a bit mad isn't it?' she says, dropping my hand.

Suddenly I feel less tired and the thought of a swim is welcome.

'Can we get in?' I say, and she turns to look at me in surprise.

'Alex, I've learned to swim. I'm pretty good now.'

She hesitates for a moment, but then a smile appears and she almost looks excited. I'd forgotten that Alex wasn't always the spiky grudge-bearer she seems to be now and I'm taken right back to the past, to when we were planning our escape.

We were in her room one evening after coming back from a day spent cycling around the loch. She had a map spread out on the floor and we sat, talking about where we were planning to go. She had a felt-tip pen and was busy drawing rings around all the places she wanted to visit. Our skin was singing from another day in the sun. Scotland was enjoying an unusual heatwave for those weeks I was there and everyone was sunburnt. I remember how excited she was, how excited I was.

Alex was braver than me, though. She was prepared to say goodbye to her lovely parents to take off with me in her brother's battered old car. Two friends on a road trip, two lovers on a road trip, not that anyone knew how close we'd become. I think William perhaps guessed at that point, but he would never judge or say anything. I wanted nothing more in the whole world than to climb into her car and never look back, but I was still terrified of what my own parents would say. They controlled and demanded, expected, but rarely rewarded. And yet, I still felt drawn home as if they owned me.

I look at her face now, her eyes shining.

I push down the memory and how it still affects me and force a smile.

'Let's get in,' I say.

We swim in our underwear because I don't have my swimsuit and refuse to rummage in the owners' drawers for a loan.

Of course there's a moment of self-consciousness when we undress by the edge of the pool, when we expose our thickened middles, nothing quite in the same place as it had been in the past. One good thing about getting older, though, is the ability to care less what others think. In my youth, even if we weren't in direct competition with our friends, then we were certainly comparing ourselves. My female friendships post fifty are infused with a sense of solidarity. We have seen some life, taken some knocks and we are all about lifting each other up.

Alex quickly defuses the situation by saying that we both look pretty good for a couple of old women and then we jump in, laughing, and hide any wobbly bits we have, under the water. Bardo sits at the side watching us as we swim back and forth. Alex is happy to do a couple of widths of the pool, but I take in a few lengths. My body feels relieved to move and stretch out after so long sitting at the driver's seat over the last couple of days.

I left home last Saturday and it's now Wednesday, I calculate. Home seems a very long way from us here. We have managed to cocoon ourselves into a bubble and it will be hard to leave it when I have to. And I will have to. Leo and I still need to talk; I owe him that, despite his head and heart being all over the place. It's also important that I make an effort with Diana, like Alex suggested. I am determined that we will be on the same team by the time the baby comes. For now though, I just want to enjoy being with Alex for as long as possible.

We do sleep after our swim. There are guest robes on hooks by the pool and the loungers are inviting. Alex makes up cool glasses of sparkling water and we stretch out. I'm ready to talk. It feels like a golden opportunity, but as I try to think of the best way to start our long-awaited conversation, I feel my eyelids drooping and I'm asleep in moments.

It's the smell of cooking that wakes me. The rich aroma of onions, garlic and oregano brings me out of my sleep and I sit up on the lounger and rub my eyes. My hair feels horrible after the swim. A combination of leaving it to dry without brushing it and the chlorine from the pool has left it in a bit of a mess. I run my hands through it, make a quick plait at the nape of my neck, tie my robe a little tighter and go through to the kitchen to find Alex.

She is at the hob on the island stirring something in a pan. She has earbuds in, listening to music. I know it's music because she's swaying in time with whatever she's hearing. She doesn't see me in the doorway and I watch her for a while. She's dressed again, in black trousers and a pink blouse and it looks as if she's blow-dried her hair into little Eighties flicks. There are so many things I want to say to her and my heart aches to. I want to tell her she's beautiful, that despite the steely exterior she has, I know how soft she can be inside. She can be fun and kind and incredibly sexy. My mouth dries with that thought, because it's been fifty-two years and our time together, in that way, is a long distant memory.

She looks up and catches my eye and there's a moment, just a tiny moment, where I wonder if she's contemplating the same things I am. Then she smiles and takes her earbuds out, reaches for her phone to turn the music off.

'I'm making a spag bol, which is pretty much all I can make these days. If you want to shower and change, then the guest rooms are down to the left off the hallway. Your room has teal and gold elephants on the wallpaper; you can't miss it. I was thinking we could eat this and get a taxi into the city, have a couple of cocktails. What do you think?'

'I think that sounds great,' I say, and walk away to find my room. Bardo trots down the hallway behind me for a bit, but then seems to change his mind and turns back to his owner. I'm not sure if he likes me. He will allow a quick pet from me, but then seems to move away. I think he's still sizing me up. But then I think Alex is doing the same thing.

17

I'm not dressed for this, I realise, the second we join the back of the short queue to get into the cocktail bar. I'm not used to coming to places like this. My long gypsy skirt and floral blouse are so out of sync with the plunging necklines and tight trousers of the other people here. It's youth, I realise, and I shouldn't be wearing the same clothes – that would be weird – but Alex seems to have it right with her outfit. She didn't change after dinner and even though she's dressed fairly casually in her black trousers and a pale pink, cotton blouse, her statement jewellery of long gold chains and colourful bracelets bring her far more up to date than me. She's also navigated the cobbled street we've walked up in high-heeled shoes, although I had to pull her up and out of the taxi that dropped us off by the gardens at the end of the lane.

'Can't we just go to the pub next door?' I ask, and she laughs.

'No, they do such wonderful cocktails in here; you'll love it.'

'I feel uncomfortable though.'

'Connie, why do you worry about what you look like? I'm sure no one cares.'

'I don't, usually,' I say, with a bitter edge to my voice. I can't really keep up in Alex's world, but then, I never could.

I always felt a bit like the spare part. I suppose that was why I was so keen to get on the road together then, because apart from the expected gentle ribbing between friends, Alex never judged me, not really.

We file in behind the others and wait to see if there's a table for us. It's surprisingly busy for a Wednesday evening.

A young man with a gorgeous ginger beard and a bright blue shirt appears. We're shown to a booth in the corner and menus are placed down in front of us.

'Can you tell Rachel that Lex is here?' Alex asks him and he nods and then disappears.

I put my glasses on and glance through the menu for something simple and palatable. What I'd really like is a glass of wine or a gin.

A woman appears from behind the bar. She's in her sixties I would guess, tall and willowy, reminding me of Vic. Her blonde hair is in a pixie cut and I notice she has a skirt on not dissimilar to mine, but she's teamed it with a jacket and that makes it look more chic. She wears a long string of pearls around her neck and a delighted expression on her face.

'Lex!' she says. 'It's bloody lovely to see you.'

Alex gets up and the two women hug tightly. She really does have friends everywhere. I wonder if it's only her inner circle that gets to call her Lex. I also wonder if she'll allow me to do the same.

'Join us,' Alex says, and I feel that tug of something unpleasant. It's the same tug I felt whenever Alex would invite others out with us, when I would really just want her all to myself. I'd dearly love to be back at the bungalow now with a cup of tea, curled up on the sofa, curled up with her.

'Go on then, I will,' she says, turning to me. 'Rachel Ewart.'

She extends her arm and I get up to shake her hand. I'm about to tell her I'm called Connie, but Alex gets in there first.

'This is Lady Constance Fitzgerald,' she says with a smirk, and I cringe. I also notice Rachel's eyes flick to Alex and then back to me with some sort of knowing behind them.

'Connie,' I say, as the waiter arrives to take our order.

'I'll come and get them, Graham,' Rachel says, and we all sit down. I glance at the menu again, with no idea what to have, so I ask Rachel what she recommends.

'Are you a gin lady?' she asks.

'Alex is the only lady here,' I reply with a laugh and Rachel looks at me, bemused. 'But, yes, gin I do like.'

'I'd recommend the White Lady then, funnily enough: Beefeater gin, triple sec, lemon, sugar, egg white. It's a simple, silky and delicious gin-laced classic with a sour finish.'

'Perfect for you, Connie,' Alex says. 'I'll have the Last Stand,' she adds.

'Of course you will,' I say, watching Rachel trying not to smirk. 'What's in that, then? Something cool and spiky with a hint of resentment?'

Rachel snorts. 'Okay, you two, I'll get the drinks,' she says and I can hear her laughing as she walks to the bar.

'Touché, Con,' Alex says. 'You always gave as good as you got.'

I don't say a word, but hold a gentle smile back from my lips.

A little later Rachel arrives with a tray and places three drinks down on the table. Mine looks elegant with a froth, which must be the egg white, and a twist of lemon peel tucked over the rim of the cocktail glass. Alex's looks just as lovely and I can smell the citrus from across the table. Rachel has something in a tall glass with ice and lemon.

'Just a Coke for me as I'm working,' she says, and we raise our glasses and toast, to good times.

'This place is lovely,' I say. 'It's warm and inviting, even for an old woman like me who's more used to the pub.'

'Thank you, Connie. There's absolutely no age discrimination here, well, unless you're under eighteen of course. I've had this place for about five years and we've made it pretty decent.'

'And this is delicious,' I say, taking another sip.

'Better than the pub?' she asks with a grin.

I raise my glass to her in response.

'So, the exhibition was a success then, Lex?' Rachel says. 'I heard it was a sell-out. Will that make things easier, do you think?'

Alex looks uncomfortable for a moment, but then she seems to rally herself.

'Did you hear that from Hank?' she asks.

'No, haven't heard from him in ages. It was from Imogen. She phoned before she flew back to the States, said there were red dots everywhere.'

I'm watching Alex during this exchange and I see the moment she visibly relaxes.

'Yeah, it was all good,' she says, but I don't miss the pointed look she then gives Rachel who busies herself with her drink.

'Apart from those paintings not for sale of course,' I say. The gin has made me want to do some digging and having Rachel here as a buffer could prove to be very useful.

'What wasn't for sale?' she asks, and Alex stares straight at me.

'Well, I had my eye on a lovely portrait of a young woman, but was told it wasn't for sale. Sitter one, I think it was called.

And then there was a gorgeous landscape of Loch Ness at sunset. It reminded me, a little, of a painting a dear friend gave me years ago, funnily enough. That wasn't for sale either.'

'That portrait had already been accounted for, I'm afraid.'

'There wasn't a sticker next to it,' I say.

'An oversight, that's all,' she says.

'And the landscape?'

'Well, that one has never been for sale. It should be in a pair, but unfortunately its companion disappeared years ago without a word or a trace.'

Her eyes are still on mine as I let her words sink in.

'Shame to have lost the other one, Lex,' Rachel says. 'How did that happen?'

'Stolen away, I'm afraid to say. The two together could have been wonderful, very valuable, but mine, on its own, to be honest, is worthless.'

I pick my drink up and take a sip, let the cool gin and warm triple sec flood my mouth.

'I hope you find it,' Rachel says, getting up. 'I'm going to get you both the same again and then leave you to it.'

Rachel disappears behind the bar and it's just me and Alex.

'I'm sorry,' I say.

'What are you sorry for, Connie?' she asks, with a weariness to her voice.

'I'm sorry I left. I didn't want to, you know, but I had to. I had no choice. And then I came back, but you were gone.' I take another sip and then a deep breath. 'I was pregnant and I panicked.' It's so odd to be saying these words to Alex after all these years of keeping them to myself. It doesn't feel liberating though. I just feel a great gaping sadness for all that has passed.

'I do know you had a baby,' she says. 'I came to find you. I guessed you might be pregnant after you left, something William said, and still I came to find you. Your parents didn't know where you were and I had to assume you'd gone off to have the baby alone.'

'You came to find me?' I can't believe it. 'You spoke to my parents?' That is unimaginable.

'I spoke to your mother and she was pure desperate, said she didn't know where you were and that it was her fault. Then your dad appeared. He was so angry and he made it very clear that they hoped you wouldn't come back. Something was off between them, that was for sure.'

'My mother is still alive, I believe, but Dad died a few years ago,' I say, trying to digest all that's been said. My mother being desperate, well, that's one word for it. The thought that Alex had come looking for me is both wonderful and also profoundly sad.

'The father,' I begin. 'He was nobody, not important.'

'But you see, that's just not true, is it. You have a son and that says differently.'

I try very hard never to think about Simon's father, but Alex is right in a way: he was important as he managed to shape most of the rest of my life in his one brutal act, but it's just not in the way that Alex thinks. I have a sudden need to unburden myself and I open my mouth to tell her what happened, so that she will see how unimportant he really should be, but she's got her hand raised to stop me.

'I have no wish to hear about it. Just leave it.'

Rachel reappears with more drinks and looks from one of us to the other.

'Cheer up, you two,' she says placing the drinks on the table. 'The night is young.'

'But, sadly, we are not,' I say.

'Speak for yourself,' Alex retorts, tipping the remainder of her drink into her mouth and reaching for the other.

'These are on the house, of course,' Rachel says, and we thank her before she returns to work.

'What shall we drink to?' Alex asks.

'Missed opportunities?' I suggest, still feeling the melancholy of our words.

'To shaking off the past and embracing the future,' she says, without much enthusiasm.

I raise my glass, happy to think about a future that might have Alex in it, but not convinced it's possible.

18

Alex is in the shower and I'm in the kitchen making a cup of tea when her phone rings. She left it on the worktop when she went to bed last night and I'm just about to put it onto charge when it starts vibrating. She keeps it on silent for some reason. Hank's name flashes on the screen and I deliberate over whether to answer or not. I swipe my finger across. It might be important, about the paintings and the deliveries.

'Hello, Alex's phone,' I say, feeling a bit silly and there's silence on the line for a moment.

'Hi,' he says, tentatively. 'Is that Connie?'

'Yes,' I say, delighted that after being so dismissed at the exhibition, Alex then must have told him who I was.

'Is she there?' he asks, and for just a second I'm embarrassed to say she's in the shower and how that sounds. I switched to non-alcoholic drinks last night, but Alex continued with the cocktails, and she was becoming morose when I finally persuaded her to get a taxi back to the house. She flopped down on the covers and promptly started snoring. I took off her shoes and resisted the urge to lie down next to her. Other than a request for a large coffee this morning, she's not said much else and I don't think she remembers holding my hand in the taxi on the way home.

'She's in the shower, Hank. Can I get her to call you back, or do you want me to pass on a message?'

'No,' he says slowly.

I'm not completely sure, because I don't know him, but he sounds a bit pissed off.

'Actually, can you tell her I've arranged the courier for Friday. If she can just be at the house then, that will be all she needs to do, and then we're done.'

'Well, *we* have eight of them,' I say. 'Actually it's seven because we dropped one off yesterday. I don't think she'll make it back by Friday, that's tomorrow, she definitely won't be back by then, we're still in Preston.'

'What?' he says sharply. 'You're doing what?'

'We're on a road trip delivering some of the paintings. Alex said she liked to deliver them herself and give that personal touch and what with your ankle problem…'

There's an ominous silence on the line and for a moment I think he's hung up, then he barks out a hollow laugh.

'But Lex has never even driven across town to deliver a painting,' he says, his voice confused. 'She's playing with you, Con—'

He never gets to finish what he's saying because that is when her phone dies. I reach for the charging lead and plug it in, stare at the blank screen while my mind catches up with what he has said and the phone decides if it has enough juice to start up again. Alex doesn't deliver her own paintings, which means she's chosen to do this with me. I'm not doing her a favour at all. A warmth begins to swell through me at the idea she has manufactured this trip so she can be with me, and then I have to push the smile from my face, because Alex appears in the doorway with a towel wrapped around her hair. I don't want her to know that she's been rumbled.

'I need paracetamol for my head and then I just need to pack. You nearly ready, Connie?' She sweeps her phone and the lead from the counter. 'I'll charge this in my room,' she says.

'Okay, I'll just finish my tea and we can get back on the road.'

I decide not to tell her that Hank has phoned. When he phones back she can answer it herself. I'd like to carry her secret for a little longer, because when she finds out I know she fabricated this trip, I will definitely get sulky Alex back.

I pack our bags back into the van and watch Alex for signs that she's spoken to him, but other than her being a little twitchy, which is pretty standard for her, I can't really tell if she has.

We make sure the house is secure before we get going. Bardo pees in the same place as he did when we turned up yesterday, a sort of arrival and departure territorial marking, but I ignore it this time the same as Alex does; he's her dog after all.

'Can I use your phone for navigation, Connie?' Alex asks me. 'I forgot to plug mine back in and it's still dead.'

I reach behind me for my bag, pull mine out and hand it to her, then reverse out of the driveway and we're on our way.

'It's in Rufford, just outside Southport,' she says, but it's not somewhere I'm familiar with. 'Not far, though. Do you want to buy some wool while we're still here?'

Alex finds a large warehouse on the road out of the town and I stop to buy a ball of pink wool. It's the colour of the walls in the cocktail bar from last night. Not sure how baby-friendly that thought is, but I shall enjoy telling my grandchild, when they're old enough, about that summer Alex and I went on a road trip and how the baby blanket was born. I catch my breath at the thought that my grandchild might come to know Alex. Nana Alex, Granny Alex, but I'm getting way ahead of myself. We leave Preston on the A59 and cross the River Ribble again.

'Keep right here,' Alex says. 'The fifty-nine towards Liverpool.'

In all the time I've travelled, I've always navigated my own way; stopping to look at paper maps in the past before satnav and Google were a thing, asking people for directions, just taking a chance and turning round if it didn't feel right. Having someone beside me telling me the exact way to go is both comforting and also a bit disappointing. There's little chance of stumbling down a blind alley and finding something or somewhere unexpected.

The land is flat on this stretch of road and the sky is huge. There's not a cloud in sight and we have the windows down. Bardo is ignoring his own bed and is back on my seats; the radio is on and Alex is drawing again. She's using charcoal. Her fingers are black and she keeps inadvertently wiping them on the seat. I try very hard not to mention it. Despite this, my sense of contentment is palpable and I hum along to the tunes on the radio.

Bliss, this is what this is: bliss.

'Can we drive down to the beach in Southport after we drop the painting off? I really want to see the sea, and let Bardo have a dip,' Alex says, and then resumes her work. She seems very well, and really has been these last few days. I still haven't raised the thorny subject of her illness. Maybe she's in remission, maybe I should just ask her what it is she's got and be done with it. Maybe Morag was mistaken.

I slow down as we come into Rufford and I'm glad when Alex tells me to turn off the main road – I've seen enough fields and hedging for a while. I realise as she directs me into the car park that it's a National Trust property – Rufford Old Hall. I can just see the building through the trees, a Tudor property and not big by National Trust standards, but very attractive all the same.

'Not a man of the cloth this time then?' I ask, as I come to a stop. The van isn't sounding quite right, like there's something in the engine waiting to give up. But it is still going, so that's good enough for now.

'I couldn't possibly say. You know the rules, Connie.' She grins widely and then turns round to climb into the back of the van, wincing as she goes.

'Are you okay? Is it your leg? Your hip? Where's the pain?' I prompt, speculatively.

'In my head. I should never have had that last cocktail last night.'

I pass her a bottle of water and she takes a hefty swig.

'It's for a portrait exhibition that they're having here in a couple of months' time, actually. I can tell you that. It's not sold; it's on loan,' she says, pulling the larger paintings out of the way to get to the smaller ones.

How I thought I could ever sleep in this van with all these in the way, I don't know.

'It's called Sitter One,' she says and she slips out of the van with a thump and disappears into the trees. I don't know if she's joking or not, and have to assume she must be.

When she's been gone for a few minutes, I grab a bungee

cord and fashion a lead for Bardo. I'm not going to make the same mistake I did at the palace and have him messing somewhere inappropriate. He looks incensed as I clip it to his collar.

'Don't give me that look,' I say, as he grudgingly follows me out of the van. 'You're not going to just run off wherever you like.'

I pick up my phone from where Alex has left it on her seat and tap in Simon's name. I haven't spoken to him for a couple of days and I ought to check in with him. He picks up after just a couple of rings and I lock Ruby up and walk Bardo into the trees.

'Hello, Mum, where are you?' he says, and I smile into the phone.

'Currently, I'm in a National Trust car park in Rufford.'

'Still delivering paintings?'

'Yep, still doing that. We've been to York and Preston and after we leave Southport, we're heading into Wales.'

'I spoke to Leo again, Mum. Is the wedding off? He said you left your engagement ring with Fiona.'

'I don't know, Simon. I only left the ring because it belongs to Fiona's mother, a fact that I was unaware of until she told me. Leo hasn't been honest about what he wants and I suggested a few days apart to think things through.'

'And you jump straight in your van on a disappearing act again.'

'That's not quite what happened,' I say, even though it's exactly what I did.

'And who is this friend of yours? I've never heard you talk about an artist friend,' he asks suspiciously.

'Alex Mackenzie,' I say. 'Alexandra Mackenzie,' I clarify,

before he can jump to the wrong conclusion, except that it would be the right conclusion.

'You need to come back and talk to him, not just bugger off on a holiday.'

'It's not a holiday; I'm helping a friend with deliveries. I'll talk to Leo when I get back.'

'And when will that be? You've been gone five days already.'

I think with the journey ahead, we might be another week at least, and I've got to get Alex home and then drive back, but I choose not to say that at the moment.

'What's really bothering you, Simon?'

'I'm worried about Leo. He's really down about it all.'

'Leo needs time to decide if he wants a life moving forward or a replacement wife.' I don't go further into it as I know how much respect Simon has for Leo and I'm not sure he'd take my side. That thought sits heavy. 'If you want to help, you can pop round to the flat and water my plants. I've got to go, but please give Diana my love and can you tell her I'm crocheting her a baby blanket?'

'Really? Didn't know you knew how to crochet.'

'I'm full of surprises. Goodbye for now, Simon, I'll phone you when I'm coming home,' I say and hang up. I don't think I've ever hung up on Simon, but his words stick in my ears. He's worried about Leo. However I try to justify my actions to myself, I mostly just feel guilty.

Alex arrives back then and I pocket my phone and try to shove my guilt in there with it.

'Let's get going,' she says, climbing back into the passenger seat with a groan she tries hard to suppress. I look back at the rest of the paintings behind me. We're only two down, there's still six to go, but this makes me happy. We have slipped into an easiness that I never thought we'd achieve. I think it's time to throw open some windows and blow the dust from our past. I wind mine back down and start the engine.

'Can you look up and see if there's a wool shop in Southport?' I say.

'You know you need to actually crochet with it, not just buy it.'

'I know, I'll catch up when we stop later.'

'Head south towards Ormskirk,' she says after I hand her my phone and there's a moment of scrolling. 'Maureen's Fabrics sells wool.'

'Another of your friends?'

'No, I don't know Maureen. I'm on Google Maps and the shop looks like it will have what we need.'

I feel a little flutter at the sound of *we*.

The shop does turn out to be perfect, with a large selection of wool. Alex comes inside this time and brings Bardo with her. The shop assistant makes a huge fuss of him and he rolls on his back to have his tummy rubbed. He doesn't do that for me.

Alex chooses a ball of moss green wool for me. She says it's the colour of all the miles of hedging we've passed. I'm beginning to think this blanket might be a bit of a mess, but maybe I can unify the colours with a complimentary border when I'm done. We walk back to where I've parked the van and climb inside.

'Come on then,' she says. 'I need a huge coffee and then I want to dip my toes in the ocean.'

'I can offer you the Irish Sea if that'll do.'

'Aye, that will do nicely,' she says.

The beach at Southport is beautifully sandy and stretches as far as I can see. The tide is out way beyond the end of the pier. With the sun glinting across the expanse, it's impossible to see where the beach meets the water. I park over the road next to a branch of the restaurant *Frankie and Benny's* and we take a couple of camping chairs from the van with us.

'We're going to have to find some shade for Bardo,' I say.

'Agreed,' says Alex. 'Let's head for the pier.'

The promenade is busy with weekday holidaymakers and day trippers. Living in a seaside town, this is commonplace to me, but Alex seems surprised at the number of people turning up to the beach in the great weather we've been enjoying.

'Inverness is touristy and busy,' I say to her after she makes a comment about the crowds.

'Not the bit that I lived in,' she says.

'Lived? Have you moved house in the few days you've been with me?' I laugh.

'Slip of the tongue,' she says.

When we're onto the sand it doesn't matter how many tourists are about, as there's miles of the stuff and we chuck our chairs down in the shade of the pier. I lay a blanket down for Bardo and fill a plastic bowl with water from a bottle I've carried.

'You're very resourceful, aren't you,' Alex says, sitting down in her chair and pulling her hat over her eyes. 'I'm going to sleep until the sea comes to find me,' she says.

'I'm going to walk to the shops and get that coffee you were after and maybe some sandwiches. Any requests?'

'Anything,' she says, lazily, lifting the corner of her hat. Then she hesitates for a second before saying, 'and thanks, Connie. I'm actually having a really nice time.' Then she drops the hat back.

The sun is managing to dodge the clouds and we spend a couple of pleasant hours on the beach. I buy large coffees and sandwiches from *Subway* and we discuss the next step on our road trip. Alex has put a two-hour cap on any drive now and chooses Bala on the edge of Snowdonia National Park as a great place to stop on our way to Aberystwyth. I pick up the blanket and begin crocheting, catching up with the apricot wool from York. I hold the pink and the new moss green up against it and they actually sit well together with the colours from the previous rows. Alex has her legs stretched out, the hem of her skirt pulled up over her knees and her head resting back on the edge of the chair, eyes closed again. Bardo has had a run and a swim, and he's now sparko in the shade underneath her chair.

'Look at us,' I say. 'Who would have thought all those years ago that we'd be sitting on a beach, aged seventy, crocheting.' I laugh, but Alex doesn't. She looks thoughtful though.

'I did, Connie; I always thought we'd be doing exactly this.'

'And how right you were,' I say, determined not to bring down the mood despite my thoughtless comment. It seems that no matter where we are and how comfortable we seem in each other's company, we're only ever a few, ill-thought words away from disquiet. What we need, I think, is a full-blown row, but I'm not going to start it. Alex gets out of her chair and begins to walk towards the sea. The tide has been steadily coming in so she doesn't have too far to go.

'I want to see three more rows by the time I get back, unless you want to swim?' she says.

I need to pick up a swimming costume somewhere soon. This is the second opportunity for a swim and I can't believe I didn't think to pack one. Then again, I wasn't expecting to be swimming in Peterborough. That seems like a very long time ago now.

'No, you go ahead; I'll carry on with this,' I say.

I watch her as she walks down to the water's edge, her red hair glorious in the sun, her skirt hitched into her knickers. She steps into the sea and shrieks as the cold water splashes up her legs. Then she stands and stares out towards the horizon. I'd give anything to know what she's thinking right now, but I'll have to content myself and assume she's as happy as she says she is, because I don't think *I've* been so happy in decades. I turn my attention back to my project.

By the time we're ready to leave I have a few rows completed with love from Lancashire.

19

Driving over the border into North Wales gives me a little thrill. Having spent a couple of years living and working in the pretty market town of Ruthin, more than five years ago, it's so lovely to be back. The countryside opens up around us and the scenery is stunning. I've always been captivated by the rugged mountains and spring-green hills peppered with grazing sheep, where the often gloomy sky meets the land and then the beauty of a shaft of sunlight breaks through. I've driven this road so many times before – in wind and pelting rain, in snow and bleak frost, but to drive it in the sunshine with Alex next to me is perfect.

We stop for fuel before we arrive in Bala at four, and Alex gets Bardo out for a wee. She insisted we stay here for the night to give me a break, but I'm thinking it's the van that needs a break really.

'We can have an easy night and leave early in the morning,' she says, as she points to a parking space outside a convenience store in the high street. 'I've found a lodge overlooking the lake and thought we could grab something for dinner, then we won't have to come back out again.'

Another expensive room for the night. I wonder if

Alex has the ability to slum it. I pull into the space and we get out.

'I'd like to see if I can buy some more wool,' I say. 'I'm really keen to get one ball in each place we go.'

'Not sure you're going to get much joy here,' she says, looking up and down the high street. 'Maybe the charity shop, though. Let's grab some food and then have a look.'

We pick up a bag of stir-fry veg and a sachet of sauce, some noodles and some frozen king prawns. Alex takes a couple of bottles of wine and a large bag of cashew nuts.

'Don't look at me like that,' she says, although I'm sure I wasn't giving her any kind of look. 'I'm quite often in pain and the wine helps to dull it.'

'Alex, you're a grown woman; you can do whatever you want. I'm not judging.' And I'm not judging because I picked up a couple of bottles myself. I'll keep them in the van for a rainy day.

The charity shop proves to be a success, as there's a basket of yarn on the counter. I choose a ball of spring-green-coloured wool and pay the woman serving.

'You have a project in mind?' she asks.

'I do. I'm crocheting a blanket for my grandchild, due in December.'

'How lovely,' she says, and I feel a warmth flood me. It *is* lovely, and reminds me that I want to be in a good place when he or she arrives. I do want to be settled, I want to be happy, I want to be ready.

'You'll need a lot more than the one ball if it's to cover the whole baby,' she says laughing. I look round at Alex who is touching the collar of a jacket, her face impassive.

'I'm buying one ball in each place we stop. We're on a road trip. My friend Alex is an artist.'

'Well, that sounds like a lot of fun, ladies, and a wonderful idea for the blanket. I'm glad it will have a little of Bala in it.'

'Oh, I need a swimming costume,' I say, suddenly remembering.

'I've actually got two, new in. But one's a young girl's size. Let me have a look,' she says disappearing through the door at the back of the shop. Alex wrinkles her nose.

'I hope it's not been worn,' she says, and I roll my eyes at her.

'I wouldn't worry if it has been. I'm sure it's washed.'

'Hmm, don't count on it,' she says.

'It's a medium, whatever that means, and it's a bit bright.' The woman reappears with something red in her hand. Red with blue polka dots on it. I can hear Alex sniggering behind me.

I take it from her and drape it across my body to check for a fit.

'Don't you have a branch of Zoggs or Speedo round here?' Alex asks, but doesn't get a response from either of us.

'I'll take it,' I say, pulling out my purse again.

'A fiver for a new swimsuit is perfect,' I say, tucking it into my bag with the wool. I'm surprisingly excited to get back to adding to the rows I've already completed. It's really beginning to take shape and I allow myself the idea of a scenario where Diana takes it from me with a grateful hand, a smile on her face as warm as the one from the woman behind the counter.

'Good luck with your blanket,' she says as we leave.

The road is narrow on the south side of the vast lake and the sunlight is fractured as it comes through the trees. I take off my sunglasses as they don't seem to be helping and the dappled light is tricky. After a couple of miles we arrive at the lakeside lodges. Three cedar-boarded cabins are nestled in the trees with a garden of ferns and angelica. Alex points to a parking space outside the first lodge.

'How have you managed to secure one of these?' I ask, as I pull into it. 'They must book by the week surely.'

'They do only book by the week, but I got lucky, because the people staying in this one had to leave early, so it's free for a few nights. I said I'd pay for the remaining days, and sweet-talked the lad on an e-mail. Don't forget, Connie, I've put the work in here. I've been through every hotel and B&B in the area. This is incredibly lucky.'

And incredibly expensive, I think, as we take our bags down the steps to the door. There's a veranda overlooking the lake with comfortable chairs. I know where we'll be spending the evening.

There is only one bed.

'I'll be more than comfortable on the sofa,' I say quickly.

'Okay,' Alex says without bothering to argue. I'm not sure how I feel about that, but try to squash any disappointment.

We make our food and take it out onto the veranda to catch the last of the sun. Bardo is the king of finding a ray of sunshine and he settles in its full glare. It's been a busy and tiring few days and we've got plenty more to come, but right now, I feel relaxed and happy with my glass of wine and bowl of comfort food.

'Where are we dropping the painting tomorrow?' I ask, resting my head back against the chair and watching the ripples across the water. There are paddleboarders and kayakers out on the lake, their trails sparkling as they move across the surface. I'm determined to swim in the sea tomorrow in Aberystwyth. All this driving is not doing my joints any good.

'It's three actually, a private collector in Machynlleth.'

'Wow, three! A Welsh collector of Scottish art. Is that unusual?'

'She's Scottish, married to a Welshman and wanting a bit of home around the place. She's bought from me before when she lived in Dundee.'

'That's great then. Alex, you're very successful. I'm so impressed.'

She scoffs and finishes her glass. I've barely started mine and intend to keep it that way; although, it's not that far a drive to Aberystwyth, I'd still like to do it with a clear head.

'You don't think you're successful?' I ask her.

'Define success, Con,' she answers.

'Selling all your paintings for a lot of money?'

'But, does it make me happy, and is it even enough money? That's the question.'

'How much money do you need? I'm pretty sure that amount would set me up for the rest of my life,' I say, but she scoffs again.

'Well, you and me are different, clearly.'

There's an unpleasant and bitter edge to her voice now and she leans forwards and tips more wine into her glass. She's hardly touched her food.

'Have you spoken to Hank?' I ask her, and she looks across at me, her expression sharp. 'About the paintings, I mean. He's your business partner, isn't he? Is he happy that you're hand delivering some of them? I suppose he encourages that personal touch?' I pick what I say carefully, my intention to drag some truth out of her.

For a long moment I don't think she's going to respond and she takes a long draw from her wine before she does.

'Yeah,' she says, slowly. 'He is my business partner, and of course he knows I'm on the road. Why wouldn't he?' she says, a little defensively. 'It was his idea, in fact. Now, I don't want to think about all that; I just want to enjoy my time away.'

I wonder why she's lying. It can't just be embarrassment about this trip, surely. I'm delighted she made it happen. Or has she actually spoken to him? I haven't heard her on the phone at all, but that doesn't mean she hasn't been. What she's saying isn't making much sense. I try to remember what it was, exactly, that Hank said to me. '*You're doing what?*' He was surprised, almost scornful I think. Perhaps the wine has got to Alex, maybe the sun today too.

'Are you happy, living in that huge house by yourself?' I continue, keen to pursue some conversation now I've started, even if she's shut down about Hank. I wonder if he's a controlling business partner, perhaps she's trying to become more independent. What does she need him for anyway?

She sighs and then drinks some more wine. Her words are becoming slurred.

'No,' she says. 'I'm not. It's too big for me on my own. I don't even like the house. I mean who needs ten bedrooms?' she asks, but I know she doesn't need an answer to that.

'How did you meet him – Lord Linton?' I say, unable to keep the amusement out of my voice when I say his name. He sounds like a fictional character: either a swashbuckling hero or a cad. I'm inclined to think the latter.

'I met him in Venice a few years ago. We were both at the Peggy Guggenheim Collection.'

'I don't know what that is,' I say.

'It's a museum of modern art on the Grand Canal in Venice. It doesn't really matter, but that was where I met him. I was travelling with a friend...' she pauses, but doesn't catch my eye '...and I met Sebastian who was there with his wife. We realised we had a mutual friend – another artist we knew – Helena – and we got chatting. Then he appeared again a while later at Helena's party in Edinburgh. She has one of my early paintings and Sebastian was complimentary about it, said he could inject some oomph into my stagnant career. He was a prolific collector and entrepreneur; he had property, status, a name. I'll be honest, and this is difficult to admit, I was swept off my feet.'

'I thought you said he had a wife.'

'He left her for me. Imagine me with a man, Con, just imagine that,' she says, splashing more wine in her glass and then drinking the lot in one go.

'No thanks,' I say quietly.

'Then again, imagine *you* with a man,' she says, laughing now. 'But, the funniest thing about that is I always had to imagine you with a man, didn't I.'

I put my own glass on the table and sit back uncomfortably in my chair. We might be here now, at that point that we've been heading towards for the last few days. Here comes the row.

'Did you love him?' I ask. Why not chuck in another grenade?

She stares at me, blankly. 'I admired him, to start with,' she says, simply. 'But I never loved him, not really.'

'I'm confused,' I say. 'He swept you off your feet; he left his wife and ignited your career. I assume you had sex?' God, maybe I'm more drunk than I thought.

'Connie, have you ever had sex that you didn't really want?'

'Yes,' I answer quickly.

'With someone you didn't really love?'

'Yes,' I say again.

'Anyway,' she continues. 'Nothing is ever as it seems, is it. You weren't, he wasn't, maybe I'm not.'

Her eyes are beginning to droop and I don't want a row; not now, I decide, not drunk.

'I'm going for a quick dip while it's still light,' I say.

'Out there? Is it safe?' she asks, rousing herself for a moment.

And there it is, the night of our eighteenth birthday party. I wonder if she's right back there the same as I am.

I'd felt awkward and out of place and only William was really talking to me. Alex was like the sun to our planets and we orbited around her. It wasn't just me – everyone seemed half in love with her. She was funny, beautiful, full of energy and completely in her element. The alcohol was flowing, but while others became sleepy or argumentative, Alex became brighter, funnier, more beautiful. I'd never in my life met anyone like her.

We'd set up on the banks of the loch. Bottles of whisky pilfered from parent's cabinets, something called Buckfast wine that was vile, and double strength cider were all being downed at an alarming rate. People had started to wade into the water; they were splashing about, swimming, some fully clothed and others down to their underwear. I couldn't swim, had never learned and had no intention of joining them, but I'd had a drink, my tongue had loosened – I told them it was my birthday too. It all happened pretty quickly after that. Arms were around me, I was lifted up in the air and carried into the water. My protestations were ignored, or certainly misunderstood. The music was loud and so was everyone else. Perhaps they thought I was worried about getting my hair wet, or my clothes ruined. I don't think anyone would have actually wanted me to drown. I was thrown further out than I think anyone intended – there wasn't much of me in those days – and immediately I was struggling.

It was only Alex who realised. She said she saw me thrashing about and she swam out to get me. All I remember was her arms around me and then my head clear of the water as she pulled me back to the shore. She wasn't one of those who had thrown me in and was furious with the others. The party evaporated after that, until it was just Alex and me sitting in front of the fire. She'd shut off the music, draped her jumper around my shoulders and as we watched the flames flickering and jumping in front of us, we really began to talk.

We made a connection that night, one that spanned five decades.

'It looks very still, but I'll be careful. There are others out on the water.'

I go inside to find my bag and then slip into the polka-dot costume. It does look rather ridiculous, I have to admit. Maybe I'll buy another at the next opportunity. I can hear Alex sniggering as I walk past her and down the steps to the water's edge. I leave a towel in the grass and step into the cool water. I don't want to stay in for long. Alex wouldn't be in a position to help me if I needed it and the light is disappearing. I enjoy a few strokes, following the line of the shore rather than out into the depths. I swim past the other lodges with guests also sitting, eating and drinking on their verandas, reminding me that we're not actually alone and Alex's voice can travel. Thank goodness we didn't quite have that argument.

I leave the water and sit, wrapped in my towel for a while in the grass, watching the clouds roll across the sky in waves and the sun sink below the distant hills.

When I walk back up to the lodge, Alex is no longer sitting out on the balcony and her bedroom door is closed. Bardo must be in there with her.

I rummage in the van for my sleeping bag and pillow and stretch out on the sofa. It's actually quite a decent size and comfortable. I pick up the blanket and continue with the pink and then the moss green. I intend to catch up to the spring-green, but I'm just too tired to do the number of rows needed. I manage to cast on the newest wool and have to leave it there.

'A bit of love from Bala, little one,' I say, this grandchild of mine becoming a permanent fixture in my mind. Then I turn out the light and sink into a comfortable sleep, wondering what tomorrow will reveal.

20

We drive into Machynlleth at nine, passing rows of pretty, tiny white cottages with doors you'd surely have to stoop to get through. Places are boarded up and some are for sale. There's a sadness about them somehow, for the past lives they housed, now gone forever. There's a splash of colour further along with houses painted in pastel, a war memorial opposite a churchyard and then, surprisingly, after our conversation last night, the Museum of Modern Art.

'Do you want to stop?' I ask Alex as we get closer. 'I could stay outside with Bardo if you like.' I don't know why I say this as she's never bothered about walking into places with her dog. She couldn't care less what people think. She's been quiet this morning, other than navigating with my phone – hers seems to be permanently dead – and I wonder if talking about Lord Linton has set her back. She seems to open up with alcohol and shut back down with a hangover.

'No,' she says. 'I really want to get these paintings delivered and then get to Aberystwyth.'

I'm not sure why there's such a big rush now, but I carry on through the high street where the shops are bigger, brighter and more abundant, until Alex tells me to turn left at the clock tower. She takes us up through residential streets until we're on a bend and she points at a driveway leading up into the trees.

The house is made from beautiful Welsh stone and has a balcony at the front. I can only imagine they have the most amazing views up towards the hills. The garden is full of rhododendrons and azaleas, with a glorious Japanese maple. The sun continues to shine and this feels very much like a little slice of paradise. I help her carry the paintings to the front door, where she takes a key from a safe stuck to the wall, reading the security number from a message on her phone. She pulls it out of her bag, switches it on, reads the number, then turns it off again before dropping it back into her bag. Not permanently dead then.

The house has a stone porch and Alex unlocks and opens the door where we stack the paintings inside. Then, she locks up and replaces the key in the safe.

'They're not back until this afternoon, but she told me to leave them,' she says, massaging her hip with the palm of her hand. 'Three more offloaded, we're getting through them, aren't we.'

We are getting through them and we've barely begun to talk, not properly. I have a horrible feeling we'll be on our way back to Inverness, having never really had the row we need to have. And then what?

Alex calls for Bardo to come out of the van and he hops down willingly. He has a good sniff about and then cocks his leg against a tree before hopping back in. I have to say, he is a very good dog.

When we're all back in the van, we leave the house and

head towards the A487. Aberystwyth is only eighteen miles away. It doesn't seem as if we're going to be spending too much time in the van today.

There's no need for navigation; this road is pretty much all there is through this part of mid Wales. We pass very little, other than a few isolated properties along the way and then a petrol station where I decide to pick up some chocolate. I don't need fuel. The needle, I notice, shows a good half a tank. I do make a mental note to get the van in for a service when I get back, though. When I get back – that is such an odd thought. It really does feel as if this is my reality now: being on the road with Alex.

'Someone called Leo phoned you,' she says, when I get back in. 'I didn't answer it,' she says.

'He's a friend,' I say, even though she didn't ask. She looks at me as if she can see the lie sitting on my lips.

'Whatever,' she says. Alex can still do a hint of the surly teenager.

Dark clouds roll over as we make the last few miles into Aberystwyth. The threat of rain is very clear in the darkening mass.

'I could do with a big breakfast,' Alex says. 'What about you?'

It's ten-thirty and we only had a cup of coffee in the lodge and some chocolate in the van. Alex finds a café and we park up on the road at North Beach and walk into town.

As expected she doesn't ask, but just walks in with Bardo. The owner doesn't seem bothered though and makes a fuss of him, but does give us a table at the back of the café away from the window. Perhaps he doesn't like to advertise the fact that he's dog-friendly.

Alex orders a huge gut-buster breakfast with everything, but I choose a toasted tea cake and a latte.

'Are you on a diet?' she asks after the waiter disappears.

'It's all I want at the moment, and anyway, I plan on stuffing my face with fish and chips in the van while looking at the sea through heavy rain later, as nature intended. We're on the Welsh coast and there is nothing I'd like to do more. I'm saving my appetite.'

In the end, Alex eats less than half of what she's ordered and most of that was dropping bits under the table for the dog. The waiter looks disappointed when he takes her plate away, as if he gets paid by the mouthful. I sincerely hope he doesn't.

'It was delicious, thank you,' I say, to his retreating figure.

We leave and walk back down to the sea afterwards and sit in the van looking at the waves.

'What's the plan, Alex? Are we here for fun today? Where's your next painting to be delivered?'

'This is a pit stop really. The painting is for someone in Llandovery, but I'm still trying to keep the journeys down to just under two hours.' I drag my map out from under my seat and open it up.

'This is a bit of a long short cut isn't it? We could have just headed down the four-seventy,' I say, tracing my finger down the paper.

'Well, your phone gave both options and one went straight through here,' she says, her tone defensive.

'But—'

'For Christ's sake, Connie, I just thought you'd like to come to Aberystwyth; my mistake, clearly.'

She levers herself back out of the van, drops to the pavement and begins to walk towards the beach, Bardo hot on her heels.

'Why don't you go and buy some wool and get your bloody blanket done!' she snaps.

She disappears down the steps and onto the sand, while I watch her go. I am so stupid. I suddenly remember why she might suggest we detour here. It was on our list of places to come when we planned our trip in 1970.

We were in her uncle's boat one day, out on the loch and Alex suddenly said that she wished we could keep going and not look back. I made some stupid joke about the loch having an end and that we wouldn't get far, but she took great lengths to explain that we could sail right out of the end into Loch Oich and then into the Caledonian Canal and beyond. But she agreed we wouldn't get far in her uncle's boat with limited fuel and really she could hardly steal it. She said she'd been thinking about borrowing her brother's Morris Minor and suddenly we had a plan in motion. We stretched a paper map of the UK out on her bedroom floor and drew rings around the places we wanted to go with a red felt-tipped pen. Aberystwyth was on Alex's list because her friend had been there on a family holiday and hadn't stopped talking about it. Alex did think her friend's enthusiasm was mainly because she'd snogged a lad from the arcade, but we stuck it on the list anyway. Our travel aspirations weren't terribly exotic at the time.

Neither of us were going to tell our parents. Her brother was working away on a building site in Carlisle and wasn't using his car. He wouldn't have minded anyway, apparently. I had saved the small amount of money my aunt had given me for cleaning the hotel, and Alex was planning on raiding her piggy bank and then selling her art on the road. We were irresponsible and stupid and so in love that we couldn't bear to hang around until someone noticed.

I can picture that map with the red ring around this town we're now leaving. Alex wasn't gone for long. The rain arrived and put her off of her sulk, so she soon came back. I put the radio on now, and Alex picks up her sketchbook. I keep glancing her way to see what she's drawing, but she has her book turned towards her, like a child trying to hide their schoolwork. Annoyance radiates from her and it's a sulky drive as we head south.

We leave the rain behind us and the clouds roll away as we drive through the pretty town of Lampeter. The Welsh flag is flying along the side of the road and bunting hangs from houses and shops. It seems to cheer Alex up a bit and she lowers her drawing and asks if I wouldn't mind stopping for a takeaway coffee.

'Left at the mini roundabout,' she says. 'Pull in here.'

I manage a first-class parallel park into a bay and can't help smiling to myself as I switch off the engine.

'There you go,' she says bluntly, pointing to the shop next to us. *Calico Kate*, the sign reads and there's a sewing machine in the window. 'You can get some of your wool while I grab some coffees.' She crosses the road and disappears inside the café opposite. I push the door open to the fabric shop and am delighted to see shelves stacked with wool. The blanket is really taking shape now and I choose a soft sand-coloured wool, reminiscent of the beach at Aberystwyth. It is hard to only buy one ball with all the colours on offer, but that is the rule I've set myself, and anyway, I don't crochet fast enough to buy any more.

I'm happy to see that Alex has bought pastries out with her as I missed my fish and chip lunch and it seems a long time since I nibbled on that tea cake. We set off again leaving the town and its pretty ice-cream-coloured houses behind us, the sky becoming darker still over the hills beyond. We're losing light fast, despite the fact it isn't that late, and I switch on my headlights.

Alex still isn't talking; in fact she's stuffing her cake into her face and gulping her coffee, but the atmosphere has lifted and as we cross the River Towy just outside Llandovery, she's almost lost the scowl.

She directs us out of the town before we've really got into it and then south on the A40, through a tiny hamlet called Bethlehem and onto the tightest of roads. It's already rained here because my tyres squelch in a puddle of mud as I take the bend, and for a moment I think I'm going to get stuck, but luckily the tyre gets purchase and eventually we arrive at a converted chapel. The front garden is a collection of old gravestones, which I think is a little gruesome, but the building has been renovated and is a substantial family home. Alex takes a painting from the back and doesn't say anything, but disappears around the side of the house. I take out the blanket and begin a row in the lemon wool that I casted on last night, and the clouds let go of the downpour they've been holding on to. The house disappears from view as the windscreen is battered with huge raindrops. I continue to crochet and try not to think about getting back round that tight, muddy bend. Bardo has curled up in the spot that Alex has vacated and is watching me with no intention of getting out.

'Yes, I know I've messed up with Alex again. What would you do to win her over?' I ask, but he just lowers his head onto his paws. 'Well, you're no use, are you.'

Alex is gone for nearly half an hour and I'm beginning to wonder if she's hanging the damn thing when she reappears with dripping hair at the side window. She seems more agile today and climbs in without any need of assistance, which is just as well as I don't fancy getting wet. Bardo climbs between the seats and makes himself comfortable on my sleeping bag. I moved it onto the seat when I was putting stuff in the cupboard and forgot to put it back. I'm about to make him move, but decide that reprimanding the dog of someone I'd like to win over is a bad idea. I'll just have to shake the hairs off later.

She sits for a moment catching her breath and I bag my blanket and hook ready to get going.

'Can you check the map and get us out of here? The roads won't get any easier with this downpour,' I say, handing my phone over and pulling away from the house. I take the bend in a considered arc, narrowly avoiding losing a wing mirror to the hedge. Alex fiddles with my phone while I take us back up to the point where I remember turning left.

'Left here,' she says.

'I think it must be right, because I thought we turned left to get to the chapel,' I say, but, in truth, I'm not one hundred per cent sure.

'No, it's left,' she says again, still looking at my phone. And I turn left because she's the one with technology on her side and really, my memory isn't what it used to be. This road does look familiar, well, if hedges and trees can be familiar.

'So, it's four-thirty now. Are we stopping somewhere or

carrying on?' I ask, hoping she's going to suggest stopping until the rain eases at least.

'I thought we could try for Bristol. It's two hours ish, and then we're in a better position to be heading down towards Truro tomorrow. But, only if you think you can manage it. Can you manage it, Connie?' She asks in such a way that makes me feel I have no choice. I remember her doing this before. A question that really isn't a question, more of a demand, a suggestion that comes with a heavy dose of expectation. 'I've booked us a couple of rooms at The Bristol,' she adds as if to sweeten the deal. I'm not taken in though. I'd be happier with sleeping in the van here and have Alex in a good mood, but, of course, I don't suggest this.

'Sure, if you think it's best,' I say.

We trundle along slowly as the wipers are ineffectually clearing the rain from the screen and I can barely see further than a few feet in front of me. If something comes the other way, I'll be hard pushed to reverse into a passing bay. Alex isn't looking ahead; she has her eyes firmly on my phone, repeatedly stabbing at the screen.

'Are you sure this is right?' I ask, after a sharp left and immediate sharp right. 'We definitely didn't do those bends on the way to the chapel.'

'Well, we're going a different way now.'

'We're trying to get back up to the A40 towards Abergavenny, yes? It skims the top of the Brecon Beacons.' I try to see the screen, but like her artwork, she has it turned away from me, which is a bit of a cheek, bearing in mind it's my phone. 'I think we're *on* the Brecon Beacons,' I say, taking another bend onto an even tighter lane. In fact it's more of a muddy track. We haven't passed any buildings or signs for main roads for miles and as we splash through another muddy puddle, I'm wondering how much tighter this track can get. The wing mirrors are clipping the hedging and the overhanging trees are scraping the roof. This lane clearly doesn't get much traffic.

'To be honest, Connie, I'm not exactly sure where we are and the signal dropped off a while ago.'

'I'm going to turn around,' I say, pushing down my irritation. 'We're just heading further towards a dead end, I think.' There's a small gap in the hedging and what could be a passing place, so I pull into it and put the van in reverse. The wheels spin and muddy water flies out behind us. I can feel Alex's eyes on me, but I ignore her and keep trying even though I can feel the back of the van sinking.

'I think you need to stop, Con,' she says. 'You're just going in further.'

'One last try,' I say, with my foot to the floor. And then the engine dies.

21

'Well, this is just marvellous,' Alex says in a dangerously low and deceptively calm voice. She opens her door and climbs out. She's not remotely bothered about getting wet and trudges round to the back of the van. I climb out to join her and we both stand peering into the muddy mess.

I step into the lane and glance up it and down it, but really, there's little point; we haven't passed anything other than vegetation for ages. The lane peters out up ahead and not in a way that suggests a nice comfy farmhouse is waiting around the corner.

'So, what now?' Alex asks, even though she's been the driving force up until this point.

'I'm going to make a cup of tea and have a think about what's best,' I say, opening up the side door of the van and filling the kettle with water from the bottle. I use just enough for two cups, which leaves us with, what I hope, is sufficient to see us through the night, because Alex hasn't reached that conclusion yet, even though I knew it as soon as I saw the mud flying everywhere.

'Not everything will be solved with a cup of tea,' she says, her voice beginning to rise now that the reality of our situation is settling in. '*You* said the van was perfectly roadworthy and would get us where we needed to be. In fact, *you* promised. Unsurprisingly, *your* promises, Connie, are, as ever, meaningless,' she says with a snap.

'Alex, you're being incredibly unfair. You knew what I was driving when you asked me for my help. And I didn't hesitate—'

'You did actually; you did hesitate,' she says, her arms folded across her chest.

'Anyone would have. You were asking me to drive for hundreds of miles for you. And I am!' I snap back. 'We'll walk up the lane at first light and find help, then we'll just get the van fixed up and be on our way.'

'No, Connie, *we* won't. I thought this was a good idea and yes, I needed some help, but really, I think it's time to call it a day.'

'You didn't need help. You only asked me to do this so you could find small ways to punish me,' I say with a cold voice.

'Don't be ridiculous, of course I didn't. Do you really think I'm harbouring some sort of resentment after all these years? Get over yourself, Constance!' Alex walks away from the van, insisting she is going to find a house and a landline, but Bardo doesn't follow her; he seems to have more sense. He looks up at me from the nest he's made himself in the back of the van with an expression that suggests I should be doing something. I watch her progress until she comes to a stop in the darkening gloom of the tree-covered lane. She changes her mind and tuts loudly. Then she turns back, her face a picture of resentment, and walks round to the passenger door where she climbs back inside.

I try not to think about the mud she's brought in with her. I sit down on the edge of the side door and pull my feet out of my shoes, then pop them into a carrier bag and tie the handles before tucking them behind my seat. Then I swing round and up to the stove, where I continue to make tea for two, regardless of whether Alex wants one or not. Sitting back in the driver's seat I sip at mine and leave hers on the dashboard, where she seethes at it, but eventually she picks it up and grudgingly drinks it.

She tries repeatedly to get a signal on my phone, until I suggest she turns it off to conserve the life of the battery and, when she ignores me and continues to stab at it, I snatch it from her hand.

'We'll need it in the morning when we have to walk for help,' I say. 'Try your own phone.'

She pulls her's from her bag, spends a few moments looking at it, then puts it back.

The sky isn't just dark from clouds now; the day is gone and we have the night ahead of us in the van. I rummage among our provisions. We have half a bag of nuts, some chocolate biscuits and, more importantly, the bottles of wine I picked up in Bala, in a secret stash under the seat. I grab the battery-powered camping lamp and hang it from the rear-view mirror.

Pulling my crochet onto my lap and settling back into the driver's seat, I begin to work with the wool I bought in Lampeter while Alex gazes out into the darkness, her arms folded firmly across her chest.

After half an hour, the tea gone and my stomach beginning to rumble, I push the blanket back in my bag and retrieve the wine and snacks. I don't ask Alex if she wants one, I just pour, and when we both have a glass of red in our hands and a fistful of nuts each, the atmosphere settles and we sink properly into our seats. *Say it now*, I think. *Say it now while she has nowhere to disappear off to*. I take another gulp of wine.

'How long have you got?' I ask.

'Until what?'

'You can stop being brave and pretending. Morag told me.'

'Morag? Told you what?'

Alex does genuinely look perplexed.

'Will's wife, you know, William and Morag.'

'Aye, I know who they are. And how do you come to know Morag? I know full well you know William of course.' This last she says with venom. She really doesn't like him.

'She said you were ill. She stopped me from going home after you snubbed me because she said you were terminally ill.'

'What!' Alex snorts and wipes some wine from her chin. 'Why in God's name did that old boot tell you that?'

'Well, she didn't actually say terminal, but she did say ill and that you'd had some devastating news.'

'Christ! The woman is a bloody nightmare. Her and Will are well suited. I'm not ill.'

'What about the visit to the doctor?'

'It was to talk about a possible injection in my hip. I have arthritis; I'm not bloody dying.'

'Why would she say that then? What about the devastating news?' I ask, as Alex pops some peanuts into her mouth and doesn't answer. Finally she stops chewing.

'She's a busybody, a gossip. Any news I have is none of her business.'

'Is it mine?' I ask gently.

'No,' she says quickly. 'No, it's not.'

I swallow down the disappointment and try to focus on the good news instead.

'I thought you were on borrowed time; that's why I agreed to this trip.'

'No you didn't; you wanted to be cooped up in a van with me for a few days to see if there was anything still between us.'

It's my turn to splutter out my wine, and I choke on a mouthful before wiping my lips with the back of my hand. I should feel embarrassed, but I don't, and of course she's right. Didn't I know this as soon as she said she was coming with me? She always did have a great way of clearing away the bullshit.

'Yes, that is true, but also because I felt I owed you for that disappearing act all those years ago.'

Alex lets out a long ragged breath and for a moment I think she's crying, but she isn't.

'You left, Con; you bloody left me. How do you think I felt after the time we spent together and the time we were planning to spend together? A note saying you had to go home for a bit and could I wait for you? You have a fling and disappear? That was it. That was what I was worth, what *we* were worth?'

I open my mouth to tell her that her timeline is off and to say sorry again, but she continues.

'I needed you! You were the one person who saw who I was and embraced it. You encouraged me; you were the ambassador for my art. I would never have done that without your encouragement. My family didn't get it, thought I had ideas well above my station, but you gave me the confidence to push forward with it. I *did* think we'd grow old with our knitting or the like, but after a long life together, not a fifty-two-year absence and then a *ta da*, I'm back. You broke my heart. Where do we go from there? How can we get from that to where we are now and for it to be okay?'

She runs out of steam and sinks back in her seat.

'I don't know,' I say pathetically. 'So, at least you're not harbouring some fifty-two-year resentment,' I try, and am rewarded with the merest of smiles.

'Aye, well, you know me.'

'I should have been honest with you back then, not run off home like a child.'

'A child, carrying a child.'

'If I had told you at the time that I was pregnant, what would you have done?' I ask the question I've waited a long time to ask. Alex sighs and turns to look at me.

'I honestly don't know. I might have asked you to give it up; I might have suggested we strap it in the back seat and take it with us.'

'*It* is Simon,' I say.

'Yes, well, you know I've never been maternal.'

'I did travel with him when he was a small child, and also when he was a bigger child. I was looking for you, I think.'

'I didn't go anywhere for a while; I was always at home.'

'You weren't when I came back. Your dad told me you'd gone away. I thought you'd taken our map and done the journey alone.'

'I was in Dundee, Connie, at uni.'

'Well, he didn't tell me that. He just said you were a walloper, whatever that is, and that you'd buggered off to waste your life away.'

'An idiot,' she says. 'He was annoyed that I was studying art, said it was a waste of an opportunity.'

'Well, he was wrong, clearly,' I say, motioning over my

shoulder at the last of the paintings stacked in the back. 'Look at you now.' I raise my glass to her, but she doesn't reciprocate.

'Yeah, look at me now,' she says, despondently, but then, she seems to rally. 'Look at us both! You were the golden child, set for university and a career in whatever took your fancy. Or maybe the wife to a prominent figure in the world of finance or law, politics or – I don't know – any kind of rich mans' game. And you did what? You went to Scotland, got knocked up, and ran away.'

I'm about to interrupt, but she continues.

'And I wasn't set for any of those things, but I did catch a break and went on to become an artist – and a dead brilliant one.'

She seems to run out of steam again and sinks back in her seat, pulling her cardigan closer around herself. It is getting colder in here.

'Yes, what a turn-around,' I say. 'But, I always knew you'd be successful. You're so talented.'

'You're missing the point, Con. You have a family, a life with people who surround you, who have your best interests at heart, who don't want to exploit you. Maybe not your daughter-in-law to be fair, but others. And, you're going to be a grandmother, so the family continues. I have absolutely nothing. Maybe I made poor choices.'

'What are you talking about? You have an amazing talent, a successful business; we've yet to find somewhere in this country where you don't have friends.'

Alex waves a hand at me dismissively and takes another fistful of nuts from the packet.

'Acquaintances, Connie, there's a difference.'

I turn back in my seat. She's a bit drunk again, becoming maudlin.

'Why did you do it, Connie?' she says, suddenly. 'Why did you sleep with William?'

22

'What?' I spin round to look at her, but her face is firmly on the dark night beyond the windscreen.

'We had something good, really good if my memory serves me well. I thought we were going to break away from the negativity and oppression our families exerted over us. I thought we were going to get out of Dodge, do something amazing, travel, be in love, be untouchable, a force to be reckoned with.'

That jigsaw piece finally slots into place in my head and I want to laugh. I don't, of course. Now is certainly not the time.

'I did not sleep with William,' I say, simply. 'How could you think I would sleep with our friend?'

She doesn't answer, but is hopefully processing what I've told her.

'Alex, I never told you why my parents sent me to Scotland because I was so ashamed. I should have told you, but I just couldn't.'

She picks up the wine bottle, wedged by the handbrake, and refills both of our glasses.

'I thought we were deeply in love and that you had sex with our best pal,' she says. 'What could be more shameful than that?'

I put my glass by my feet; I really don't want any more to drink tonight. This is so important; I've waited a long time to say these words. I want to do it with a clear head. I want Alex to stop drinking too, because I have a horrible feeling that she might not remember any of this in the morning.

'I was pregnant before I left London, not that I knew it at the time of course,' I begin, and Alex turns to me, her face a picture of surprise. 'Of course I didn't sleep with William.' I watch her as everything she thinks she knows slides away.

'Who the hell is Simon's father then?'

'I had an encounter with a man.' I can't bring myself to tell her I was assaulted. I just don't think I could say the words. 'It's why I was sent to Scotland, to get me out of the picture until things blew over. He was a married man with kids, a friend of my parents.' I swallow a hard lump and pick up my wine. Sod the sobriety, I need a drink.

'Christ, Connie, why didn't you tell me?'

'Like I said, I was ashamed. I didn't know I was pregnant for weeks. It didn't occur to me until I starting feeling sick. I thought it was a mix of nerves and being in love.' I laugh, but it comes out as a hollow bark. 'When I left Scotland,' I continue, keen to move on to safer territory, 'I went straight home, because that's what I always did. I was a good girl who did as she was told and always went home. My father wasn't there, luckily. My mother was furious.'

I remember that day as if it was just last week. I arrived back to my mother drinking a cocktail at three in the afternoon and it clearly wasn't her first. I had realised at this point that she had a problem with alcohol and that it was probably caused by my draconian father. It was a mistake to not let her know I was on my way; we didn't have the sort of home you just turned up to, even if you actually lived there. She was not pleased to see me. I took the opportunity to tell her about my predicament and to remind her of the truth that led me to my situation, but she was too flustered to listen. She helped me pack some more things and gave me some cash, quite a lot of cash actually, then told me to get myself sorted before my father came home.

She never specified what she thought I should do to get myself sorted, but I left with my suitcase and the money and hovered back at the train station contemplating returning to Scotland. I'd never felt so alone and frightened in my life. To me, Alex was a strong and independent young woman and I was pregnant and on a completely different path suddenly to the one we had planned.

'They were fond of sending you away, weren't they,' she says, when I relay some of this to her.

'Yes, always keen to cut off those not towing the family line.'

'So where did you go?'

'I got on the next train out of the station and ended up in Bournemouth. I didn't have a plan; that was just where the journey took me. I stayed in a grubby B&B for a couple of nights, then got myself a job in a restaurant kitchen and found a hostel to crash in. At that point I knew I'd never go home.'

Alex takes my hand into her lap and squeezes it.

'I'm so sorry, Con, how awful for you.'

'It *was* awful not being with you, but really, that was the time I grew up. I was getting steadily more pregnant and the chance to get rid of it had long gone.' I look to gauge her reaction, but her face is steady; she's just listening. 'I did look at that cash my mother had thrust at me as a means to get back to you, like it had never happened, but I just couldn't do it. Mostly because I was too scared to. I thought it would hurt; I didn't know where to go to do it anyway. I buried my head about it and just looked to survive. Eventually I found a house share with an older woman, Cheryl, who was wonderful. She helped me through the difficult time of having a baby. It seems like another world now. Simon was six months old when I got on another train to see you. I was so in love with my baby that I had a mad moment where I was convinced you'd have to love him too. That's when I spoke to your family, turned around and came back again. You had gone off on an adventure and I was a single mum.'

'Christ, Connie! Those early days must have been hard. You were eighteen with a baby. How did you cope?'

'I took each day as it came. Did some casual jobs: cleaning offices, ironing, a fair amount of bar work, couple of factory shifts. I shared child care with the women I worked with and Cheryl helped me out too. And I saved and saved, took donations of clothes for Simon and eventually managed to rent a small, one-bed flat.'

'That's a tragic story, Con,' she says.

'It's an everyday story for thousands of women. Not tragic, just life.'

'Did you get any help from the father?' she asks tentatively, but I close that line of enquiry down quickly.

'No, I never saw him again.'

She seems to realise that I don't want to talk about it so changes the direction of the conversation. She was always good at doing that too.

'Can't believe I thought you slept with Will. I was vile to him and he just took it.'

'He thinks you were mad with him for driving me to the railway station,' I say, as a snort of laughter erupts. 'Christ, Alex, what were we playing at?'

She begins to chuckle, just in the back of her throat to start with and then a barking laugh comes out, making Bardo glance up from his recumbent position on my sleeping bag. He decides he's heard it all before and goes back to sleep. I feel a weight lift from my head, my shoulders; in fact, my whole body. It's so good to talk, to tell, to explain.

'How wrong of your parents to blame you and send you away, push you off like it was your fault. And then the only support your mother offers you is cash.'

'Oh, Alex, it doesn't matter anymore. I just wanted you to know the truth finally. My mother isn't a terrible person; I think she did what she had to do to survive in her world. Dad controlled her and she lived on pretty little eggshells, never wanting to rock the boat.

'So, when did you first start travelling? When did you buy your first van?'

'It was when Simon was at school. His mates were going on holiday and we'd never really had one. A friend of mine offered us the use of her camper van for a weekend away, and I was hooked. We used it a few times, until I was desperate to get my own and make our trips longer. I'd trained as a bookkeeper by then and worked for an electrical company doing payroll. I saved and bought my own really crappy van. We never took it too far in fear that it would break down, but surprisingly it never did. I loved being on the road and Simon did too. He loved making friends wherever we ended up in the school holidays. As he got older and I saved more, we got a modern van and went further afield. We made it into northern France and over to Ireland on the ferry. I'd pick him up after school on a Friday and we'd just take off. There was a bit of a dry spell in his teens when he'd rather be with his local friends, but then when he was older still and more independent, I began to go off on my own. When he left home for uni and then when he was gone permanently, I took off for weeks on end, working as I went. After all those years juggling jobs I was good at the travelling life.'

We finish the wine and then after donning our shoes, the three of us go outside for a wee. Bardo cocks his leg against a tree and then we take it in turns to do the same– well not quite the same– although Alex gives it a fair attempt while laughing uproariously.

For the first time on this trip we are going to have to sleep in the van, and I begin the process of rearranging the furniture to make the bed, move the remaining paintings and tidy up. I pull out sleeping bags and pillows. It seems funny now that I put two in with the thought that Leo and I might go away together.

Leo. I'm still not looking forward to that inevitable conversation, but it must be done. For now though, I have to navigate the tricky situation of me, Alex and one bed. She doesn't seem fazed at all, and after cleaning her teeth out of the window, this five-star-hotel woman wriggles into one of the bags, plumps the pillow and lies down on the bed.

'This will be cosy,' she says.

'I can always sleep in the front,' I say, 'if you're uncomfortable.'

'Don't be ridiculous, Con, get in your bag. I need you for warmth.'

This is true. The temperature has plummeted and despite the warmth I've enjoyed from drinking the wine, I'm keen to get in my sleeping bag now. Alex scoots over and I lie down next to her, then she turns over and moves back against me, her body curved into mine. The potentially awkward situation is alleviated when Bardo jumps up and squeezes in by our feet.

'Connie,' Alex says. 'I'm so sorry for what you went through, and I wish I could have gone through it with you.' There's a moment of silence and then she says, 'night, Con,'

I lie there, barely breathing, the smell of her perfume invading my senses. I suddenly feel emotional and have to take very quiet, shallow breaths to stop the tears from coming. This is what I've dreamed about. This is what I thought my future would be like fifty-two years ago. And here we are, now, together. A montage of images flickers through my mind like a silent movie. Us together as girls in Scotland, and then imagined pictures of us as middle-aged women and older. The stuff we would have done, the places we would have visited, the things we would have seen. I could weep for the loss of those years together, but instead, I'm going to have to be incredibly grateful for what we will have now.

Eventually I fall into the most satisfying and contented sleep of my life.

23

I wake before Alex and lie staring at the ceiling of the van, digesting our conversation from last night and feeling a wonderful lightness that I haven't experienced in many years. She's lying next to me on the narrow bed, cocooned in her sleeping bag, but still her body is curled into mine. I know now that there can never be a reconciliation with Leo; there will be no wedding. I've probably known it for longer than I've accepted it. No matter what happens with Alex, I can't continue to live this half-life I've been attempting to do for so long, pleasing others, not really looking at what it is that makes *me* truly happy. That weight has been lifted from my shoulders and also from my heart. I am not the same person I was yesterday and it's an odd but enlightening feeling.

My bladder ruins the mood, of course, and I unzip my sleeping bag and try hard to get up without waking Alex. She stirs, turns over and curls back up again. I grab our handy bag with tissues and hand sanitiser and climb out of the van to find a sheltered spot in the trees. I let Bardo out too and he runs down the lane to find his own sheltered spot. I whistle for him as I walk back to the van, but he doesn't come. Instead I hear a volley of barks in the distance. It doesn't sound aggressive, more playful, and I wonder if he's found a rabbit.

'Not now, Bardo,' I mutter. 'I need to make some coffee.' I begin to walk in the direction that he headed, but don't get far before I see him racing around with a black Labrador. Then I notice the owner – a tall man in a wax jacket and wellies making his way down the lane towards me.

'Morning there,' he calls and waves a hand. His Labrador bounds over to me and happily accepts my fingers stroking his head. He's been in the wet bushes, I realise a little late, as I pull my sodden hand away. Bardo has too – his coat is soaking.

'Can you help us at all, please? My friend and I managed to get lost and then the van got stuck in the mud here last night. I've no signal on my phone, so can't call for help.'

'You spent the night here? Goodness, well then yes of course,' he says. 'My neighbour is a farmer and has a tractor. I'm sure he wouldn't mind pulling you out.'

He assures me he'll head straight back and send his neighbour out to help us, then he disappears.

Alex is whistling and attempting to get the kettle going when I open the door of the van. I watch her for a second as she fiddles, unsuccessfully, with the gas ring. She turns when she sees me and breaks into a grin that makes me so happy.

'How do you work this wretched thing?' she asks, flapping the kettle at me. I take it from her and get it going.

'We're getting pulled out. Bardo found a dog walker who's going to help us. We'd better be quick with this and make sure we're ready.'

Half an hour later we hear the distinct sounds of a tractor chugging down the lane. Gavin, the farmer, is an amiable chap and soon has the van hooked up to a rope attached to his tractor. He has his son with him, who gets into the van, even though I've told them I've driven from Inverness and am more than capable. They both look at the bank of sprayed mud and suggest we get out of their way. To be fair, I'm more than grateful to them both, and Alex and I climb in beside the farmer as he pulls the van out of the mud and reattaches the rope to the front to pull us up the lane.

His farmhouse is warm and inviting. He has a teenage daughter called Maddy and she offers us tea and toast and use of their bathroom while Gavin takes a look at the van.

'You've run out of fuel, love,' he tells me when I go outside to join him. Bardo and the Lab are tearing around the yard together, which means he'll be happily exhausted for the next leg of our journey.

'But, I'm pretty sure we had about half a tank, last time I looked.'

'It's your fuel gauge that's faulty. It does show half a tank, but I can tell you, it's empty. A quick fix at a garage should do it. I've popped some fuel in to get you to the nearest petrol station.'

'I'm so grateful to you,' I say. 'You've been so kind, thank you.'

We head back inside where Maddy insists we have a slice of her homemade lemon drizzle cake before we go. Alex has been sitting at the kitchen table with her, talking about art and showing her the sketchbook she's spent days doodling in. Maddy is intrigued and attempting her own artwork with a piece of Alex's charcoal. She's actually pretty good and has a fair likeness of the view from the kitchen window. There is noticeably no Mrs Farmer around and Alex, in true form, asks her where her mother is. I cringe at her direct question, but Maddy doesn't seem at all worried as she tells us her mother died ten years ago from cancer when Maddy was only five. There is contentment in this house though. You can feel the warmth between father and daughter, between brother and sister, even though my heart breaks a little for them.

Alex tears a page from her sketchbook and hands it to the teenager.

'It's just something I've been doodling on the journey,' she tells her, but when I sneak a look, I see a beautiful study of the Welsh countryside. Maddy is d

elighted and we leave with the three of them waving from the doorway and promises from me that if they're ever in Brighton then there's a meal on me.

We pick our way back to the main road, slowly and carefully, and stop in Merthyr Tydfil to fill up with fuel. I phone ahead to a garage I know in Bristol and book the van in for a check and then we head down towards Cardiff and the M4.

The radio is on and the windows are open as the sun arrives with mid-morning. It's been a roller coaster of weather as we've headed down the country, impossible to know what's coming next. Bardo is sitting on Alex's lap with his head resting on the top of the door, his ears flapping in the wind. There's a comfortable air between us and we chit-chat about the news on the radio and make up silly stories about the lives of the people in the vehicles that overtake us. I'm driving slowly and carefully, being very fuel-conscious, and I feel a pang for our imagined life. This is how it would have been if we'd made it onto the road when we were eighteen. I try to shake off the nostalgia and keep in the moment, to stop fantasising about what might have been and try to enjoy what we have now. You can't ever go back.

We cross the River Severn and arrive outside The Bristol

Hotel on the riverfront at two. I drop Alex off with her bag and her dog and she insists we take the remaining two paintings inside and that the hotel keeps them locked and safe for the duration of our stay. They agree to this without any problem, and also to accommodating Bardo, which tells me exactly how much Alex is paying for the night here.

The garage isn't far and the owner, Julie, promises to give Ruby a good all-over check and let me know if there are problems other than the fuel gauge. She's hopeful to have it ready for the morning, but says that if not, we can use one of her cars to take into Cornwall. I've known Julie for years and trust her implicitly, not something I can say about every garage I've frequented in my time.

Julie offers to get one of the lads to drive me back to the hotel, but I thank her and decide to walk. It's such a lovely day and my limbs could do with a stretch. I find myself at St Nicholas Market, somewhere I've been many times before, and I decide to get some wool from the haberdashery shop inside. I choose an icy blue shade, which is almost exactly the colour of Alex's eyes, but I definitely won't be telling her that. I slip the ball into my bag and begin walking back to the hotel.

Alex is in the bar and on her phone having a heated conversation when I arrive. There's clearly nothing wrong with the device at all. I hold back and try to listen in, which I'm not particularly proud about, but there's definitely something she's not telling me. Unfortunately I can't make out what she's saying as her accent has thickened and her words are coming fast. I walk over to the bar and order a coffee.

'Everything okay?' I ask, when she joins me a short while later. 'I see your phone is working again.'

'Oh, fine,' she says, breezily waving her hand to prove it, but she looks tense, a muscle twitching in her jaw. 'It's just being temperamental. I've taken Bardo out and he's sleeping now. Your bag is in your room if you need anything.'

I hesitate before I answer, suddenly disappointed not to be sharing a room after a wonderful night curled up together in the van, but I have to remind myself that Alex booked this before our Brecon Beacon adventure. Also, one row and then a minor reconciliation really doesn't mean anything permanent.

'I've got everything I need in my handbag,' I say. 'Look, do you fancy getting a boat round to the Pump House for lunch? They do a great gin and tonic in there, and there's no driving until tomorrow. We can be proper tourists. We can take the dog; I've got water and a bag of his biscuits.'

Alex slips her phone into her pocket and pulls the smile back to her lips. She was always good at burying a problem, pushing it under the bed and pretending it wasn't happening. The only problem is that she can never keep her brave face on for long. Eventually her mood will darken unless I can get her to talk about it. She might have a quietly glittering career and a large house with a bank balance to match, but she's still that eighteen-year-old with the same serious expression that she can't hide from me, when faced with a problem. I just wish she'd tell me what it is.

We leave the hotel with Bardo and walk the short distance along the street to the landing place to catch the boat. Bristol is busy. All the restaurants along the waterfront are packed with people having lunch and I'm beginning to wonder if we'll be able to just walk into the Pump House and grab a table. I don't have contacts like Alex does.

The ferry takes us past the arthouse cinema and the restaurants, the art centre and the amphitheatre, the huge building housing the M Shed on the left, partly obscured by the four cranes anchored out the front. Simon used to love the history of Bristol Museum when he was younger. If we were jumping in the van and taking off for a weekend, Bristol was often his first choice.

I try to engage Alex, pointing out the pretty coloured houses of Melville Heights and Brunel's SS *Great Britain*, but I hear how I sound – a poor imitation of the actual commentary going on behind us – and anyway, Alex is scrolling through her phone. Bardo seems interested though. He's sitting on her lap, staring over the side and wagging his tail at the ducks we pass.

We disembark at the Pump House and are lucky that a couple are just vacating their table so I pounce on it as soon as they leave.

I buy us drinks and order big fat burgers with chips, and we settle down for a pleasant lunch in the sunshine, watching paddleboarders floating past while Bardo takes a great interest in the ducks again.

'Are you going to tell me what's going on?' I ask her once we both have a drink inside us. I decide to jump in with both feet. 'Is it about Hank? Because I took a call from him the other day.'

Her head snaps up at that and she looks shocked.

'What? When? What did he say? What did *you* say?'

'Well, you said you'd spoken to him, so he must have said about the courier he'd arranged for Friday. I told him it was unlikely you'd be back and clearly you weren't. I told him we were dealing with eight of them by delivering them ourselves. We got cut off though because your phone died.'

Alex lifts her hands to her face and begins to massage her temples, small circular movements that are meant to soothe, but with the pressure she's applying she might take her skin off.

'Why didn't you tell me?' she asks through her hands and I open my mouth to answer. 'No, it doesn't matter. It won't make any difference now anyway.'

'I didn't say anything because I didn't want you to be embarrassed.'

She takes her hands away and stares at me across the table.

'Embarrassed? Why would I be embarrassed?'

'Hank told me you never deliver your paintings, so I knew you chose to be on the road with me, that you never really needed my help.'

Never mind her, I'm the one who's embarrassed now. She continues to stare at me, her expression becoming incredulous.

'You think that's what this is about? That that's all I have to worry about?'

'I don't know, Alex,' I say, feeling the afternoon slipping away, the sunny lunch and warm boozy glow evaporating. 'You won't talk to me.'

'It's just… complicated,' she says, standing up. She picks up our empty glasses and Bardo follows her inside the bar.

'And none of my business, I guess,' I say under my breath.

By the time Alex comes back with more gin, she seems to have softened a bit so the afternoon isn't a complete disaster. She doesn't mention Hank, and I salvage what I can with chit-chat about our onward journey down into the West Country.

It's been a while since I was in Cornwall and I'd like us to make it down to Land's End. It would be wonderful to traverse the country with her. Perhaps we can take in the

North York Moors on our way back up, maybe stop at Whitby for the best fish at the Magpie Café. We could cut across to Anglesey and jump on a ferry to Dublin – I'd love to take her to Galway and do a tour of Ireland. My heart is bursting with the possibilities and opportunities still open to us. My head, I'm afraid to say, is telling me I have business at home, but I push it to one side for now. I know, ultimately, I won't be able to push away my responsibilities for ever, but just for now I'd like to enjoy that feeling of hope, for me and this wonderfully stubborn, infuriatingly gorgeous woman.

That's if I can just get her to open up.

24

Later, buoyed up by the gin I've had, I contemplate taking her hand as we walk back to the hotel, but I resist that urge. I couldn't find the words to get her to open up and even our small talk was strained. Alex was never the easiest person to have a face-to-face, uncomfortable conversation with. I always used to feel wrong-footed and worried about saying the wrong thing. Our currency was action. The things we would do for one another. She'd clean one of the hotel rooms with me; I'd help her set up a painting space in an old shed in their garden. She'd pick out clothes for me when we went shopping; I'd make cakes with her younger siblings when we had to babysit. That was when we talked, and also in the dark, under the covers when we'd find a way to be together.

The sun is disappearing now and the lights begin to twinkle on the boats and along the waterfront. We follow the river back round, past bars and restaurants, tucked-away cafés and beautifully painted moored barges, then along the Millennium Promenade to the shops. Alex is swaying as she walks and not just from her usual hip pain. She's consumed more than me and she's a bit drunk. As if to prove my thoughts, she swerves left towards a chain bar, drinkers out on the pavement, heavy bass coming from inside.

'Let's have a nightcap,' she says.

'We could do that at the hotel, get the dog back,' I suggest, but she's already gone inside and I quickly follow behind her with Bardo's lead tightly in my hand. She heads straight to the bar and orders herself a large whisky then turns to me to ask what I want.

'I'll have a Diet Coke please,' I say, but she snorts.

'Another whisky,' she tells the barman. He looks up to see what I think.

'Diet Coke,' I confirm and he nods at me.

'God you can be joyless at times, Connie,' she slurs.

'Don't see much joy in being so drunk you can barely walk or string a sentence together,' I retort and then watch as Alex pulls her purse out, spilling coins all over the bar.

'Hey,' I say. 'What are you doing?' How can she be so drunk? I wonder now how many times she went to the bar and maybe came back with a double gin instead of a single, or had a shot of something while she was inside. I whip out my card and tap the contactless machine while scooping her money back into her purse. 'Let's take these outside.'

'No glasses outside,' the barman says, reaching for a couple of plastic cups. 'Sorry,' he says handing them to me.

'Don't worry, it's probably for the best,' I say, gesturing to my swaying friend. 'Have you got a couple of plastic bowls I can take too, please?'

He looks at me strangely for a moment and then nods, disappears through the door to the kitchen and comes back with two disposable bowls, which he hands to me.

We walk back out into the cool evening air. The sun has

completely disappeared now and I pull my cardigan closer. We find a couple of seats away from the rest of the drinkers and Alex sits down heavily before knocking back half her drink. I'm about to tell her to take it steady, but decide against it. She's beyond the point of no return. All I can hope now is to get her back to the hotel in one piece.

I fish the bottle of water out of my bag and the container of dog biscuits, then fill both bowls for Bardo. He eats and drinks and then settles by my feet.

'So, are you going to tell me what's really going on?' I ask her. She's usually more forthcoming when she's drunk, but I might have missed the boat this time.

She sighs for so long she has to fill her lungs back up again before she can speak.

'I've got to move out of the house,' she says, taking me by surprise.

'Why?'

'Because Sebastian and I were never married; he wouldn't marry me. It was too complicated with his property, his name, his children. The house belongs to his family and they've finally come calling.'

Instinctively, I glance at her rings glittering in the outside lighting and she follows my gaze.

'An expensive prop that will have to be sold,' she says, holding out her hand and admiring the diamonds, as if for the last time.

'Why did you tell people you were married? What was the point of that?'

'It was his idea, so I could command a higher price for my art. He was so well known in that world and he could influence collectors. Everyone wanted a piece of Lord Linton and wouldn't it be great to have some work by his wife? He suggested it as a bit of fun, and I was happy to play the part. He did it for me.'

She doesn't look as if she was happy to play the part; in fact she looks a bit disgusted.

'He must have really loved you,' I say, kindly, and fill her empty glass with water from the bottle. I'm pleased to see that she drinks it without really thinking about it.

'I think he was a bit obsessed with me, to be honest,' she says, wiping her mouth with the back of her hand. 'God knows why.'

I lean on the table a little closer to her. I know why. I'm a bit obsessed with her myself.

'I know it sounds like I used him, but it wasn't really like that. I was in a mess financially and he wanted to help me. He turned things around for me, well, at that point at least. I was very fond of him,' she says wistfully and I notice her eyes are starting to droop.

I begin to collect up our things and she leans her head in her hand, elbow propped on the table to take the weight.

'The trouble is,' she says, through squinted eyes and swaying head, 'him dying when he did was not great timing. He'd suggested a trust for me; it would set me up for life, he said. He never got around to it. He was a bit of a drinker and often didn't get around to those things he promised. Not that he should have; I really didn't deserve it.'

I can imagine Alex drinking her way through the last couple of years of her life. That sort of lifestyle would probably have involved parties and events. How easy it would have been to overindulge, for it to become a habit.

'So, what will you do now? Get a place of your own? You must have made a fortune with all your paintings.'

She laughs then, a proper belly laugh, but as I watch her face convulse, there's a moment when I realise she could just as well be crying.

'Con, basically I have nothing. I've lived way beyond my means for far too long and retribution has come knocking. I paid my parent's mortgage off, helped my siblings when I wasn't realistically in a position to do so, pretty much gave everything I had away. I was so desperate for them to see they were wrong and that the life of an artist was fruitful and rewarding. I thought I'd just produce some more paintings and get back on track, but it didn't happen. My parents, it turns out, were quite right – the up and down life of an artist is not easy. Fortune and misfortune are both at the behest of other people.

'Then, when I met Sebastian, he offered me a way out of my predicament, but it came with a lifestyle I had no business indulging in. He wasn't a steady sort of man really. I don't own any of the proceeds of the sale of the paintings. Hank is not my business partner as everyone seems to think he is – he's a friend of a friend, a man who has helped organise the sale of my work and to make sure the proceeds get to the people I owe money to. And he's just found out that I've basically stolen some of my own artwork and sold it behind his back. I've had private arrangements for those paintings that we're delivering. He's apoplectic.'

'Bloody hell! How have you managed to let things get to that? How long have you been having financial problems and – God, Alex – why are we staying in such expensive places?'

'I wanted to impress you,' she says simply and without a shred of embarrassment. 'I wanted that original rich chick from that posh London house and posh London family to think I'd done well.'

'I do think you've done well. I think you're bloody amazing and it has nothing to do with money. I live in a one-bed flat in Brighton and drive a camper van. That is my reality and has been for most of my adult life. I don't measure success in monetary terms and never have done.'

We sit for a while in a silence that is punctuated with the chat from those around us and from the music coming from inside, but it still feels palpable. I need to get us back to the hotel and get Alex to bed.

'What are you going to do?' I ask her as I begin to collect our things. I pour the remainder of Bardo's water away and tuck his biscuits back in my bag after letting one fall into his waiting mouth. He lets me rub behind his ears.

'This,' she says, swinging her arms around. 'This is what I'll do. Get on the road, paint, sell stuff as I go. No one can take away my ability, my talent.'

It doesn't sound like quite the impassioned speech, what with the slurring and the bitter edge to her voice.

'You can come and stay with me for a bit, if you want,' I say, but she doesn't answer. Instead she gets up and begins to pace between the tables like she's lost something. Bardo gets up to see what she's doing. People are looking, surprised at this drunk woman staggering around near them.

'Alex, let's go,' I say, taking her arm and bringing her back to the table to retrieve my bag and the dog. We begin the walk back to the hotel, away from the bar. It's only nine-thirty and families are still out finishing meals and enjoying a walk through the city. I'm dragging a seventy-year-old and a spaniel and would quite like a magic wand to get us back to the hotel.

'Con,' she says suddenly, whipping her head up to look at me. 'I don't feel very well.'

I steer her quickly to a clump of bushes at the edge of a square garden. Houses line all sides, but I don't have time to worry about what people think, if they're looking out of their windows. I hold her hair back while she empties the contents of her stomach under some perfectly clipped hedging. I glance behind me, but no one seems to be looking as Alex heaves and coughs, although Bardo looks away in disgust. When she's finished I hand her a tissue and she wipes her mouth and turns to look at me.

'Sorry, Con,' she says, her words still slurred.

'Let's get you back to the hotel.'

I slip my cardigan around her shoulders and take her arm. Despite what has just transpired I'm delighted to have her close to me. I love her. The thought appears in my head without any of the usual nonsense of whether she feels the same way, whether she even cares about me. I realise it doesn't matter either way. There is absolutely no question, I love her. As we make our way down the street towards the hotel it strikes me that this both pleases me and terrifies me at the same time.

Alex falls onto her bed when I get her back to her room, but I make her sit up and drink some water, then pull her shoes and trousers off, remove all her jewellery and tuck her in under the covers with just her pants, her top and my cardigan still on. The dog ignores his bed and jumps up beside her, turning round twice before settling into the crook between her bottom and her legs. I sit with her for a while. She's curled up away from me, and I watch her shoulders rise and fall as she slips into sleep. Then, I take a blanket from the top shelf in her wardrobe and settle in the armchair by the window where I intend to keep an eye on her. In five minutes, I'm asleep myself.

25

I have Ruby back by ten and I'm packed up ready to go. I took Bardo with me for the exercise. I've transferred money from my savings account to cover the bill, retrieved Alex's remaining paintings and stacked them in the back. They feel like stolen goods now and even though they're wrapped, I still cover them with a blanket. I need to get to the bottom of how much money she owes and who she owes it to, although I doubt she'll be forthcoming. I've decided from now on we sleep in the van because it's free or, if Alex is averse to that, it will be cheap bed and breakfasts. She has to stop spending money she doesn't have.

She's applying make-up when I go into her room through the interconnecting door. The door that only yesterday gave me a thrill, but now is no more than a convenience. I realised as I was walking to pick up the van that because I love her, my childish infatuation has to stop. Something more has happened on this trip. Probably more than we ever shared in the past. I'm keen to get on with delivering paintings and then to make decisions about our future, because for the first time since I saw her again at the exhibition, I know that she features in my future in every way. Not the yearned-for figure of the past, but the solid and very real presence of now. And she needs me; that is clear.

'How are you feeling?' I ask her, leaning against the doorframe, watching as she brushes mascara onto her eyelashes and fixes all of her jewellery back into place.

'Fine,' she says, as if there's no reason why she would be anything other than fine. I have lots of questions about her situation, but decide to save it for now. She might say she's fine, but I'll bet her head is thumping at the very least.

'Do you want to get breakfast before we go, or pick something up for on the way?' Personally I'm keen to get on the road to Cornwall. I can picture us on the beach at Portreath or walking the cliff paths near St Ann's.

'No, let's go,' she says.

In reception she begins to walk towards the desk, pulling her purse from her bag, but I gently touch her arm.

'It's sorted,' I say.

She frowns for a moment and begins to open her purse, but then seems to change her mind and sets her face to resignation. She doesn't thank me – she doesn't need to – but I can tell that last night's conversation is coming back to her and she's not happy about it. I want to help her; I want to remind her that I suggested she can come and live with me for a bit, or forever, but I bite my tongue. I want to recapture the closeness we've managed over the last couple of days before I encourage her towards any sort of commitment.

We drive out of Bristol towards the M5 and the van feels good. Julie at the garage gave me a list of the tweaks she'd made and the fuel gauge now indicates the amount of petrol we actually have. If Ruby can just get us down to Cornwall and back to Brighton, I'll be happy for now.

Alex finally admits to a hangover when she begs me to take her to a drive-through McDonald's at the services. Then we eat as we drive, the windows down, the radio on and Alex sighing with pleasure at the benefits of a greasy breakfast, while slipping titbits of her bacon to Bardo who's abandoned the back seat in favour of the food up the front.

We have a painting to drop just outside Bridgwater, and I get her to look up where I can buy some wool while we're there.

'I like being on the road,' Alex says as we pass the sign for Clevedon and Nailsea.

'You don't miss the Highlands? I thought you were welded to that place.'

'I love home and I won't deny it, but I'm happy to be on the road with you, Con,' she says, and then turns to look out through the open window. I'm glad she can't see the huge smile on my face and I try hard to get rid of it before she turns back.

The house is just outside the town centre on a new-build estate. I don't know why this surprises me, but it does. Alex directs me off the main road and into the maze of houses. There's an eclectic mix of properties, all built with an attractive use of something similar to Bath stone. We end up in a small close of six identical houses. They're all large with double garages and pristine front gardens.

'Number three,' Alex says and I pull over. There is nothing but fields beyond this cul-de-sac and it's eerily quiet. 'She's a wedding planner and events organiser,' Alex says as she rummages for the painting. 'We'll probably have a coffee if you want to disappear and get your wool. I'll keep Bardo with me so you can do your own thing. Clarissa won't mind.'

'That sounds like a great idea.'

'And then if we keep to the two-hour rule, we can stop in Bude for a meal. Perhaps you can look up somewhere special?'

'Fish and chips on Summerleaze Beach,' I say, and watch as her face drops. 'Alex, we don't need to eat in fancy restaurants and, besides, I didn't get my fish and chips in Wales, so I'm definitely getting them in Cornwall.'

'Okay, okay,' she says, climbing out of the van with the largest painting. I get out to help her.

'What's that one?' I ask.

'Loch Lomond,' she says, but I can't remember seeing it.

'We need to talk properly about your money situation,' I say, and she turns to give me a sharp look.

'Do *we* indeed?'

I laugh at the expression on her face and decide, in that moment, that I'm going to give her back my painting. It might not make a huge difference to what is owed or what she wants to keep, but it might help a little bit, especially if she tries to sell the two together.

'You can't put me off with that face,' I say, provocatively. 'Not now.' For a second I think about walking those four steps there are between us and kissing her, but I hesitate, lose my nerve and she's turning, and then walking away. She calls over her shoulder that an hour would be good, and then she disappears up the pathway to the front door, Bardo trotting obediently beside her. I drive away feeling a bit bereft and a little like I haven't got her yet, not really, not properly. It's exactly how I felt fifty-two years ago, but can you ever really have Alexandra Mackenzie?

★

The wool shop is quiet, and I chat to the woman serving for a few minutes as my eyes roam over the colours. I tell her about the baby blanket and how I'm travelling with my artist girlfriend into Cornwall to deliver the last of her paintings. She doesn't seem at all fazed at the mention of a girlfriend and for the first time I realise I will be introducing Alex to my family as exactly that. I wonder what Simon will think. I worry that he's so attached to Leo that he won't accept any other scenario.

I buy a couple of balls of wool, breaking my *only one in each place rule*, a soft peach and an ochre colour. This baby's blanket is going to either be lovely by the time I've finished with it, or an amateurish mess. Stepping outside again I see a newsagent's over the road and decide to buy some sweets for the journey. The sun is warm on my face. The slight breeze lifts the hair from my neck and I pull it back into a bun. It feels so good to be alive. It's as if this part of my life has opened up again with possibilities. I pop in and buy some fudge and a box of shortbread for Simon and Diana. I suddenly very much want to be part of their lives. Not the peripheral figure hovering at the edges, which I've become the last few years. I can't blame Leo – he's struggling with his own emotions and, really, he is a good man. But, it has become incredibly clear to me over the last few days that he is not what I want. I want Alex, or certainly I want me, the person I am when I'm with her. The question is: do I need her to achieve that and does she want me? I buy her a stick of rock while I'm in the shop as a silly gift and then I get back in the van to go and pick her up. My stomach is bubbling with anticipation for this next part of our journey.

My phone rings as I pull back onto the driveway of the

big house. Alex is standing outside talking to the owner, the wedding planner. I watch her in full conversational flow. She looks every inch the professional as she talks animatedly with Clarissa. You wouldn't know she's in a financial mess, has stolen her own artwork and is now homeless. I suddenly want to heal her. I want to take away the physical pain she's in and resolve her financial situation too. She could come and live with me in Brighton. She could paint and I could look after us. Maybe all she needs is to know that someone is there for her. When I arrived in Scotland, I had nothing and was in a bit of a mess. Alex put me back together then and now, I want to do the same for her.

'Hello,' I say distractedly into the phone without looking at the screen.

'Mum,' Simon says. 'Where are you?'

'Bridgwater,' I say with a chuckle. Simon doesn't change at all. There's a silence and then his voice comes again with a quiet urgency.

'Good, not too far away then.'

'What's up, Simon? Is everything okay?'

'Mum, it's Grandma. She's at the end of her life and I know you probably don't want to, but *I'd* really like you to come. She's in a nursing home in Kent and they really don't think she has long. I've got that bloody sales meeting in Prague tomorrow; I think it's time for you to step up.'

I watch Alex give the woman a warm hug and then turn towards the van, waving at me in what seems to me to be such a tender gesture. I hear the silence on the phone and try to gather my thoughts.

'Who?' I say, my brain not comprehending.

'Grandma,' he says again, but more urgently this time.

'Simon, you don't have a grandmother. Who are you talking about?'

'For goodness' sake, Mum, your own mother: Elizabeth Fitzgerald. The woman who gave birth to you.'

'Please be clear what you're saying, because I haven't seen Elizabeth Fitzgerald for all the years you've been alive,' I say, desperately trying to get a grasp on the situation. Alex is walking towards the van now, her hip swinging out to the right as she goes, but there's a lightness to her steps despite the pain I know she's in.

'Well, yes, of course I know, and that's a shame to be honest, because I've been in contact with her for the last ten years.'

26

We leave Bridgwater on the A39 heading towards Minehead. Bardo is curled up in the back again now the food has gone and the radio is giving us the news headlines, but I can't hear them because Alex is talking incessantly at me.

'Connie, you know I'm the last one to offer up my unsolicited opinion,' she says, and my response is to scoff. 'But I think you should go to the home.'

'Why would I do that? Why would I bother after all these years? We drew our battle lines fifty-two years ago. I'm not going to back down now. It goes against everything I stand for.'

'What utter bollocks! What do you stand for? You stand for being a bloody good mother who puts her family above her own happiness. You don't stand for decades-long grudges against decrepit old women. *Simon* is asking for you to be there, for *him*. Are you going to stop being his mother because your own is suddenly in the equation? I doubt it.'

My fingers grip the steering wheel and my foot is to the floor. Admittedly, it usually is to the floor, otherwise we'd never get anywhere, but the road is becoming windy, and I should probably slow down. Alex clearly agrees.

'And, you need to slow down, Connie.'

I ease my foot off the accelerator and my heart rate seems to slow with it.

'She might want to make amends with you. Would you let her go to her grave without the chance of doing that?'

'Oh, stop being so Scottish. I'm from the emotionless south and I don't care.'

'Rubbish, you're the most emotional person I know. Look, Connie, your mother let you down when you needed her; I get that, but if she's going to die, then maybe there's things you'd like to say to her.'

'She gave me money and told me to go before my father came home. What sort of mother does that? Anything could have happened to me. She didn't care, only about what the neighbours thought. I was an embarrassment.'

'And look at you now. A wonderful mother for all these years, single-handed, living an amazing life that I can only wish I'd been a part of, and a soon-to-be grandmother. You rose above it and did what was best for you and your son. My parents pretty much told me I was on my own if I wanted to pursue a career in art. I showed them how wrong they were.'

'It's not the same thing, Alex.'

'I think it is. Parents make choices based on what they think is best for their children. Sometimes they choose poorly. What do you choose for Simon, now?'

'What do you mean?'

'Well, does he have to sit by his grandmother's bedside on his own as she dies? Is that something you want for him?'

'How does she get to have a grandson? She didn't want to know before he was born. How bloody dare she have a ten-year relationship with him!'

We drive into the village of Holford and I slow down a

little more. I'm becoming increasingly aware of the distance growing behind me to home, to Simon, to my mother.

My mother. She wanted me to go to university and I chose to have Simon instead. She wasn't remotely sympathetic. She saw her own life of compromise and didn't want the same for me. She married at nineteen when she was pregnant and hoped that I would dodge that same bullet. The difference was that she chose the man she had her child with and I didn't get to choose at all.

'Connie, pull over for a minute. You're all over the place.'

There's a pub, the Plough, on the left and I pull over across some white lines outside the front, clearly telling me I shouldn't really be parking there. Alex leans over to turn off the ignition and then takes my hand.

'I'm sorry,' she says. 'Of course it's up to you and I'm sure you know best. But, I would say that people usually regret the things they don't do, not the things they do.'

I feel the truth in her words, but just can't reconcile the thought of popping in to visit my dying mother.

'To do it, I would have to give up all my justifications for a life-long estrangement, for ostracising them from our lives, for keeping a grandson from them, for not attending my father's funeral,' I say, my voice becoming quieter the longer my list goes on. Because the truth is that guilt bites at me. Maybe not daily – most of the time I can sit quite comfortably on my moral high ground – but when I occasionally let those thoughts in, it never takes long to overwhelm me. The more time that passes, the easier it is to try and ignore the very real truth – that, actually, I'm not really a very good person at all.

'Not completely ostracising; don't forget, Simon has been

in touch for the last ten years. Maybe you should go back so you can tell him off,' Alex says with the mildest of laughs. I do appreciate her attempt to lighten the moment. 'We can drive back together. I'll come into the nursing home with you if you want. Show your mother how wonderful you are, how forgiving, and that you and Simon are a united front. Your daughter-in-law will thank you for it.'

'I doubt that,' I say sourly. I pick up a bottle of water I've got stashed behind my seat and take a gulp, contemplate what it really means that Simon has been in contact and not told me about it before. 'If he's been seeing her for ten years, that means he probably got in contact when my father died,' I say.

'Perhaps,' Alex says simply. 'How did you know when your father died? Have you been in contact with other family members over the years? Do you *have* many other family members?'

'I have been in contact occasionally with my dad's brother, my Uncle Henry, but he died a couple of years ago. There was no love lost between him and his brother. Henry found Dad problematic and didn't have much to do with him. He tracked me down when Simon was about eight through one of my old school friends that I'd stayed in touch with. We exchanged phone numbers and addresses and he promised he'd only bother me with good or important news. He'd sometimes send me some money, but I always put it into Simon's savings account. It was so important to me to be independent. He was the one who told me Dad had died and he did try and get me to go to the funeral, but I couldn't bring myself to see my mother. I couldn't bear for her to reinvent the past and pretend we could have a relationship just because my father had gone. She had never been strong enough to leave him or maybe, deep down, she didn't want to. I expect that Henry was the conduit between Mum and Simon. There wasn't really anyone else.'

'Where is your mother?'

'She's in Parkview Nursing Home in Kent. Simon has sent me the address.'

Alex, who is still using my phone for navigation, begins to tap away at the screen.

'If we head back now, we can be there by seven.

'Hmm,' I grunt, noncommittally.

'When nursing homes say, 'come now', there isn't much time, they usually mean it, you know. I was half an hour away from getting to my dad's bedside when he died. I'll never forgive myself for that.'

'For goodness' sake, okay then,' I say, but an anxious feeling envelops me at my words. I don't really want to go. 'What about the last painting?'

'Don't worry, I'll stick it in the post,' she says with a grin.

I turn to look at her and shake my head then put the van in reverse and do a U-turn in the side road. I sigh as we head back the way we've come.

'What is it? Are you worried you've made the wrong decision?'

'No, not really, I'm just pissed off I still haven't had my fish and chips,' I say with a wry smile.

I am actually incredibly sad to see the promise of Cornwall fading away from sight in the rear-view mirror. Now Alex and I seem to be, if not quite on the same page, then certainly in the same book. I had a lovely image of us together in the West Country. I just hope we'll have another opportunity.

*

We're in the car park at the nursing home by seven-fifteen.

'What about Bardo?' I ask Alex as I find a parking space and reverse into it. We're around the side of the building, under a tree.

'He's got water, the van is in complete shade and the window by the wall is down. I'll just see you in there and then come back out while you visit with your mum.'

She takes my arm and we make our way up the path to the main entrance past the neatly clipped shrubs and rows of lurid begonias. This part of the building looks new and, inside, the reception area has the smell of freshly laid carpet. There's a quiet and almost sombre air to the place and two staff members dressed in navy trousers and pale blue polo shirts look up as we walk in.

'I'm here to see Elizabeth Fitzgerald,' I say to one of the receptionists who glances down at her computer screen.

'Are you a family member?' she asks me.

'I'm her daughter,' I say, and her eyes flick from the screen to me. Her colleague's eyes also travel to me. I'm pretty sure they're trained not to show any kind of judgement, but these two weren't quick enough to wipe it from their faces. She rallies though, and swaps the surprise for a well-practised and warm smile.

'Great,' she says gently. 'If you can both sign in here. It's just so we know who's in the building in case of an evacuation.' She pushes a book towards me and I quickly write down my name and the registration number of my vehicle. Alex declines the pen and tells them she's not coming in any further. Then I notice Simon. He's walking through a door at the end of the corridor leading from the area. He has his phone in his hand and an anxious look on his face. His expression softens when he sees me though and I'm grateful to Alex, then, because she's right. I need to be here for my son.

'Mum, you came, thank you for that,' he says.

'I came for you, not for her,' I say, rather unkindly and the two pairs of eyes watch me from behind the desk.

'And because I made her,' Alex says behind us.

'Alex, sorry,' I say, moving apart from my son. 'Simon, this is my friend Alex. Alex, my son, Simon.'

'So you're the man she left me for,' Alex says.

'You're the artist,' Simon says, and their words converge, although I hear all of it.

'Sorry?' he says, bemused.

'Yes,' she says, as I squirm like a teenager. 'I'm the artist. I'm sorry to hear about your grandmother. It sounds like you had a few years getting to know her, though. I hope they were good ones,' she says.

'Thank you, Alex,' he says. 'They were.'

They both turn to look at me then and I feel ridiculously small and insignificant, no longer in control of those around me. Alex looks disappointed as if she didn't quite get the introduction she was hoping for.

'I'll go and wait out with the van and Bardo,' she says and, without waiting for a response, she walks back out through the main door.

'How come you've never mentioned *her* before?' Simon asks in a tone that suggests he has something to be wary of. Instinctively he senses a threat, which almost makes me laugh. I've avoided introducing him to anyone over the years. He's never had the '*Come and meet so and so*' introductions. Any relationships I've had have been fleeting and private. Simon was the one who introduced me to Leo. In fact there's been a couple of times he's pointed me in the direction of a nice man he works with, but I've always declined the offers of coffee, theatre trips, meals out and once, oddly, a day at Thorpe Park. It was only Leo who I'd said yes to and I'm still wondering if I'd just run out of steam to say no.

'She's a very old friend I haven't seen for years. But tell me about you and Elizabeth. I think that's a bit more important don't you? You certainly didn't mention anything about her.' I try to keep my tone as light as possible. My feelings of annoyance are directed at me not him. I'm ashamed that he felt he had to get in contact and wasn't able to tell me about it. Then I remember the silent eyes beside us and take Simon's arm and walk him a little way away. I'm sure these women are used to all kinds of family dramas in this place, I tell myself, trying to ignore the whispering coming from them.

'Well, I did say several times over the years that I wanted to meet my grandparents. You can't say that I didn't. But, you just kept shutting your ears to the matter. You made it more than clear you didn't want any kind of reconciliation, but when I split up with Nikki, I was lonely and sad, and you were away. I did some digging and found a recent obituary for my grandfather.'

I hadn't anticipated how hard this would be to hear, and I have to keep my breathing steady to stop myself from becoming emotional.

'Mum, I went to the funeral to meet my family, such as they were.'

There it is, the first tear slides down my face and I wipe it away.

'Look,' he says. 'I know that you didn't get on with your parents, but it's not like they ever did anything bad to me.'

And absolutely nothing to help either, I think, but sensibly I keep my mouth shut. The problem is, I realise, that I blame everything on my parents. Even though I never really told them the truth about that night, I still expected them to guess what actually happened. *He* was their friend after all. And to be sent away like a naughty girl and then having to leave Alex and return home. Being dismissed with a wad of cash and then losing Alex for fifty-two years. I blame them for it all, and that is going to be incredibly difficult to let go of.

'She's been here for three years,' he says. 'She had a stroke and then after a few weeks in hospital it was clear she wasn't going to make a miraculous recovery, so Diana and I helped to choose this place for her to move into, not too far from us.'

'You and Diana?' I say sharply.

'Yes, she's my wife!'

Suddenly, Diana's cutting remark and her look at the restaurant on my birthday make a lot more sense. I feel a bubble of anger rise up in me for all that was going on behind my back.

'Mum, someone had to do it. She was completely on her own and she made me her next of kin.'

I scour my memory for all the times that Simon would raise the thorny subject of my mother and after every rejection from me, I do remember a time when he stopped talking about her altogether. I thought he'd just resigned himself to my way of thinking. I should have known him better.

'So, what's wrong with her now?' I ask.

'The stroke weakened her, and she's mostly been in bed since then. She's got pneumonia now and that's pretty much it, I'm afraid. She's not really with it, but do you want to come and see her?' Simon asks me, and I have to fight the urge to tell him that of course I don't want to see her. *Do it for him*, I tell myself. *Once she's gone it won't matter anyway.*

'Okay,' I say, 'just for a moment.'

27

The room is surprisingly light. Maybe I imagined I'd be walking into her bedroom, her curtains pulled closed, on one of her late afternoon naps with just her velvet bedside lamp lit. One of her cocktail parties would do that to her – leave her needing beauty sleep to recharge her batteries ready for the next one.

I look everywhere but the bed.

She has a corner room with two windows: one looking out over the gardens at the front and one over the car park at the side. I glance down and see Ruby in her spot and Alex with the side door open, sitting on the ledge, Bardo drinking from his plastic bowl by her feet. Alex has her phone out and is tapping away on the screen. I lean against the window ledge and turn back to face the room. It's surprisingly hotel-like for end of life. I think I'd been expecting a more hospital-like set-up, but this room has plush carpets and curtains and some dark wood furniture. The only nod in a medical direction is a chart on the wall and one of those hospital-type tables on wheels that swings round and across the bed when needed. My mother's is firmly against the wall.

Simon walks straight in and over to her bed, picks up her

lifeless hand and sits down in the chair beside her. I take a step closer.

The woman in the bed is not my mother, or not as I remember her. Where is the rouge, the perfectly coiffured hair, the painted fingernails? This woman is elderly, decrepit, with an oxygen mask strapped to her face. I take another step. Her hair is short and white, barely more than a few wisps across her scalp. She's eighty-nine years old, but looks surprisingly older.

I feel a twinge of guilt and also annoyance. Guilt that I haven't seen her sooner, meaning Simon had to take on her care, and annoyance that she looks so pathetic that I'll have to be the bigger person. Who could possibly not forgive a woman on her death bed? I suddenly very much wish I hadn't come.

Simon hovers for a moment and it's so strange to see him hold the hand of a woman I've not seen for so long: a stranger. Then he says he needs to phone Diana as she hadn't been feeling well. He wants to check on her.

'What's wrong, not the baby?' I ask, kicking myself for not asking about her before. I need to get my head back to what's important.

'No, I think it's just the effects of pregnancy,' he says.

'*Just* is a big word,' I say. 'Pregnancy wreaks havoc on your body, but I know you'll be looking after her. Give her my love,' I add as the door swings closed behind him and I'm alone with Elizabeth Fitzgerald.

I walk over to the bed and sit down in the chair that Simon has just vacated. I lean my elbows on my knees and stare at her, take in the lines on her face, her slack jaw, the way her thin hair is tucked around her ears. I wouldn't know this woman if she was able to pass me in the street. I can't imagine this woman sipping cocktails and laughing at jokes that handsome men make. It's impossible to think that she danced and sang, read me stories when I was a small child, painted her nails and made up her face to always be the most beautiful woman in the room.

I choke back a sob when I think of all the times she has tried to contact me over the years, written letters that other family members passed on, left messages on my answering machine that I would delete before listening to more than her first couple of words. The imagined image of her at my father's funeral is too much and I lean forward.

'Mum,' I say. 'It's me, it's Constance.'

Her chest rises and falls rapidly, her lungs desperately trying to keep her alive, but that is the only movement from her body. All of a sudden I have so much I want to say to her. I take a deep breath.

I will never know what Dad did to make you so distant and unfeeling. I won't know why I always played second place to your friends, shopping and drinks parties. I thought I was quite easy to love and would have been very loving in return. I don't regret not answering your calls and letters; it was all about self-preservation.

Because, you let me down. When I needed you the most you chose to send me away. I know that you realise what really happened that night, because I saw it on your face before you shut it down, before you decided it was better for all concerned if it was a matter that could be packed away on a train and out of sight.

When I came back from Scotland – I won't say home because it was clear I wasn't welcome – that was your opportunity to make amends, to find some way to help your only child and you couldn't even do that. Throwing cash at me and sending me away again was an unforgivable thing to do to me. I needed you and you couldn't bring yourself to put me first.

You are so lucky to have had that time with Simon, and you didn't deserve it. I adore my son with a deep and unflinching love that you could not possibly understand.

This is the speech I've run through in my head for years. This is what I wanted to say if I ever saw her again, but now, sitting by her side, I realise that I will have to be the bigger person yet again. And, perhaps I'm not such a bad person after all.

I lean forward and take her hand in mine, careful not to harm the papery skin or catch her wedding ring that hangs loose on her finger. Suddenly a glimpse of a memory works its way into my brain. Me as a small child holding my mother's hand. We had a game, how could I forget? Three squeezes from her: *I Love You*. Four squeezes from me: *I Love You Too*.

A sob bursts up from me and tears come unbidden, flowing down my cheeks in torrents. My mother's eyes suddenly open. She doesn't turn and look at me, but stares up, seemingly vacant. I quickly squeeze her hand three times.

'Mum,' I say. 'I love you and I forgive you.'

28

I walk out of her room and back down to the reception area on wobbly legs, my head full of regret and sadness. I don't get much time to process it though because there are two people sitting side by side on the bank of plush sofas next to the reception desk: Alex and Leo.

They both look up as I approach, Alex's smile warm and friendly, Leo's a little more apprehensive. His left leg is jiggling up and down, his hands folded tightly in his lap. Two strangers who have no idea they share a connection.

'Leo, what are you doing here?' I say, as lightly as I can. Alex immediately turns to look at him and I see every emotion behind her eyes as she takes him in.

'I came to see you of course. Simon phoned me to say you were here. I didn't think you'd come to be honest. I know there was no love lost between you and your family, but it's wonderful to see you're here to forgive.'

'Leo,' I say. 'I'm sorry but I don't have the headspace for this at the moment. Can I call you tomorrow? I've only just got back from my trip.' I keep my voice as light as I can, the tone you'd use with a friend, *just* a friend.

'Ah, yes, your trip. So lovely to give your friend a helping hand. So like you, Connie. You've always been such a kind and generous woman. And so forgiving too,' he adds, in a way that makes me want to shrink. Alex stares at me pointedly; now is the time for an introduction that I don't want to make.

'Why don't you go *now*, and I'll phone you tomorrow?' I suggest, feeling ever more anxious. I don't want to be in this position where I'm introducing my ex-fiancé to the love of my life.

'I'm Alex,' she says, turning and holding out her hand. 'I'm the friend.'

Leo takes her hand instinctively and there's a long ten seconds of silence while every wraps their heads around the situation. I'd much rather be back by my mother's bedside right now. Whatever else Leo is, he's a very intuitive judge of character. He reads people so easily, apart from when he's trying to mould them into his late wife, of course. To help his thought process along, Alex pushes her arm through mine, linking us together.

'Lovely to meet you,' Leo says. 'So, you're an artist, I hear.'

'Yes,' I jump in. 'Alex painted the picture of Loch Ness that's on my living room wall.'

'Oh? The one that used to be above your bed?'

'Yes,' I say, nearly choking. 'That's the one.'

Alex snorts beside me. 'How is your mother?' she asks, finally getting back to the reason we're all here.

'She's pretty much out of it to be honest. I sat with her for a bit, but it's not like she can hear me.'

'Don't they say that your hearing is the last thing to go before you do? Maybe she *can* hear you,' Alex says.

'I've heard that, too,' says Leo. 'Keep talking if that's what you want to do.'

He stares pointedly at me and there's an awkward moment where the three of us reach for something to say.

'I need to check on the dog,' Alex says suddenly. 'Won't be long.'

She doesn't wait for a response, but leaves us standing in the middle of the reception area. Leo turns to me.

'I am sorry, Connie,' he says simply and sadly.

'We've had a lovely time together and you've been a very good friend to me. I was very sorry to hear about the sad passing of your wife; that must have been incredibly difficult for you to deal with. Fiona told me a very little of your sadness.' I take hold of his hand as a flash of pain crosses his expression, but he nods and it's gone. I let my hand drop to my side. 'I do think, though, that we rushed into the whole marriage thing and that perhaps we shouldn't have done that.' I pause to allow him to say what he thinks and I brace myself for some sort of protestation.

'I agree completely. It was rushed into and not thought out properly. I *was* devastated after losing Brenda, and you're probably right about me pushing to try and replace her. To be honest, Connie, I don't think we really work. You're more of a free spirit than me. I like being at home with my comforts, with my daughter. I think I need to look after someone and you're far too independent. I want to be with someone who likes the same things and you're not really that person.'

'Right,' I say, a little taken aback. This was not what I was expecting at all.

'And, I did want to speak to you sooner, but you've been preoccupied, on the road with your friend.'

'Yes, I'm sorry I just took off without talking to you. I was hurt that you hadn't mentioned me to Fiona and about the ring too. I should have given you a chance to explain.'

And keen to go and see Alex, I think. My ego could do with a little crushing, it serves me right, frankly. It's not as if Leo has rushed off to find someone else.

'I wasn't thinking, Connie.'

'It doesn't matter now. I just wish you all the very best, I really do,' I say, taking his hand again and squeezing it. I realise that we haven't used the words, *it's over*, but we both know that it is.

'Will you be okay?' he asks. 'I'll cancel the wedding venue and all of that, just leave it to me.'

'Thank you, and I will be, I'll be just fine.'

He leans forward to kiss my cheek and I catch sight of Alex out of the corner of my eye. She's walking towards us, her expression unreadable.

'Well, I'll leave you to it,' Leo says, stepping back from me and dropping his hand. Relief radiates from him, in fact I don't think I've ever seen him so animated. 'Nice to meet you,' he says to Alex, and she nods in response.

We both watch him as he walks away, a noticeable spring in his step.

'Well, that was weird,' Alex says. 'Are you done for now? I'm happy to wait outside for a bit longer if not.'

'No, I'm done. Said what I came to for now and might come back, might not. Simon should be around still, he's not going away until tomorrow morning.'

Simon chooses that moment to reappear. He has a coffee cup in his hand and a troubled look on his face. I loosen my arm from Alex and stick my hand in my pocket.

'Everything all right?' I ask him.

'Been on the phone to Diana. Is it normal to feel this tired when you're halfway through a pregnancy?' He looks at Alex as he says this.

'Don't ask me,' she says. 'I've never been inclined to put myself through it.'

'Yes, it is,' I jump in quickly. 'The *whole* thing is bloody tiring. She'll have to learn to get on with it.' As soon as the words leave my lips I want to claw them back. I know it's incredibly unfeeling of me and Alex raises her eyebrows at me. 'Sorry,' I say directly to Simon. 'I don't know why I said that; I'm just a bit tired myself.'

'I was going to ask if you'll keep an eye on Diana while I'm away—'

'Of course I will,' I interrupt. 'Of course, and Elizabeth too. I'm going now, but I'll probably come back tomorrow,' I say, desperate for him not to think I'm completely heartless.

'If she's still with us,' he says.

'Well, yes, but you'll phone me if there's any change?'

'Sure.'

'And, Simon, I promise you, I'll be wherever Diana needs me.'

His face softens and he pulls me into a hug.

'Have you seen Leo? He was here.'

'Yes,' I say, quickly. 'We had a chat. Look, we've got to go now, but I'll speak to you later.'

He looks at Alex for a moment before he tells her it was nice to meet her, but he doesn't look as if it was a nice experience. I need some breathing space to work all of this out. Simon heads back to my mother, and Alex and I leave. I am exhausted.

29

The journey back to Brighton is slow and quiet. I don't know how to feel about what has transpired. My mother hasn't been in my life for such a long time that it was so strange to see her again. Perhaps I will have to re-evaluate what I think I know about her. Maybe I should have listened to Simon and reconnected earlier when we could have really talked, but once I'd made my decision to drop my parents out of my life, it became increasingly difficult to reach out.

I suppose Simon holds all the answers now, or certainly some answers for the last ten years. I have to accept that he wanted to meet his grandmother and that he felt he had to do it behind my back. I feel terrible about that. Would I have talked him out of it if he'd told me at the time? I probably would have tried. And now there's a whole ten years that I know nothing about, which is my own fault. I wonder what they talked about, what that ten-year shared experience was like for them both. I wonder if she talked about me. It's odd to think that the catalyst for my meeting Alex and the estrangement from my parents is all wrapped up in my son. He is the reason for everything.

I turn the key in the lock of my flat and invite Alex inside. It's the most surreal experience to have this woman in a space that I've called home for a few years. She seems to dither in the doorway as if she's unsure whether to come in or not, but eventually she steps inside, Bardo trotting after her, and I close the door behind them.

'Shall I make a cup of tea?' she asks, in an odd detached voice. 'Do you need to have a rest? You've been through quite an experience.'

A rest? She makes me sound like an old woman. An experience? I'd quite like to shake off the last few hours of my life and never revisit them. I want to open a bottle of wine and take it and, possibly, Alex to bed.

'Let's open some wine,' I say, and then I panic that I've said my thoughts out loud. But Alex doesn't look horrified; she just looks exhausted too.

I pull a bottle from the makeshift rack I've constructed in the gap between the dishwasher and the under-sink cupboard and I take a couple of glasses from the shelf. Alex is standing in the middle of the living room scrutinising my painting, *her* painting, while Bardo makes a circuit, sniffing everything at his height. Alex turns to take the glass of wine from me, her face expressionless.

'Still looks good doesn't it,' she says, but it's not a question.

My eyes move around the small space: my tatty sofa with an old blanket thrown over to cover the worst of the worn bits, the armchair that doesn't match, the rug in front of the ugly gas fire that I never light because it smells, the coffee table with my to-be-read pile almost obscuring the view of the TV on the stand in the corner, my collection of plants crowding the windowsill and the blind above that never shuts fully because they're in the way, the uninspiring view down to the car park below.

It's not that I'm ashamed of my home particularly, but it is interesting to try and see it through Alex's eyes. She hasn't taken her attention off the painting though.

She gulps at her wine as if she's nervous. I choose the sofa and leave Alex to make her own choice, but Bardo leaps up onto the armchair, turns twice and promptly falls asleep. She sits down next to me, her eyes still on the painting. I'm about to tell her she can have it and sell it with the other one, but my phone buzzes on the coffee table.

'It's Simon again,' Alex says, removing her eyes from the painting to stare at my phone. 'It's a message.'

I pick it up and open it quickly, expecting news about my mother. Maybe she's gone, and if she has, I don't know what to think about that.

Mum, Grandma is holding on. Hope you can pop in tomorrow. Don't really want her to die alone. We'll have a proper chat when I'm back from Prague on Thursday. Love you x

'Oh, Simon,' I say to my phone and text back that I love him too. I don't want any bad feeling between us. Goodness knows what he's going to think when he hears about Leo, though. I glance at Alex and see she's finished her wine. I've not even started mine. I don't want her to get drunk again, I want to talk, and I actually want to kiss her. A heat rushes to my cheeks and I feel as if I'm eighteen again.

'Can I have some more wine?' Alex asks, turning her gaze from the painting to fix it on me.

'Sure, help yourself, it's in the kitchen.' I say, glancing up from my phone.

After she's gone, I drop it back onto the table, and walk to the bathroom. I use the loo, wash my hands and stare at myself in the mirror. My hair is working its way out of the bun I put it in and I contemplate setting it free, but I don't want to walk back into the room, looking as if I've made any sort of effort. For the same reason I don't put on any lipstick or concealer under my eyes.

Less than two weeks ago I became seventy. I had a fiancé, had found out I was going to be a grandmother and was looking my retirement years squarely in the face. I was finally settling down, becoming the person other people thought I should be and told myself I was happy. I didn't talk to my mother, hadn't confronted the worst thing that had ever happened to me and had lost forever, my one true love.

Everything has changed now, well, most things have changed. I'm certainly in a very different place than I was. I will not be that young woman frightened in the bathroom. I am the owner of all my wishes and desires now.

Alex is standing in the kitchen doorway, her wine in one hand and her phone in the other.

'Do you fancy a takeaway?' I ask her. I think I need to get some food inside her before she drinks too much. She may very well have filled her glass, but it's half empty again now. She puts it down on the table with her phone and walks towards me. Her eyes are bright and for a moment I think she could be furious, but it's gone in a flash.

'I fancy *you*,' she says, boldly, her face inches from mine. Her warm breath blows against my skin. And here it is, my now-or-never moment, just like it was fifty-two years ago in her uncle's boat on the loch. Alex used the same words then. Words I'd been desperate to hear for weeks. I'd felt like a yo-yo, being drawn close to her and then spun away. But, that day on the boat, she'd finally told me what I wanted to hear and then she'd kissed me, fiercely, and I wanted to disappear into her and never resurface.

I slide her hand into mine. My mind is whirring with the what and the where and the how. Maybe I should get us to the bedroom; perhaps we can sink down onto the sofa. Not the floor, she'd never get up again. While I'm thinking, though, Alex is acting and she slides her other hand up my arm and to my face where she cups my chin and brings her lips to mine. And then I'm not thinking at all.

30

The sound of a supermarket delivery van wakes me. Its continued beeping as it reverses into the parking bay cuts through my sleep. My head is thick and my mouth is dry. As I come to, the previous evening appears in flashes. My mother in hospital, Alex here in my flat, no food, but wine – God, lots of wine. And as my surroundings come more into focus, I remember that kiss, that deeply delicious kiss and then what came next.

I'm lying on my back with my arms by my sides, palms turned up, relaxed. I usually sleep on my side in a foetal position, my hands tucked into my chest, which, at eighteen, my mother told me was a mistake. You'll prematurely wrinkle your *décolletage*, she'd said. Always worried about the least important things, my mother.

I turn my head slowly to my left, not wanting to move too much and wake Alex. I'm going to make us coffee and a huge breakfast. We will walk down to the seafront and sit on the stones. We can stroll through the Pavilion Gardens hand in hand, declare ourselves to the world at last. I'll tell Simon when he gets back, and I think he'll be okay about it. He wants me to be settled and happy. I'll show him how happy

I actually am. And then I remember my mother again in her hospital bed, possibly taking her last breaths.

Beside me my bed is empty, I realise, the covers pulled up to the pillow and I have to reorganise my thoughts, make sure I haven't made the whole thing up. But, no, what we experienced last night cannot be made up. It's as real as the ticking of my bedside clock. Eight-thirty it reads. Perhaps Alex has beaten me to it and is making coffee.

I push back the covers, exposing my naked body. Stretching out my arms and legs I shiver as more memories of last night appear. I can't seem to wipe the smug smile off my face. I pull my dressing gown from the hook on the back of the door and tie it around myself, then walk through to the kitchen. Alex isn't there; Bardo isn't curled up in the chair. Could she have gone out to get coffee, to walk the dog? She might well have, as she likes a coffee with all the works: sugar, syrup, froth, and if nothing else, Bardo will need a wee.

Desperate for some caffeine myself, I fill the kettle anyway. I'll make a quick espresso and still have whatever she brings back. I rinse out the glasses we used last night and that reminds me that my head is hurting, so I swallow a couple of paracetamol.

Eight-forty-five my microwave tells me and I feel the first twitch of unease. She won't have got lost will she? My phone is on the table still and I snatch it up to check. Nothing from Simon and nothing from Alex either. I send a message to her. Tell her that if she's buying coffee to make mine a large. The kettle clicks off in the kitchen and I turn, sliding my phone into my pocket. The kitchen door is open and I can see straight through to the living room. It takes me a second to see what is wrong. Something glaring is missing. The painting isn't hanging on the wall.

I pace the flat like a mad dog, sniffing the air, checking all the places that Alex has been. No cardigan over the kitchen chair, no bag dropped onto the floor by the sofa, no sign of her using the bathroom and most obvious of all signs, if needed, is the enormous gaping space on the wall. My bloody painting. I fish out my phone again and call her, but it goes straight to voicemail, so I cut it off, take a few deep breaths and try again. I need to give her the benefit of the doubt. Anything could have happened. There could be any number of easy, obvious and acceptable explanations.

I can't think of one.

'Hi, Alex, it's me. Just wondering where you are. Call me back, please.'

I imagine her listening to this, my voice sounding needy, pathetic and a bit desperate. I'm back in the bedroom, pulling on clothes and running a brush through my hair. Then I'm in the bathroom, cleaning my teeth and using the loo. I pull on a pair of trainers so I can comfortably walk the streets to look for her, although I can't imagine she'd get far with a giant painting under her arm. She'll be at the railway station; she has no other transport. I glance out of the window with the sudden thought that she's taken the van, but it's still there in the car park below. I'm starting to feel sick and I gulp down some water before heading for the front door.

That's when I see it, on the table in the hallway. The place I keep takeaway menus and keys, a scented candle and now there's a photo of me and Leo and a note attached to it. In the photo, he's holding my hand and grinning at the engagement ring on my finger. Where did she find this? It wasn't as if it was pinned to the fridge. But, I remember now, sliding it into the paperback I was reading when I lost my bookmark. I'm pretty sure it was on the kitchen windowsill. It must have looked to her like a treasured possession. I turn it over to read the date I remember him writing on the back. His sloping handwriting is tucked neatly in the bottom left-hand corner.

May 2022 when you made me the happiest man alive

The note simply says, *Connie, you haven't changed a bit!* I grab my keys and lock up the flat behind me.

I don't walk, but jump in the van and head straight for the station, looking out at everyone I pass for a flame-haired woman with a painting under her arm and an obedient dog trotting at her heels. What time did she leave? How far has she got? Maybe it wouldn't matter to Alex that Leo and I are no longer together, I didn't tell her about him. I didn't want to give her any other reason to think badly of me and yet I've managed that perfectly. How foolish of me to think I could jump from one person to the next without repercussions. Did I really think that because we are older that the rules don't apply?

I get to the station and pull up outside, then phone her again while I lock up the van. I'm on a double yellow line, but I'm going to have to chance it.

She's not on the platform, she's not in the loo, she's not in the shop and the last train to London left twenty minutes ago. I've lost her.

I walk slowly back to the van and a traffic warden is walking away. There's a ticket stuck firmly to Ruby's windscreen.

'Well, that's just bloody marvellous,' I say, and the traffic warden shrugs.

I pull the ticket from the screen and get back in the van, sit with my hands on the steering wheel. I'm going to have to let her go, I realise. I can hardly chase her to London and intercept her train; I'd never make it anyway. I can't believe she took the painting. I have nothing of her now, do I? I check the back pocket of the passenger seat and then the back of the van, but she's taken everything with her. The last painting has gone too. It really is as if she was never here. This must have been what it was like for her when I left Scotland. Quite the payback, if that's what she was going for.

Starting the engine I pull away from the kerb and am about to turn onto the main road when my phone rings from the passenger seat. I stamp on the brake and grab it, sliding my finger across the screen to answer.

'Alex,' I say. 'Where are you?' But, it isn't Alex, it's Diana.

'Connie? It's Diana,' she says in the smallest voice I've ever heard her use. 'Can you come and get me?'

'Where are you?' I ask. 'What's the matter?'

'I'm at home. I'm bleeding. I think I'm losing the baby.'

31

Two care facilities in twenty-four hours, except this time I'm in the beginning of life part of the system rather than the end of life. I vehemently hope this is the beginning of life still and not the end. Diana phoned ahead. She has consultant led care because of the IVF they've had. She was clutching her tiny baby bump on the way here and talking about what wonderful things they can do now to save premature lives while the tears flowed down her face, her teeth gritted against the discomfort. I kept my mouth firmly closed. She's only twenty weeks and I'm pretty sure that's not conducive with life outside of the womb.

I'm under strict instructions not to phone Simon. There's nothing he can do, Diana has said. It was obvious she didn't want him to worry. I didn't want to phone him anyway. My one job was to look after his wife and growing child. So far, not so good. She took my hand as we walked inside the building and I squeezed it tightly – three times.

'Everything will be fine, sweetheart,' I had said, both of us accepting these new roles we'd been handed: me, caring mother-in-law and her the grateful daughter-in-law.

*

It's been only ten minutes since we arrived, but still I've been pacing the waiting room, counting the birds sitting on the telephone wire outside the window and picking the skin around my nails. Alex has been forgotten for now.

'Is it Diana Fitzgerald?' a nurse asks. I turn away from the window and Diana stands up. 'Do you want to follow me through?' she says.

'Shall I stay here?' I ask Diana, but her answer is to take my hand again and pull me with her.

It should be her mother and father here, but I know she doesn't have a great relationship with her parents, and they're in Birmingham anyway. I'm the closest and it's my job. She'd been trying to get through to me while I was phoning Alex. I hope I haven't failed her.

Diana climbs onto the couch and begins to answer all of the questions that are asked of her. I hover by her side, not in the way, but near enough to take her hand if I'm needed.

'Are you Mum?' the midwife asks me.

'Mother-in-law,' I say.

'Oh, that's nice,' she says, pressing a plastic device against Diana's belly and moving it around.

The sudden whomping sound of the baby's heartbeat is hugely comforting and I gulp back an emotional lump in my throat.

'Heartbeat sounds good,' the midwife says. 'It is quite common to bleed during pregnancy, but we can check a couple of things with a scan. You haven't had your twenty-week scan yet have you?' She looks through Diana's pregnancy notes as she says this.

'No, I'm booked in for next week.'

'Okay, well let's do it now and we can save you another journey. I'll get my colleague.'

'Simon is missing this,' Diana says, as the midwife leaves the room.

'He'd much rather know you're okay, though, love,' I say.

'Yeah, you're right.'

This is not a phrase I've ever heard leave Diana's lips, but I manage to keep my smile inwards. The midwife prepares the machine and I suddenly realise that she's not out of the woods yet. That heart is beating, but there could be more to find. I take her hand and it's so different from holding my mother's yesterday. I'll go back, I decide. I'll go back once I have Diana settled. There's more I want to tell my mum, much more I want to say. I suddenly very much want to give her those missing years.

The midwife returns with her colleague and they set up the machine.

The sonographer squirts gel onto Diana's belly and picks up the probe from the side of the machine. She applies gel to the end before pressing it gently against Diana's skin. She repositions and tries again while tapping the buttons on the machine. She has the monitor turned away. Without the sound of the baby's heart to comfort her, Diana suddenly looks as worried as she did earlier. I hold her hand tighter.

'Right, well, here is your baby,' she says at last, turning the screen round so we can see. It takes me a moment to grasp what I'm looking at and then it's clear. I can see the head and two tiny hands formed into fists. Then as she moves the probe we can see its spine and legs too. I am overcome with emotion.

'Oh my goodness, Diana, your perfect baby,' I say as tears appear on my cheeks. She's crying too, through a huge smile.

'I can't believe it,' she says. 'Connie, I'm glad you're here. I really thought I was losing it.'

'Your placenta is lying a little lower than we would like, but that isn't anything to worry about at the moment. It should move up as you grow over the next few weeks, but we'll keep an eye on you. There's a possibility you may have to have a C-section, but we will know in plenty of time and prepare for that. So, nothing to worry about now, and probably nothing to worry about at all. Do you want to know the sex?'

'Oh, Simon should be here for this,' I say. 'I could step out if you want to know and tell him later?'

'No, don't go. I do want to find out, but please stay. Why shouldn't you get to know a little more about your grandchild?'

The sonographer glances between us both, undecided.

'I can write it down if you're unsure.'

'No, I think we'll find out thank you,' Diana says, and looks at me with an expression that says: we need this.

'All right,' the sonographer says, rolling the probe back over Diana's belly again. 'I think if you look here...'

'Do you want to come back to mine for a cup of tea, or do you want me to take you home?' I ask Diana when we're back in the van. 'I think Simon would – no – *I* would like to keep an eye on you for a bit, if that's okay. But, we can go to yours.'

'I'd like to go to yours,' she says. 'Your flat is so cosy.'

This is the first time she's ever said this. I always thought she looked disdainfully at my things. Have I got it all wrong?

'Great, let's go then.'

She smiles and nods, and then turns her head to look out of the window, her hand resting on her bump.

'Are you pleased, now you know what you're having?' I ask her as we leave the hospital car park.

'I'm thrilled,' she says. 'I mean, it shouldn't matter, if the baby is healthy, but I am pleased, yes.'

'I've been crocheting you a blanket,' I tell her. 'I'll show you what I've done so far when we get back.'

'Simon told me. That's such a lovely thing to do, thank you.'

'It needs a lot more work, but I collected the wool as I journeyed down the country. It's got stripes from lots of different locations. I hope you don't think it's a mess.'

'I probably will, but I'll keep it to myself; we don't want to spoil this new-found friendship, do we.'

I turn my head sharply to look at her, but am delighted to see that she's grinning.

'Had you for a second,' she says.

At the flat, I fill the kettle and plump the cushions on the sofa for her. She settles down and I hand her the baby blanket.

'Oh, Connie, I love it. You'll have to tell me where all the wool came from. What a well-travelled blanket.'

I go back into the kitchen to make the tea. I'm feeling a bit twitchy about my mother. I really did want to go and see her, but I don't want to leave Diana. I take the tea through and tell her I'm going to make a quick phone call, then disappear into the hallway.

'Hello, I'm Elizabeth Fitzgerald's daughter, just wanted to check in on her.'

The receptionist asks me to wait and I fiddle with the note from Alex on the table. Just the sight of it makes me feel sick. To think I've lost her again after all this time. I have so much I need to resolve and it would be so nice if I could tick one thing off my list, but I very much doubt Alex will be forthcoming anytime soon. To have Diana here and the two of us to be talking is wonderful, and I'm grateful for that, at least.

'Constance Fitzgerald?' A voice comes on the line and I screw up Alex's note and drop it on the table.

'Yes, I'm here,' I say. 'Just wondered how my mother is doing.'

'I'm afraid I have some news, and it's that she passed away ten minutes ago. We were about to phone your son. Two nurses were with her; she wasn't alone and it was peaceful.' The voice is gentle and soothing, but the words are deafening, devastating.

When I hang up I hover in the hallway and stare at the screwed-up piece of paper for a moment, thinking about Alex's words on that note.

Connie, you haven't changed a bit!

I walk back into the kitchen, my legs like lead, and stand for a second, looking out towards the sea through the window. It's the only decent view I have from this flat. Seagulls are swooping down towards the beach and I can only assume they're scavenging. Someone is going to lose their fish and chips. The sun is high in the sky and there is only the merest wisp of a cloud across the huge expanse of blue. I open the lid of the bin.

'I haven't done the right things, I know. I seem to be repeating some of the mistakes I made all those years ago, but I'm ready to change now, Alex, and I really wished you had stayed so you could see.' I drop the piece of paper inside.

32

'My mother's gone,' I tell Diana when I curl my legs up underneath me and sit back in the armchair. I'll regret it in a bit when I want to move, but for now, folding myself up seems the natural thing to do. 'I should have been there really, but—'

'But, you were with me,' Diana says. 'I'm sorry, Connie.'

'Don't be. I wanted to be with you. You're important to me. Not because of the baby, but as well as the baby. I hope you know that.'

'I do,' she says, 'especially now.' She still has the crocheted blanket in her hands and she runs her fingers along the stripes. 'You did go and see her, though. That's important – something you can carry with you.'

We are silent for a while, sipping our tea, lost in our own thoughts.

'I've been difficult, I know,' Diana says. 'I found it quite hard seeing you being such a brilliant mum to Simon. My parents didn't want me – I'm sure you know. It's not like they've ever made it a secret. And then to find Simon, who is so lovely to me, and to see how you both are together, is tricky for me. That's a hard thing to admit to, being jealous of your mother-in-law. Most of my friends say that they wish their husbands loved their mothers as much as Simon does. I just wanted all of his love. It's pathetic. And,' she continues, looking very much like she wishes she didn't have to, 'I'm a bit worried that he might love the baby more than me. God!' she says, putting her hands over her eyes. It's heartbreakingly childish and makes me want to give her a hug. 'I'm such a bad person, how can I possibly be a good mother, like you are?'

'Diana, you'll be a wonderful mother and Simon adores you, that won't change when you have the baby. In fact, he'll love you all the more. But me, well, thank you for saying I'm a good mother, but I'm not a good daughter – that's the truth. My mother was eighty-nine and just died alone in hospital. My father died ten years ago and I didn't go to his funeral. And I didn't, because… because I was so bloody ashamed of myself. I thought that if I didn't think about them then they would just go away. And look, turns out, I was right.'

I don't even realise I'm crying until Diana gets up and hands me a tissue. I take it and dab my eyes and blow my nose. The thing I've waited my entire adult life to happen, has now happened. I've lived as if my parents didn't exist and now they don't. Will it be enough that I saw my mother before she died, or will I always live this guilty half-life?

'What happened Connie? With your parents?'

I look across at Diana and contemplate brushing it all away, fobbing her off and saying it was nothing, but I have a sudden desire to talk to her and perhaps we need this; a confidence between us, but I can't tell her everything, that would be too much of a burden.

'When I was eighteen I had a fling with a friend of my parents. He was forty and married with two children. I had flirted with him a bit at one of my parents' parties. I'd had a couple of drinks and thought I'd practise my skills to try on the boys I knew. I was so square, had no idea what I was doing. He was actually quite drunk and something happened between us in the bathroom.' I pause for a moment to hear this half truth in my mouth, but I can't possibly leave her knowing something she'd feel compelled to keep from Simon. 'It was unfortunate,' I continue, 'because his wife was waiting outside to use the loo and started shrieking at me when he opened the door. My parents appeared and it was clear to all what had happened. He told them all I'd thrown myself at him and that he barely knew what he was doing because he was so drunk. And, because they thought I was becoming a bit wild after seeing me drinking at another of their parties, and the fact my grades had slipped a bit because I wasn't trying hard at school, and because they wanted everything to be hushed up – he was a GP, you know – they believed it was all my doing. They were all talking at each other, at me and, to be honest, I just wanted them to stop. So, I agreed that it was on me, it was my fault, and they believed me, but how they could have I'll never know, because I was a complete mess.'

'Christ, Connie, that is awful. I'm sorry.'

Diana looks so troubled, I wonder if I should stop. Is she really the person to offload onto?

'Maybe I shouldn't be talking about this with you.'

'I think you need to talk about it, to be honest,' she says.

'My parents sent me straight away to Scotland to work in my aunt's hotel for a few weeks until it all blew over, like *I* was the problem, and to them I suppose I was. I was irrationally angry with them for not guessing the truth even though I hadn't offered it. Anyway, while I was there I met someone, who turned my head.'

'Simon's father?' Diana asks, clutching the blanket to her chest, her face hopeful. I really shouldn't have started this.

'No, a woman actually: Alexandra Mackenzie.' I watch her expression change to surprise and then to the possibility that this story does have a happy ending. How disappointed she's going to be.

'The woman you've been travelling with? Simon said you'd been delivering her paintings.'

'Yes, that's her, but it's the first time I've seen her since that summer. We were eighteen and we spent the next six weeks falling in love. We planned to run away together, to borrow her brother's car and take off where no one would judge us. We would say we were friends, and who wouldn't believe us?'

'Who would judge?'

'It was 1970, plenty of judging going on, and let's be honest, Diana, plenty of judging going on now, too.'

'True,' she says, 'but not by me. So, you're a lesbian then?'

'No,' I say, 'well, yes, I don't know. I fell in love with a woman, that's all. I never felt the need to label it.'

'Maybe it was just a teenage crush. You'd been sent away from home; she must have felt safe.'

I think about that for a moment, that Alex was safe, and maybe she was that, too, but I know the deep love and intense passion we shared. I wasn't looking for safety, particularly. Maybe I was looking for escape, though.

'It wasn't just a crush; she was the love of my life.'

'Have you been with other women?' she asks me and her face is so straight and without judgement, I answer her honestly.

'No, I haven't. All my flings have been with men.'

'So, you're bisexual then?'

'I've honestly never thought about it. I fell in love with a woman when I was eighteen and was devastated not to see her again, then I was very busy being a single parent and didn't think about any sort of relationship at all. I went on a few dates and slept with a few men in my later twenties and thirties, forties *and* fifties, but Alex was honestly always on my mind and I never committed to any of those men, even the ones who clearly wanted to take it further.'

'But, have you been attracted to women?'

I'd forgotten how persistent Diana could be with a line of questions.

'Have you ever thought about a job in interrogation?' I say and she laughs. 'I have been attracted to a couple of women, but there was never anyone who was on the same page as me.'

'And now there's Leo. Where does he fit into this?'

'God, Leo, well, he doesn't fit into this anymore. He's a confused man who wanted to replace his wife after her traumatic death. He doesn't want me. He told me I'm wrong for him and he's right. We've had a parting of ways, but an amicable one. It's my fault really. I should never have said yes to marrying him.'

'Simon made that happen, didn't he. I did tell him to back off actually, but he saw Leo's loneliness and you becoming more settled and he thought he could tie it all up.'

'I can't really blame Simon; I was a bit lonely too. I was travelling less and did worry about what my remaining years would look like. Leo was very sweet to me and, I suppose, I settled for him. That's terrible to admit to. I got swept up in the idea of a companion for my later years, which was unfair of me really. Leo also didn't go in with the right intentions, so it ended up being a bad fit all round. It would never have lasted, which is a funny thing to say of a couple of seventy-year-olds.'

'So, what happened then? In Scotland I mean.'

'I found out I was pregnant and I ran back home.'

'But...'

I watch her mind turn the facts around, the timings and the outcomes. I don't need to state the obvious, and I see the moment it all falls into place.

'Oh, from the fling!' She says the word *fling* with a very direct look at me, but doesn't say anything else.

'Yes, from that,' I say. Do you want another cup of tea?' I ask her. I need a coffee.

'No thanks, I'm fine.'

'How are you feeling?'

'I feel a lot better. Bit tired, but the pain has gone.'

I make another drink and I grab some cheese and biscuits, some nuts and fruit and take them back to the living room and lay it all on the table. I bring a jug of water and a couple of glasses too.

'I'm happy to drive you home whenever you want to go.'

'Can I stay, Connie? I can sleep on the sofa.'

'Of course you can stay,' I say, then think about what a mess my spare room is. It's a job I never seem to get around to doing. 'But you shall have my bed, absolutely no arguments.'

She pours herself a glass of water and nibbles on some cheese.

'So what happened when you came home then?'

I take a deep breath before I start again.

'I came home because it felt like the right thing to do. I hadn't seen my parents for six weeks and I was ready to have an honest conversation. I needed their help and support. But my mother gave me cash and told me to go and "sort it out".'

'What? You mean get rid of Simon?'

'I don't really know, to be honest. My father wasn't there, my mother was drunk and I was still a problem that she needed to be rid of.'

'Blimey, Connie, and I thought my parents were bad. At least they do acknowledge I exist. I can see now, why you cut yourself off and didn't speak to them. You must have been so frightened and confused at the time.'

'I was both of those things, but I also desperately wanted to get back to Alex. I wanted to get back to our plan. I did think I could "sort it out" and be back in the Highlands as if I'd never been gone. Just home to grab some things, then off on our adventure. She'd never know.'

'But, you didn't because Simon is very much here. So, what? You changed your mind? Let me guess, you felt the baby move and you couldn't go through with it.'

Diana's face has softened again. She's thinking about her own pregnancy.

'Something like that I suppose. I honestly looked at all the options, including adoption. I went to Bournemouth to get away and with the help of a lovely woman, I had Simon.'

'What about Alex? What happened with her?'

'I wrote her a letter and said that family business had called me home, that I was sorry for running off, and if she'd be prepared to wait for me, I would come back to her.'

'That sounds romantic.'

'Oh, it wasn't, it was desperate and pathetic. "*Wait for me*." She never wrote back.'

'But, you didn't have Simon adopted so, you did change your mind.'

'Well, Diana, that was the part where I felt my baby moving, and oddly for the first time in my life, I felt completely in control. It felt right that I was going to be a mother. It had been chosen for me and I was going to make a bloody good job of it.'

'But, you did go back for her, didn't you. A long time later, but you did. Where is she now?'

'I don't know. She has a complicated financial situation and has to move out of where she has been living,' I say. 'But she'll be fine; she's strong.'

'And how have you left it? Does she still love you? Do you still love her?'

'I do love her, yes. But how she feels about me is anyone's guess.'

Diana shifts herself around on the sofa to get up, but she pauses on the edge for a moment.

'Connie, where's your painting of that lake?'

'Alex took it with her, so maybe how she feels about me is obvious. I have nothing of her now.'

I glance up at the wall and to the empty space. *Sunrise* and *Sunset over Loch Ness* together again and worth a pretty penny, I guess.

33

The day of my mother's funeral it rains so hard that the parched ground cannot cope and pools of water appear on grass verges and in fields. Puddles pepper the pavements and the motorway journey is terrifying from the passenger seat of Simon's car. After weeks of flip-flops and sandals, I've crammed my toes into sturdy shoes, but had contemplated wellies for just a moment.

It's been a fortnight since she died, a strange time of coming to terms with her new absence that seems weightier than the one that's lasted for so many years. I'm glad Alex talked me into seeing her and I'm happy that she had time with Simon too. I decide to take only happier memories of her with me. Those ones from my early childhood where I loved her in the easy way children love their parents. I thought she was beautiful and willed myself to be older, to be exactly like her. That's where I decide to close that book of memories.

The church isn't packed – most of my mother's friends have either passed away themselves or lost contact. I have since learned that she was pretty reclusive in the last few years of her life. She was very lucky to have been able to see Simon during that time. He was one of her only visitors.

I haven't told *my* friends as I couldn't bring myself to offer up an explanation. I feel as estranged from my mother in her death as I did in her life.

Simon and I planned my mother's funeral together. It gave us a chance to talk about her. I shared some of the more pleasant stories from my earlier childhood and he filled me in on the last ten years. He used to visit her a couple of times a month, drive up from Lewes to her nursing home and spend a few hours with her. I had always told Simon that I had run away from home when I became pregnant, that I didn't get on well with my parents and wanted to do things on my own. My mother, it seemed, had been more honest than me. I learned that she always hoped we could reconnect, which brought me a mixture of happiness, guilt and intense grief. She wished she had invited me home that day. She never forgave herself for turning me away, believed that she should have been stronger against my father and his draconian rules. I'm glad I got the opportunity to say I was sorry for those missing years, but really I can't ever forget her neglect, however regretful she was. Nothing was ever mentioned about Simon's father, so at least that can stay buried.

I get the occasional look from Diana, and the odd light touch of my arm when she's passing me. She is an intuitive person and if I thought I'd fooled her with talk of a fling then I was wrong. She doesn't talk about it though and I'm grateful for that. If Simon ever noticed the tense relationship that Diana and I had before, he never really mentioned it, but he seems to notice the truce we have made. He seems more content generally. Things are so much easier now.

My mother's will is unexpected. Simon and I have her Kensington house to sell and investments and savings to deal with. It will be the first time in my life that I won't have to think about money, but I doubt I could really change my habits from a lifetime of frugality. I said that Simon should have it all, but he dismissed the idea immediately.

'It's what parents do,' he said. 'Let her do that at least. And, anyway, you'll be passing it on to me at some point,' he added with a grin.

Alex has not been in contact in the last two weeks and her absence is like a punch in my chest.

We make our way down to the front of the church behind the coffin. Simon and Diana are either side of me. I feel like a fraud as the few who have come offer me sympathetic looks. Leo, I'm surprised to see, is sitting in the pew waiting for us.

'Connie,' he says, standing up to greet me and I hug him.

'Thank you for coming, Leo. I do appreciate it.'

'Of course, why wouldn't I come?' he says and I remember that he's here for Simon, of course he's here for Simon.

We sit down together and I try to concentrate on the service, but I can't get my head away from thoughts of Alex today. I have an enormous wish to have her by my side. I want to know what she's doing and who she's doing it with. Mostly I want to know why she left. Was it just supposed to mirror what I had done to her? Was she getting her own back? She must have been really spooked by Leo's photograph. Of course, I do see how it looks, how it was. Ultimately I was cheating on Leo with her. That is what she'll be thinking and she'll be right, in a way. I try hard to brush it aside for now.

I reach out my hand to Simon and try to remember that this will be hard for him today. He had her in his life for ten years after all.

*

The burial is a brutal affair. The grass is sodden and the rain continues to fall. Luckily the church warden seems to have a stash of black umbrellas, which he hands to us as we file outside. I hold back a chocking sob as her coffin is lowered into the ground and Simon clutches my hand. After, we make our way to the pub that Simon chose, just a short walk from the church. We have arranged for a small spread laid out for the few who bother to come back, but most just have a quick drink and then disappear.

Leo moves in my direction and I pick up my coffee and meet him halfway.

'Can I talk to you Connie?' he asks. 'Perhaps we could pop outside?'

'Of course,' I say, hoping that he's not going to renew an interest in us.

We walk out to an enclosed area that is probably meant for smokers. There are patio heaters and fairy lights in jars on the tables, blankets on the benches for those chill evenings when you want to stay outside just that little bit longer. We're the only two out here now. The rain has eased and there are just the occasional drops on the roof above us as we take a seat.

'I just wanted to say that I've met someone,' he says.

'Right,' I say, a little taken aback. This was not what I was expecting at all.

'I met her at the garden centre near Fiona's not long after you left on your trip and we hit it off immediately. She likes her home comforts, not keen on travel and she likes me very much,' he says with a blush to his cheeks.

I open my mouth to say something and then close it again.

All that agonising and those guilty feelings of wanting Alex so much while being tied to Leo who was actually happily making new plans of his own all that time. I could laugh, but I have that ache in my chest for what I've lost again.

'I'm very happy for you,' I say eventually, and I am, I really am, but a sudden wave of loneliness hits me. The loss of Alex, my mother and now, even though we weren't right together, Leo too.

'Are you going to be okay Connie?'

'I will be absolutely fine. Thanks, Leo, for your honesty, and I really am very happy for you. Make sure you introduce her to Fiona.'

He laughs at that.

'I have. They get on famously.'

I do wish he'd stop now.

'What happened to your friend?' he asks. 'She seemed nice. She's not here though is she?'

'No, she had to go home; in fact, Leo, I'm going to find Simon and go home myself. It's been quite a day.'

I say my goodbyes to him, wish him happiness and find Simon and Diana back inside.

The journey home isn't nearly as bad now that the weather has cleared and we make steady progress back down south. I'm sitting in the back with the baby blanket on my lap, another row underway.

'Connie, can I talk to you about Alex?' Diana asks, leaning around in her seat to look at me.

'Sure,' I say tentatively, glancing at the back of Simon's head as he drives.

'Okay, well, to be honest, I told Simon about her.'

'Simon knows about her already. He met her at the nursing home.'

'I mean, *really* told him about her and what she means to you.'

'Oh,' I say, quietly, glad for the distraction of my crochet and a reason to avoid Simon's gaze.

'I did wonder, Mum. There was such an intensity between the two of you. Is she the reason things didn't work out with you and Leo? Is it because he's a man? Because you have had relationships with men; certainly one man.'

Diana shifts in her seat and throws me a worried glance, but I shake my head.

'I'm not really comfortable discussing my love life with my son,' I say, reaching for a note of humour in my voice. 'But, yes, I have had relationships with men in my time, as you know, and they've been great on the whole. And I thought Leo was a very nice man and we got on well and I probably would have married him if he hadn't been looking for a replacement for Brenda. Luckily I saw that before it was too late. It wasn't just that though. I thought I needed to slow up, to settle down, to become the woman everyone expected me to be in my old age, but I wasn't being truthful to myself. I know you think a lot of him and I understand why. I guess you thought that I would love Leo as much as you do. We want different things though and I'm glad my eyes were opened to that fact, by Alex mostly. I realised how much I loved her, still loved her, and how much more myself I was when I was with her. It wasn't ever like that with anyone else I've seen over the years and I don't think it's a gender thing, I think it's an Alex thing.'

There's silence for a moment inside the car. Simon indicates and pulls onto the inside lane. We've just passed a sign for services and I assume he's planning on stopping.

'That's so heartbreaking, Connie,' Diana says. 'And, if I may say, for someone who isn't comfortable discussing her love life with her son, I think you've done admirably.'

Simon drives up the slip road, pulls into a parking space, then switches off the engine. He turns round in his seat to look at me.

'I do want you to be settled and happy – that is true,' he says. 'But not with the wrong person, or any person if you're happier on your own. I did push the whole Leo thing, I know. He ticked all the right boxes for me, but that was silly really as I wasn't the one marrying him.'

I lean forward, rest my hand on his shoulder and smile at him.

'You were looking out for me and I appreciate that. For a time, I thought Leo was completely right for me too. He's found someone else. Did you know?'

'Bloody hell, he's a fast worker,' Diana says.

'He's found his Brenda replacement, hasn't he,' Simon says.

'I wish him well,' I say.

'But, Mum, the thing is you have been reunited with the love of your life and finally, at the age of seventy, you know what you want. I think we need to do something about that.'

'Like what?' I ask him.

'We need to find Alex,' he says.

34

Grace Fitzgerald is born on a chilly Christmas Eve afternoon, while flakes of snow fall silently outside the hospital window. I'm sitting in a chair in the maternity ward with my granddaughter in my arms. She is wrapped in the blanket that I crocheted and just her face is visible from the folds of multicoloured layers. She is so beautiful; her tiny rosebud mouth is opening and closing in her sleep while she dreams about suckling. She has the faintest wisp of blonde hair like her mother. I tear my eyes away from her and look across at Diana, resting back on the pillow, serene, but exhausted.

'She's just gorgeous isn't she,' she says, and I can only nod in agreement.

'She looks like you,' I say, and Diana smiles. That's how we talk to each other now. We compliment and we care. I'm so relieved.

It was a mad rush in the end. Diana went into labour two weeks early while I was helping her fold the baby's clothes into the wardrobe in the nursery. Simon had spent the last few weeks decorating the room in a soft lemon colour as he wasn't convinced the sonographer could possibly be one hundred per cent correct, and besides he didn't want to project gender expectations onto his daughter. I'd never seen Simon so serious about anything before, but it was touching to see. The quality and colour of the carpet had been deliberated over for ages and it was interesting to see how neither of them cared about that when Diana's waters broke all over it. They left immediately and I stayed behind to clear it up. And it was a good job they did go so promptly because Grace was born only three hours later.

'What do you want to be called?' Diana asks me, as I reluctantly hand Grace over to Simon who has his arms out eager to take his daughter. 'Are you going to be Grandma like your brooch suggests?'

I laugh. The birthday gift seems a long time ago now; so much has happened.

'Yes, I like Grandma. She sounds wise and kindly.'

'Grandma Connie,' Diana says. 'So, Alex can be Granny then.'

'What?' I look across at her, surprised.

'I've found her,' she says.

'Yes, my wife's time has been well spent over the last couple of months.' Simon perches on the edge of the bed and passes Grace over to Diana to be fed.

'I couldn't help but look for her after you told me what she meant to you, what she still means to you.'

'It's been four months now. If she wanted to get in contact she would. Her number is no longer in service. I think we're probably done. Is she still in Scotland?' I ask, despite myself.

'She is living in Scotland, yes. I remembered what you told me about some of your road trip. I looked up that bar in Preston you talked about and spoke to Rachel. You could have done that Connie; she was easy to find.'

'I've done enough chasing, thank you.'

'But you and Alex are meant to be together. You told me she was the love of your life. You *have* to be together.' Diana looks exasperated, but then concentrates on latching Grace on for a feed and her expression softens. After a moment she continues. 'I got her new phone number from Rachel.'

I look at her for a moment, sorely tempted to take the number from her and rush from the room to call Alex, but I take a breath and don't.

'It's too late now, Diana. Too much has happened.' I don't say what I really want to, that I can't bear to keep chasing someone who doesn't want me.

'What will be, will be,' she says.

Later, back at home, when I finally tear myself away from Grace, Simon and Diana, I make a coffee and sit staring at the space where my painting used to hang. I decorated my Christmas tree last week and the fairy lights cast a glow across the empty wall. I have a horrible empty feeling myself, much worse than the one I've carried with me for all these years. Now I have the memory of those days we spent together to miss too.

Baby Grace is what I will centre on: gorgeous Grace and my wonderful family. I'm really very lucky to have them all. I put down the coffee and glance at my watch. It's six-thirty. In the kitchen I pour a glass of wine and take it back to the living room where I begin to flick through the TV channels. I can't decide between an animated movie or a Christmas romance. In the end I decide not to bother with either and I turn it off and pick up a book instead. Tucking my feet underneath me, I begin to turn the pages, but I'm not taking in any of the words. I chuck it back onto the coffee table and sigh.

The snow is still falling and I get up to see how deep it is now, in our communal car park. The top of my van has a layer of white covering the raspberry paintwork and I wonder how easy it will be to get to Simon and Diana's tomorrow. I'm taking Christmas lunch with me. Everything is prepared and all I need to do is chuck it in their oven in the morning. Diana has been given the all clear to go home. After all those agonising attempts to get pregnant and then the worry about her placenta, in the end, she seemed to breeze through labour and birth. Well, that's Simon's version. He's so proud of his wife, but she may have a different take on things.

My neighbour is making his way across the car park with a couple of carrier bags of shopping. He lives alone too and I'm wondering whether to invite him in to share the wine, when I notice someone else trudging through the snow with a large package under their arm. What is it with people and their last-minute Christmas shopping? I'm about to lower the blind when I notice their gait is slightly off, throwing their hip out to one side. I stop with my hand on the cord and watch as my neighbour disappears through the door below, and the other person follows.

I seem to see Alex everywhere I go now: a flash of red hair, a particular walk, her accent. I think I'm going mad.

I continue to lower the blind and turn the table lamp on, then pick my wine back up and take a mince pie out of the packet in the cupboard. And then there's a knock on my door.

I do know it's Alex. I knew it as soon as I saw her in the car park, but now I'm not sure I can open the door. I place my wine glass down onto the table and walk into the hallway, then I take a grounding breath and open the door.

'It's freezing out there,' she says, before bustling into my flat. 'I've bought something for you,' she continues, holding out the package, but I'm too dumbfounded to answer. 'Well, look I'll leave it down here for now.' She props it up against the armchair and begins to take her coat off.

'So, you just turn up unexpectedly after all these months? Just like that?'

She turns to look at me with sharp eyes, her arm only halfway out of her sleeve.

'Fifty-one years and six months sooner than you did,' she says, before throwing her coat over the back of the sofa. 'Are you going to offer me a glass of that wine?' Her eyes move to my glass on the table.

I can't stop the smile stretching across my mouth as I fill her a glass in the kitchen, but I wipe it off before I come back. This is Alex; outwardly confident and untouchable, but there's always been that little girl inside, desperately hoping someone will want to play with her.

'Where's Bardo?' I ask her.

'Staying with a friend for the moment. How's things with you?' she asks.

'So, we're doing small talk, are we?'

'Yes, it's seems easy, don't you think?'

'No, let's do big talk,' I say. 'Where the hell have you been and where's my bloody painting?'

'Cheers,' she says raising her glass.

I sit down in the armchair and Alex takes the sofa, kicking off her boots as she lifts her legs up onto the coffee table.

'I had to go back,' she says. 'Hank kept on calling; he wasn't just going to give up. I thought I could run away and take some of the money with me, but he wasn't going to let that happen. I had to pay back what I owed and now I have. So, I have nothing, but at least I'm not looking over my shoulder all the time.'

'You could have done that from here. How do you think I felt when I realised you'd gone?'

'You're asking *me* that question? I of all people know full well how you would feel, but I had to come to this as equals. You would have tried to help me and I needed to sort out this mess myself. I really wanted you to be proud of me, Con.'

'So it wasn't because you found that photo of me and Leo then?' I say.

She throws her head back and laughs loudly.

'Of course not! I wouldn't have let something as silly as a man stand in my way. No, I had unfinished business and now I don't. I am sorry about the note though; I was a bit hungover and being dramatic. I hope you'll forgive me.'

She lifts her glass to her lips and eyes me over the rim.

'Aren't you going to open your present?' she says.

'Oh,' I say. 'I haven't got anything for you, because I didn't know you were coming.'

'Your hospitality is present enough,' she says, lifting her glass again.

Getting up from the chair I pick up the package, pull the tape from the sides and tear the paper away to reveal a painting. *Sitter One.*

'It was always for you,' she says. 'I painted it not long after you left.'

I look at it for a long time and then hang it on the wall where my other painting used to be.

'I like to call it, *Lady Constance Fitzgerald,*' she says, and I slap her playfully on her arm.

'So what happened to the other painting? Did you have to sell them together?'

'No, I thought I was going to have to do that, but I didn't in the end. The exhibition made more money than anticipated and I got a few commissions from it too.'

'So, you still have the paintings then? You know I was going to give it back to you anyway; you didn't have to just take it.'

'Yes, I have them both. Sorry, Con. My head was all over the place. I do have a plan though and want your permission to sell them. I have a mad idea for a road trip.'

'Another one?'

'Yes, but this one would be quite epic and I need to fund it.'

She gets up, opens her bag and drags out a map, which she proceeds to lay across the coffee table. I watch her finger as she traces a line along the paper. She pulls out a red-felt tip and grins at me.

'I think the best time would be in the late spring, early summer. Everyone usually says autumn, but apparently there's an explosion of wild flowers across the mountains in June and they're not to be missed. The whole trip would take a few weeks, ideally, hence the idea for selling the paintings, with your permission of course,' she adds.

I feel as if there's a sudden urgency in me to try and keep hold of her.

'Will you stay tonight?' I ask her and she looks up from the map.

'I just got off the train and I doubt I can get a room anywhere so, unless you want me to sleep in the van, I would like to stay, yes.'

'And we're going to Simon and Diana's for lunch tomorrow,' I continue, wanting to pin her down.

'I know,' she says.

'How do you know?' I ask her, surprised.

'Because Diana got in contact with me,' she says ruefully. 'I didn't just turn up, Con. I needed to know you'd want to see me.'

'Well, you would have to ask me that, surely,' I say, a little annoyed by Diana's interference and Alex's assumptions.

'To be honest, she said you were miserable without me and it would be great if I could come.' She smiles broadly and smugly.

'For goodness' sake,' I say, shaking my head.

'Connie,' she says, taking my hand. 'We don't work properly without each other; I think we've established this. No more second-guessing. We love each other and I'm happy to be honest with myself, you and anyone else about that fact. It turns out that Lady Constance Fitzgerald is the love of my life and there's nothing to separate us now.'

I'm moved by the honesty of her words and they fill me with an intense relief, even though they're not quite true.

'You're going away in a few months' time. That will separate us.'

'I'm not going anywhere without you, Con! This will be the golden girls' road trip,' she says, using her fingers to show an imaginary banner in the air. 'I'm not doing it alone.'

She takes my face in her hands, pulls me forward and rests her forehead against mine.

'Now,' she says. 'Get the felt-tip pen and pinpoint everywhere you want to stop.'

EPILOGUE

SIX MONTHS LATER

I stretch the map out on my lap and move my eyes down the length of the historic Route 1 – 2369 miles, stretching from Fort Kent near the Canadian border, down the East Coast of the States through Maine, New Hampshire, Massachusetts, Rhode Island, Connecticut, New York, New Jersey, Pennsylvania, Delaware, Maryland, Washington DC, Virginia, North Carolina, South Carolina, through Florida and hopefully, if we're still alive at that point, ending in Key West.

Alex sighs beside me from the driver's seat. A couple of injections in her hip and she's renewed her driving license.

'I don't know why you bother with that paper map, it was only meant to be a nostalgic present. You've got tech that's far more likely to keep us on track.'

'I just like the feel of a map, that's all.'

'Do you want to swap and drive for a bit?' she asks.

'Why, are you feeling tired?'

We only left the beautiful town of Ogunquit half an hour ago, but then Alex *had* stuffed her face with a load of chocolate and vanilla ice cream at the Dairy King on the beach, so maybe she's feeling a bit off, if not tired.

'I'm not tired, Connie, I'd just quite like to navigate, that's all.'

'No,' I say, sternly. 'It's my turn.'

She sighs again.

'I'm better at navigating than you.'

'No, you're not. You just keep trying to get us onto interstate 95.'

'It's wider, smoother and going the same bloody way.'

'Route 1 is historic and I think it's important to be true to our journey,' I say. 'Think of all those places you've loved driving through so far. You'd have missed them all.'

She nods her assent. It's been so hard not to stop in every place we pass. The picturesque villages with pastel-painted houses and shops, sandy beaches and tucked-in rocky inlets. Alex has said on more than one occasion, *Okay, we live in Maine now.* I've felt the same myself, but the tug of where we're going next is huge and our red felt-tip pen markers along the length of the country on the paper map are calling to us.

We flew into Maine a few days ago and have covered a fair amount of road in that time. But we're not in a rush; we have no deadlines, no pressures. We have our comfortable rented RV and we have each other.

Simon drove us to the airport, with Diana insisting she come too, gorgeous baby Grace in her carry car seat between us in the back and Bardo in the boot. Simon has been trying to talk Diana into getting a dog for ages and jumped at the opportunity to look after Alex's dog while we're away. A, *try before you buy*, scenario, he'd said. Diana looked like she was softening to the idea when Bardo sat sentry to Grace's car seat.

'We'll FaceTime loads,' she'd said to me when I got a bit teary at the airport. 'You can show us where you are. I'm so excited for you both.'

When we hugged goodbye it was how it always is now: warm, tight and genuine. I can't believe it, but Diana and I have become friends. Alex babysits with me, when they need a break. We take Grace out in her pram and Alex loves being the one to push. It makes me smile to see her so enamoured with the baby, but it breaks my heart a little too, for all that time we lost.

The paintings are all gone now. That heaviness hanging over Alex has been lifted and her new work is all her own. We have *Sitter One* of course and *Sunrise* and *Sunset over Loch Ness – Gold Was the Day*. Gold was the day, indeed. They hang in my tiny living room and I think they look so grand and possibly out of place, but it's also lovely to see them hanging together again at last. I couldn't let Alex sell them to fund this trip. My inheritance has left me very comfortable and when we get back we're going to look at where we want to live and get a place together. For now, though, we're based in my Brighton flat. I've cleared out my mess of a spare room for a studio, but really, Alex paints best on the road, *en plein air*, when we take Ruby out and about. Life is wonderful and new and free.

'Right, look we're just crossing the Piscataqua River, and… wait for it…'

Alex steers us across the bridge spanning the gap between Maine and New Hampshire and I look out across the expanse of water, tracking the progress of speedboats and yachts down below. My window is down, the warmth from the May sunshine penetrating the skin on my arm resting on the edge, the breeze blowing strands of my hair around my face.

'Here, we go,' I continue. 'There, we've just crossed the state line. We're in New Hampshire now.'

I turn to see Alex's reaction and watch as her face breaks into a grin.

'I feel like I'm in a movie,' she says.

'So, are we agreed that we're sticking to Route 1? Can we say that you've moaned about this road for the drive through a whole American state, but that you're over it now and we can continue through the next fifteen of them without another word about it?'

She snorts with laughter and toots her horn, much to the surprise of the people in the car driving alongside us. Alex puts her hand up and gives them a cheery wave.

'Okay,' she says to me. 'No more moaning, but who will know which piece of road we'll be travelling when I'm behind the wheel and you're asleep?'

I relax back into my seat. The van is so plush and cosy. Initially I had reservations; I felt ridiculously unfaithful to Ruby, but dumped that idea pretty quickly. It only took a few short miles of extremely comfortable driving to forget her. I'll take her out for a good run when I get back to make it up to her.

We'll be in Boston within the hour and have booked bus and boat tours, tickets for museums, walking trips that take in the best eateries in the city and also I've arranged a day trip to Martha's Vineyard. I haven't told Alex about that yet.

'Can you believe we're finally on our planned road trip? I guess last summer was a warm-up for the real thing.'

She reaches her hand across the gap between the seats and takes hold of mine. Her warm skin soft against my own.

'It might be more than fifty-two years later than we planned it, but here we are, together. Nowhere I'd rather be.'

I rest my head back in the seat and turn to look at her: this woman who has invaded my thoughts for all these years; this infuriating, gorgeous and exceptional woman.

My first love, my last love.

ACKNOWLEDGEMENTS

A lot is talked about the tricky beast that is the second novel, so when I wrote the words *Chapter one* on what turned out to be *The Golden Girls' Road Trip* I thought, let's see.

Well, a tricky beast indeed!

It's with this thought in mind that I have several people to thank for their support and for helping me wrangle this tricky beast into shape.

Firstly, my agent, Robbie Guillory. His enthusiasm and commitment is unparalleled. He always reminds me of what is at the heart of the book when I go *off piste*.

To my editor, Rachel Faulkner-Willcocks. I'm so grateful to you for taking a chance on me and my writing.

To Bianca Gillam who is always on the end of an e-mail and puts in so much work. You are a star!

To all the team at Aria and especially to Ayo Okojie. I appreciate all that you do.

There's a reason I keep writing when it gets tough, when I wonder what on earth I'm doing and it's because of good friends and family.

The Virtual Writing Group are the absolute best! Who else could you ask 'What is the best Scottish word for an idiot?'

and have several eager and informed responses in minutes followed by an in-depth discussion!

My family allow me time and space to write and I am incredibly grateful to them for that. My husband, Richard, is so supportive and really doesn't mind at all when I fire random questions at him! He really is the font of all knowledge.

I have picked the brains of a few people while writing this book: Danielle, Bev, Marnie, but any mistakes are my own.

Finally a huge thank you to all the lovely people who have read, reviewed, rated and told a friend. I am indebted to you all.

About the Author

KATE GALLEY is the author of *The Second Chance Holiday Club*. She lives in Buckinghamshire with her husband, children and Meg, their Patterdale Terrier. Much of Kate's inspiration comes from the many varied lives of her clients as a mobile hairdresser.